D0111078

6/18

8 SECONDS
TO MIDNIGHT

8 SECONDS
TO MIDNIGHT

JOHN LEIFER

Copyrighted Material

8 Seconds to Midnight

Copyright © 2018 by John Leifer. All Rights Reserved.

No part of this publication may be reproduced, stored in a retrieval
system or transmitted, in any form or by any means—electronic,
mechanical, photocopying, recording or otherwise—without
prior written permission from the publisher, except for
the inclusion of brief quotations in a review.

This book is a work of fiction. Any references to historical events, real
people or real places are used fictitiously. Other names, characters,
places, and events are the product of the author's imagination, and any
resemblance to real events or places or
persons, living or dead, is entirely coincidental.

For information about this title or to order other books and/or
electronic media, contact the publisher:

Earhart Press
P.O. Box 6131, Overland Park, Kansas 66206
www.earhartpress.com

ISBN: 978-0-9995655-0-6 (print)
978-0-9995655-1-3 (ebook)

Printed in the United States of America

Library of Congress Control Number: 2017916425

CHAPTER ONE

AYESHA DROPPED HER HANDS TO HER KNEES, laboring to draw in enough air to quench her oxygen-starved lungs. Sweat ran down her forehead and across her cheeks before spilling onto the sidewalk. Her heart pounded in her chest. As her respirations slowly deepened, she rose, hands on her hips.

She had run with a vengeance. It was an attempt to push through the depression—to clear the ever-present fog that engulfed her following the accident. Running brought relief, like a balm applied to an open wound. With each stride, she strained to distance herself from the images of her mother's body. Yet no matter how hard she pushed, she couldn't outrun her demons. The pain was too fresh.

Nor could she escape the scrutiny of the two men seated in a parked car across from her house. She waited until her breath returned before standing up and waving to them. It was a game she played with the bodyguards, who never waved back. She knew they worked for her father, but not why he felt it necessary to protect her following the accident. It was an issue he refused to discuss with her.

She glanced at the clock on her bedroom table before letting her soaked running clothes drop to the tile floor and climbing into the shower. It was 6:15 AM, and Ayesha knew she would be late to the clinic. It was a perpetual problem for the young physician, who never missed her morning run.

Dressing quickly, she dabbed the last beads of perspiration from her forehead, made a minor adjustment to her hijab, then declared herself fit to engage the outside world. Graced with the natural beauty of her mother, it never took her long to get ready.

Ayesha grabbed the keys to her aging Toyota and walked out the door of her modest home in the F10 district of Islamabad. It was a quarter to seven, and the sun was just rising above the lush green Margalla Hills that surrounded the city. She navigated past schools, parks, and neatly manicured lawns until she reached a major boulevard lined with flowers suffused with rich, autumnal colors. Their beauty was lost on Ayesha, whose depression stripped the world of its vibrancy, replacing it with a netherworld of dull pastels.

Will it ever lift? she wondered.

Ayesha turned sharply into the doctors' parking lot at the National Islamic Hospital. It was a new facility offering patients state of the art care imbued with traditional Muslim values—a mission that resonated with Ayesha. Its administrator was a former Major General in the Army Medical College and a close friend of her father.

It was a quarter past seven when she approached the private entrance to the clinic. She glanced down the hall toward the reception area, where a single patient was waiting. Ayesha recognized the frail, elderly woman immediately.

As she stepped through the door, Ayesha's nurse greeted her with an anemic smile.

"Good morning, Dr. Naru."

Naru was her mother's maiden name. Ayesha had adopted it professionally, not to dishonor her father, but to maintain some semblance of anonymity—however thin the veil. Her full name was Ayesha Naru Malik.

"Good morning," she responded as she grabbed her lab coat from a small closet, pulled it on, and squared the collar. "I can see that Ms. Azam is waiting for me."

"Yes, doctor. The clinic opens promptly at seven o'clock."

"I'm doing my best." She knew she was under no obligation to explain herself to the staff.

"She will be in Exam Room 4."

"I'll be right there."

"There's another *visitor* waiting for you, in your office," the nurse said as she thrust Ms. Azam's chart into Ayesha's hands.

The man in Ayesha's office wasn't accustomed to being kept waiting, and he showed his displeasure the moment she opened the door.

"You're late, Doctor. The minute you are finished with your examination of Ms. Azam, I will speak to the patient alone."

The man was in remarkable shape. A narrow waist gave rise to broad, muscular shoulders. His angular features and sweeping mustache combined to give him a ruggedly handsome appearance, while his white lab coat conferred a clear mantle of authority. Only his thinning gray hair betrayed his age.

Ayesha spoke hurriedly. "I'm sorry. Let me just glance at the patient's chart, and then I'll be ready."

She blinked slowly to regain her composure, but it did not stop her from being blindsided by the question that followed.

"When will it stop haunting you? It's been almost a year since the accident."

"And why doesn't it haunt you more?" she responded reflexively, before remembering her need for deference.

"We don't have time for this conversation, nor for your self-absorption."

The man paused, studying the woman in front of him. "I'm sorry, Ayesha. We both grieve the loss of your mother. You know that, don't you?"

"You have an interesting way of expressing your concern, Father."

Her father, General Omar Malik, was no physician—as the top ranking Pakistani military officer, he was one of the most feared men in the country. And, at that moment, she could not think of a single reason why she should be helping him.

Ayesha's nurse had retreated to the reception area, where Faiza Azam was slumped in a chair. As the nurse bellowed her name, the old woman began to stir. Her movements were excruciatingly slow as she struggled to rise. Finally extricating herself, Azam shuffled toward the open door. She was covered from head to foot by a burqa.

"Follow me," the nurse ordered, as she moved too rapidly for the woman to keep pace. When she reached the fourth exam room on the right, the nurse hovered until the patient caught up.

"Dr. Naru will be in shortly." She grabbed a gown from a cupboard and dropped it on the exam table.

"Put it on," she instructed the woman on her way out the door.

The patient simply nodded. The nurse gave her a scowl, sensing that the old woman was not about to surrender her burqa, then pulled the door closed behind her.

Ayesha walked out of her office, nose down and thumbing through the pages of Faiza Azam's chart. She stopped outside of exam room #4, feeling her father's presence behind her. She knocked lightly on the door and then waited a moment before opening it. The patient, still clad in her burqa, sat awkwardly on the edge of the exam table. Ayesha entered. Her father followed and closed the door.

The patient stood, gripped her burqa with both hands, and lifted the heavy garment over her shoulders. Underneath, she wore men's trousers and a loose fitting shirt. She began to speak in a deep, raspy voice.

"Dr. Naru, General Malik, it is good to see you again."

"Ibrahim, I believe that burqa suits you well," Malik responded.

"I see you haven't lost your sense of humor, General. Even as a devoted Islamist, I think we're torturing our women with such attire. You should try it sometime. You might become an advocate for less oppressive dress."

Turning toward Malik's daughter as if to elicit support, al-Bakr said, "Wouldn't you agree, Dr. Naru?"

Too wise to take the bait, Ayesha feigned a smile. "If you gentlemen are done discussing women's fashion, I'd like to begin my examination."

She pointed to the exam table, signaling for al-Bakr to take a seat.

It was hard for Ayesha to comprehend how this frail man could be the leader of the most feared terrorist organization known to humanity—the United Islamic State. How much truth underlay the horrible atrocities of which he was accused, she wondered. And why did her father choose to do business with such a man? But her role was that of a healer, not an inquisitor.

Ayesha gently rotated al-Bakr's head from side to side. Long keloid scars crisscrossed his face and neck. One eye, which was nothing more than a piece of cosmetic glass, drooped, its socket crushed beyond repair. Along with his jaw, al-Bakr's chin had been shattered.

Though he struggled to eat or drink, often choking on half-chewed food, al-Bakr was grateful to Ayesha. His injuries had required all of her skill and more than a dozen surgeries to repair.

"So, Doctor, how do I look?"

"The mere fact that you are alive is reason enough to thank Allah."

"I am grateful to you, Doctor, but I would like to believe that you have more medical magic up your sleeve."

"I'm a reconstructive surgeon, not a miracle worker." Raising her hand to his face and tracing the outlines of a scar, she added, "We may be able to de-bulk these keloids with a minor surgical procedure, but let's wait. I'd like to see what nature can do to help you heal." She smiled at al-Bakr before taking her leave.

Both men rose to their feet as Ayesha bade them goodbye, then returned to their seats. From his elevated position on the exam table, al-Bakr looked down upon the general.

"Tell me, General. I know you love her deeply, but do you ever worry about your daughter's discretion?"

"No!" Malik bristled.

"Why does she help us? Surely filial loyalty only goes so far."

"My daughter deals with the aftermath of war. She sees a constant parade of patients whose injuries portend a lifetime of pain and suffering. Each one hopes that my daughter can somehow make them whole again."

"And she helps us because we are here to stop the carnage . . . to destroy the United States . . . the purveyor of such suffering?"

"That's part of it."

"And the other part?"

"The accident. She holds the Americans culpable for the death of her mother. But we are not here to discuss my daughter. You requested this meeting," Malik reminded al-Bakr.

Al-Bakr folded his hands as if in prayer. "Yes. It is regarding a small favor, General. One that I trust you will find easy to grant."

"Rarely do I feel as though I have a choice."

"Come now, are we not friends fighting the same war? And will not our victory bring glory to all who stand with us under heaven?"

"What is the small favor that you have gone to such elaborate lengths to request?"

"Allah calls upon us to finish what we began last year."

"Another biological weapon? Did the United Islamic State not learn a lesson from its recent failure?"

"Is that how you would describe the death of 85,000 Americans, coupled with the sheer terror inflicted upon most of the Christian world?" Al-Bakr's voice rose precipitously. "When have you enjoyed such a victory in battle?"

"You spoke of Armageddon—an apocalyptic vision that would transform the globe and create a holy Caliphate. It wasn't tens of thousands who were to die, but hundreds of millions. Only faithful Islamists, the chosen ones, were to survive. But the United States didn't perish. Its people were resurrected. Your unstoppable virus was systematically eliminated. Now the West stands poised for ever greater aggression against our country and our people. So, yes, I would call your last attack on America a failure," Malik countered.

"Have it as you will, General. Our job is to strike again and again until our vision comes to pass—the vision of a single state governed by Sharia Law. That is our obligation as faithful Muslims, and that is why I know I can count on your collaboration."

"What are you asking of me?"

"That you aid us in procuring a nuclear device. It is our intent to detonate a weapon of mass destruction in one of America's most treasured cities. We may not kill millions, but we will accomplish something far more powerful. We will kill the spirit of the American people."

"And you call that a small favor?" Malik barked.

Al-Bakr lifted himself off of the exam table and stood a few feet from the general, who remained fixed in his chair.

"I thought you would relish the idea of striking back at a country that invaded our sovereignty and exposed your complicity with the United Islamic State," al-Bakr said, referring to Malik's role in the biological attack.

"You speak of my complicity as if it is a known fact. If so, why haven't the Americans demanded my head?"

the general asked. "They may know that the intelligence services and military played a role in the biological attack, but not the complicity or identities of the individual actors."

"It's merely a matter of time. The Americans are assembling their case against you. Then you will have your day in court—and the world will learn of your misdeeds.

"By the way, General, does Ayesha know of your role in helping launch a global pandemic . . . or have you managed to convince her that you are the unfortunate victim of CIA slander? It's a good story, and it fits well with the CIA being to blame for the accident that claimed her mother's life."

Malik leaped to his feet, while al-Bakr stood fast. "Don't you dare threaten me. You speak as though your hands are untainted by blood, but it was your mind that conjured the vision for an apocalyptic attack against the West, and it was your protégé who carried it out."

"All true, and the only apology I offer is to Allah for not completing the task. But there are differences between you and me, General. Your role in the biological attack made you a target for not only the Americans, but for our president. Mughabi felt betrayed by your complicity. You now have two adversaries, and you are a highly visible target. I, on the other hand, am presumed dead."

"If that American puppet, Mughabi, thinks that I am a traitor, why do I still hold the keys to our nuclear arsenal? Why am I not rotting in Peshawar Prison?"

"Because Mughabi fears a coup from your loyalists in the military and intelligence community."

"Then our president is wiser than I thought."

"Why would I do something to further inflame the Americans—to support another grand vision of destruction likely to end in cataclysmic failure?" Malik demanded.

"Because we won't fail. We learned a great deal from our last attack. And though a nuclear weapon cannot grow into the global pandemic, as we had prayed the virus would, it can still bring America to its knees. When that happens, you will no longer be hunted. You will be raised up as an exalted military leader who helped bring an end to the imperialistic reign of the world's greatest superpower."

"It's a Herculean task to bring such a weapon into a country so well defended. The Americans have long anticipated such a threat, and they have safeguards in place to stop the very thing you wish to accomplish."

"They lack the will of God. This is not a child's escapade we are discussing. We've given great thought over many years to the challenges you refer to, which is why we don't seek to smuggle in a weapon, but rather a nuclear core."

"You are asking me to give you a plutonium core?"

"No, General, I am asking you to deliver a uranium core."

"What do you know of uranium or plutonium?" The general's words were laced with contempt.

"I know that it will be vastly more difficult to detect uranium than plutonium. I know that the core must be a minimum 90 percent weapons grade uranium-235. Do you take me to be a fool, General? Some ignorant goat-herder riding his camel through the desert?"

"No, I didn't mean to imply anything of the kind. I trust that you also know that the core will be relatively worthless without an appropriate housing to complete the weapon.

Unless perfectly compressed by a conventional explosive, it will fail to generate a self-sustaining reaction, at which point it will merely fizzle. In fact, without beryllium reflectors, a neutron gun, and other components, you will be lucky if your bomb yields a single kiloton."

"I appreciate your concerns, General, but my people are addressing these issues. All we lack is the core. Trust in Allah, General; you will be pleased with the results."

"The nuclear cores are not under my direct control."

"Yes, I know. They are under the control of General Patel, a close friend of yours, and of ours as well. We assumed that the core would come from the POF, where General Patel is the chairman."

The POF—Pakistan Ordnance Factories—referred to a collection of fourteen factories located in Wah Cantonment, only 25 miles northwest of Islamabad. The factories formed a virtual city, employing more than 27,000 people engaged in the production and distribution of weaponry.

"This will require months of planning."

Al-Bakr was only half-listening as he maneuvered to restore the burqa over his damaged body.

"You have a week, General. Then I will return for a follow-up appointment with Dr. Naru. I will expect you to have worked out all of the details."

His hand on the door, al-Bakr turned a final time toward Malik. "I trust we are in agreement."

He exited without waiting for a response.

CHAPTER TWO

A YEAR AND CHANGE HAD ELAPSED since the United Islamic State had launched a biological attack on the four busiest airports in America. By deploying a highly lethal, genetically engineered form of smallpox, the jihadists had intended to trigger a global pandemic. They almost succeeded. The only thing capable of stopping the virus was a novel vaccine that allowed a short window of post-exposure immunization. The vaccine had been developed by UIS with the intention of protecting loyal Islamists committed to the rise of a holy Caliphate.

The American people had been sheltered from the truth about how close they had come to annihilation by the government. Such knowledge could be damaging—raising the public's anxiety level while exposing the country's vulnerability to weapons of mass destruction. Beyond the president and his cabinet, only a hand-picked team of specialists at the epicenter of the epidemic knew the complete truth.

Commander John Hart, the nation's leading bio-warfare expert, had led the team responsible for liberating the vaccine from a clandestine laboratory in Pakistan. A physician, Navy Seal, and senior intelligence officer, Hart could be physically and intellectually intimidating—talents that he held in reserve to be deployed only when needed. Officially, Hart reported to Marvin Kahn, Deputy Director of Operations at the CIA, but everyone in the counter-terrorism community knew he was the president's go-to person during national crises.

Hart leaned heavily on Dr. Elizabeth Wilkins, a pre-eminent virologist who ran the Biolevel IV lab at the CDC. Accustomed to dealing with deadly pathogens, Liz had proved to be invaluable in the aftermath of the bio-attack.

Known to be brilliant, as well as possessed of a wicked sense of humor, Wilkins was well matched with Hart—both in the field and in the bedroom. After a back-and-forth courtship that played out during the biological attack, the two became engaged to be married.

John Hart was many things, but he was not subtle. The heavy thud of his boots echoed in the hall as he marched toward their apartment. For Liz, it was an early warning indicator of an incoming Seal. It provided the precious seconds she needed to light the candles on a decadent red velvet birthday cake before he walked through the door.

As he stepped across the threshold, Liz broke out in song. "Happy birthday to you, happy birthday to you, happy birthday, my dear warrior, happy birthday to you."

"Go ahead, blow them out," she encouraged.

But Hart was laughing too hard. Collecting himself, he made a wish, blew out the candles, then took the cake from Liz and set it carefully on the table. He wrapped his powerful arms around her and hugged her. His hugs were like being gripped by a python, Liz thought, as she struggled for breath. Hart eased his hold.

"You forget your own strength, cowboy. One of these days you're going to send me to the ER with broken ribs, and then there's going to be some explaining to do."

"It's called passion," he explained, "unbridled passion."

"Oh, that's what you call it. Well, why don't you and your passion go have a seat on the couch while I get things ready?"

Hart sauntered over to a long, gray couch and plopped down, while Liz poured four fingers of Macallan into a brandy snifter. She served it neat, as Hart liked it. Nothing but a few drops of water should desecrate a fine single malt. She handed him the glass. "Dinner will be ready in about thirty minutes."

Eager to investigate, Hart stood up and walked into the dining room. The table was formally set with beautiful china and sterling—one of Liz's contributions to their pending life together.

"Wow," the Commander exclaimed, "I didn't expect this."

"It's time someone pampered you," Liz called from the kitchen.

Walking into the kitchen, he started to wrap his arms around her in another constrictor-like hug, but she held him back with a spatula.

"How'd you do it?" he asked. "Your flight from Atlanta didn't land until two o'clock."

Liz was still commuting from CDC Headquarters in Atlanta. It wasn't easy building a new relationship with their work lives separated by six hundred miles.

"I ordered your cake from Buttercream Bakeshop and picked it up on the way in from the airport. But I still have some cooking to do." She raised the spatula and shook it at him for emphasis.

"I thought we were going out."

"I thought you might enjoy a home-cooked meal. And I've got a present for you. Actually, it's two presents."

Hart perked up. There was a wonderfully childlike quality to the man she loved. He could be one tough son-of-a-bitch, but he could also be winsome and playful.

"One of the presents you don't get until after dinner," she said, eyes dancing.

"And the other?" Hart asked.

"A special weekend in New York—in celebration of your fiftieth birthday and New Year's Eve. I've booked a suite at the St. Regis, and we have dinner reservations at Le Bernardin."

"Liz, that's a month's pay. I love you, darling, but how about the Holiday Inn and Black Iron Burger?"

"No, Commander. I'm in charge." She paused and looked at him closely to ensure he had capitulated. "Any more questions?"

"Just one. The first present . . . can I have it before dinner?"

"You just keep that passion of yours in check for a little while longer and let me get dinner ready, okay?"

"Where are you going?" Hart asked as Liz moved toward the bedroom.

"I need to get out of these work clothes before I start cooking. I feel grungy from the flight. I'm going to take a quick shower."

"Can I watch?" John asked with a sly smile.

"You are incorrigible," Liz sighed.

Hart retreated to the living room. "Take your time," he said, as he picked up the Macallan and turned on the evening news. Wolf Blitzer was in the *Situation Room*. Hart was relieved to see that there was no banner exclaiming "Breaking News."

Fifteen minutes later, Liz stealthy approached Hart. Engrossed in a story about the vulnerability of Pakistan's nuclear arsenal, the normally hyper-alert Commander failed to notice. It wasn't until Liz placed her hand on his shoulder that Hart shifted his gaze away from the television.

"I don't think I've ever seen you speechless before," Liz told her fiancé, whose mouth was agape.

Before him stood a goddess wearing only an apron. It covered less than half of her body. And it was a hell of a body, Hart thought. Liz looked far closer to thirty than forty-five. She slowly turned her back on the Commander, glancing over her shoulder as she spoke to the man mesmerized by her nakedness.

"Commander, I believe you were asking me about that first gift? Well, maybe I should give it to you now so you are not distracted during dinner. You don't mind if we push dinner back until eight o'clock, do you?"

"That only gives me an hour and half," Hart complained.

"Don't worry, cowboy. If you need more time, I'll give it to you," Liz said, extending her hand and leading Hart to the bedroom.

It was just after nine o'clock when they returned to the kitchen and Liz began to prepare the elaborate dinner for her lover.

"What kind of grub are you serving?" John asked.

"We're having beef tenderloin, served bloody—the way you like it—a demi-glacé sauce, whipped potatoes with wasabi and haricot verts. You've already seen dessert."

"Is that what you call it?"

"I'm talking about the cake." Liz shook her head. "You are something else."

"That's why you love me," Hart said, grinning widely. "Can I have a second helping of dessert after dinner?"

"John!"

She wanted to prepare an elegant dinner—to make everything as perfect as it had been on their first date, when John had taken her to The Inn at Fletcher Mill. That had been a magical evening, graced not only by food that was divine, but by conversation that never faltered.

Smitten after one date, they'd nonetheless had their ups and downs, including a major break-up after six months of intense dating. But in the end, they knew that nothing but death could sever the bond between them.

CHAPTER THREE

AYESHA FELT A SENSE OF DÉJÀ VU as she examined the man who had visited her clinic precisely one week before. She knew he was not here to see her, but rather to complete a discussion with her father. Even so, she felt obligated to examine his wounds.

She ran her fingers along the jagged scar bisecting al-Bakr's cheek. Her patient's survival was nothing short of miraculous. Al-Bakr had been squarely in the kill zone when a Hellfire missile exploded in the courtyard of his compound. Two of his compatriots were not so fortunate. Ahmed Al Hameed and Beibut Valikhanov, the men responsible for launching the bio-attack on America, were eviscerated by shrapnel. Only a leap of faith—a split second decision to dive for the cover of a stone wall—had saved al-Bakr.

Ayesha stretched the skin on either side of the keloid, gauging the degree of elasticity that remained.

"It's a miracle you survived," she told him.

"No, it is by the grace of Allah that I am here. He still has plans for me. Maybe someday he will allow me to enter paradise, but not while there is work to be done."

Ayesha nodded in acknowledgment, not comprehending the magnitude of the work to which her patient alluded.

"I'm pleased with how you are healing. We'll talk about reducing some of these scars soon."

"Thank you, Doctor, but they are of little concern to me."

Ayesha's father had been sitting silently in the corner of the exam room. General Malik rose to his feet, a none-too-subtle message to Ayesha that the examination was over and she needed to leave. As she moved toward the door, al-Bakr spoke.

"Thank you, Doctor. Your father and I have important matters to discuss regarding the work we do in praise of Allah. Someday you will learn of the important role your father played in restoring our great Caliphate."

"I think that's quite enough," the general interjected. "My daughter does not need to concern herself with such matters."

"It's alright, Father, I heard nothing. Now, gentlemen, I trust you will excuse me. I have a long list of patients to see." She slipped out of the room.

General Malik waited until Ayesha was out of earshot.

"What is the matter with you? We have an agreement—my daughter is to know nothing."

"And there is nothing of substance that I shared with her," al-Bakr said, unfazed by Malik's anger.

"Keep her out of it, Ibrahim."

"General, that sounds like a threat."

"It's not a threat. It's a promise. I will finish the job the Americans began with their drone if you attempt to pull my daughter into our matters. Is that clear?"

Al-Bakr sat with his legs crossed like an unperturbed Buddha.

"Yes, General, you are quite clear. Now may we resume our discussion regarding my request? I trust you and General Patel agreed to grant my small favor."

General Malik took several deep breaths before responding. Gradually, the flush of red faded from his face and the quiver disappeared from his voice. He pulled his chair closer to the examination table and spoke in a hushed tone.

"General Patel and I have considered the *small* favor you requested."

"And?" al-Bakr asked, raising his chin and looking down on Malik through his round wire spectacles.

"We will give you what you asked for—a nuclear core consisting of twenty-six kilograms of highly enriched uranium, but there are caveats."

Al-Bakr ignored the last part of his statement. "What is the hypothetical yield from such a core?"

"If properly constructed, the weapon will yield upwards of fifteen kilotons—equivalent to the bomb dropped on Hiroshima. It will be a crushing blow to the Americans, if you can pull it off."

"Why such doubt, General? Do you lack confidence in the United Islamic State?"

"As I told you at our last meeting, building a nuclear bomb is more complex than merely procuring the core. Do you think it is as simple as wrapping some explosives around a ball of uranium? We're not talking about some primitive suicide vest constructed of C4 and ball bearings. That I know you can handle."

"You sound contemptuous, General."

"Perhaps that's because I am. You pretend to be knowledgeable about beryllium reflectors, high explosive lenses and kytrons, but I am afraid that it is nothing more than fancy rhetoric coming from your mouth. Your bomb will go poof, not roar with an unholy thunder that brings down skyscrapers and vaporizes people where they stand. That's my prediction and my hesitation in complying with your request."

"And does General Patel agree with you?"

"Remember, General Patel works for me. We agree that, unless you can bolster our confidence, we have difficulty supporting an ill-conceived plan."

"Ill-conceived?"

"Yes, ill-conceived. I'm being polite; otherwise, I would call it a fool's errand."

Al-Bakr was on his feet, closing in on the general before Malik could move. "You pompous ass! You parade around in your military suit with medals dangling from your chest, yet you've never seen a day of combat. I will answer your questions, and in return you will give me the core."

Malik backed his chair away from the fiery cleric until it lodged against the wall.

Al-Bakr continued unabated. "You fool, I do not claim to possess the knowledge to build such a weapon, only the ability to bring together the requisite talent and materials to accomplish such a goal."

"But such people don't grow on trees. How do you hope to find them in America?" Malik seethed.

"We do not need to find them. We planted them there many years ago. Nuclear engineers, metallurgists, and others eager to immigrate to the land of the free and the home of the brave. Their adopted country trusted them, embraced them, and eventually hired them to work in its vast military-industrial complex. Of course, they were carefully vetted before being issued Top Secret clearances. But there was nothing to discover. They were clean. And as a result, they became privy to America's most closely guarded secrets."

"And then?" Malik questioned.

"They waited for our instructions knowing it could be months, years, even decades before they were called upon to act."

"And now that day has finally arrived . . . is that what you are claiming?" Malik asked, the anger fading from his tone.

"Yes," al-Bakr hissed. "Our men stand ready to use all of the knowledge and material they have acquired to construct a weapon of mass destruction. All they lack is the nuclear core."

"The men you claim to have planted in America are the linchpin upon which your ambitious plot succeeds or fails. Tell me more about them."

"There is nothing more you need to know. We have been planning this day for many years, and nothing is going to stop it. Surely not you and General Patel."

Malik knew his life, as well as the lives of Ayesha and General Patel, hung in the balance. He had no choice but to acquiesce.

"As I said when we began this conversation, you will get your core."

Al-Bakr stepped back, his posture becoming more relaxed. "How will we take delivery?" he asked.

"You will send three men to the POF on November 30. They will arrive at the main gate at precisely 1700 hours. They will be driving a nondescript and unmarked white van—one that matches those used by our military to transport nuclear weapons."

Malik opened a folder and pulled out a photograph of a Ford Transit van. Attached to it was the name of a rental car company.

"Your men will be dressed in the uniform of the SPF, the unit responsible for the security of all nuclear weapons. We will provide standard issue black fatigues, 9mm pistols and, of course, the requisite identification and orders authorizing the procurement and transfer of a single nuclear core."

"And once my men present the orders to the guard?"

"The sentry will follow procedure and contact Major Ali Barr. Barr is one of the senior officers responsible for the storage and transfer of nuclear weapons at POF. He's also General Patel's son-in-law and his most trusted aide. He will meet your men at the gate."

"And what if something goes wrong?"

"I can assure you that there will be no margin for error. General Patel and I stake our reputations on it."

"There's far more than your reputation at stake, General."

"I do not like to be threatened, particularly when I'm granting a very big favor."

"I wasn't threatening you. I was reminding you that your life and the life of those close to you depend upon our successful acquisition of the core."

Malik wanted desperately to reach out and choke the bastard.

"I have one more question, General, but first I suggest you let go of your anger. It's very unbecoming, and there's no point in raising concerns in the clinic."

Despite his words, al-Bakr seemed to enjoy watching the general seethe.

He continued, "What happens when the loss is discovered? How will you explain such an event to President Mughabi? And what of the Americans—aren't you concerned that Mughabi will alert them to the loss?"

"Our president will be told that three men successfully infiltrated the POF by impersonating army officers from the SPF. The perpetrators carried signed orders bearing the forged signature of General Patel. Major Barr followed protocol and executed the orders, which required the delivery of a nuclear device for transport to Gujranwala."

"Barr will be under intense scrutiny following your revelation."

"The major can handle it."

"And what of the Americans?"

"Mughabi will not utter a word for fear that such a loss will justify immediate intervention by the United States. They would seize control of our nuclear arsenal. The U.S. has been pushing to strip us of our nukes since the bio-attack, and it won't take much more provocation for them to act."

"And why would Mughabi stop them, General?"

"Because the president knows that once our country is deprived of its nuclear deterrent, nothing stands in the way of a full-out attack by India."

"It is not only Barr who will be under the magnifying glass. You and General Patel will be, too."

"We've been through this issue. You are the one who said that Mughabi already viewed me as a traitor. Yet our president did nothing to prevent my ongoing complicity with terrorists. How will that play with his constituents? I'll tell you—it won't play well. Mughabi will bite his tongue, for he has no choice. Now, if you don't mind, I'm returning to my men. Expect a package within forty-eight hours."

Before exiting the exam room, the general picked up the burqa and tossed it to al-Bakr. "You really do look lovely in black."

He walked out, leaving the door wide open for anyone to see a small disfigured man with round spectacles struggling to restore his burqa.

CHAPTER FOUR

ZAHID MAHAR BENT DOWN AND KISSED his young daughters as they lay nestled in the tiny bed festooned with images of daisies and hollyhocks. It was 4:30 AM, a full two hours before the girls would begin to stir. He hovered over them, watching their gentle breaths come and go in synchrony, savoring the moment before turning his attention to Karin.

After ten years of a childless marriage, the twins' arrival had been a precious gift from God. He thanked Allah for this blessing. But Zahid did more than offer prayers of gratitude; he also pledged unquestioning obedience to the United Islamic State.

"Tell my girls how much their father misses them. Promise me that you will tell them every day."

"Of course I will," his wife said. "But I thought you were only going to be gone a few days."

Zahid was silent, confirming Karin's fears. Because he was a soldier of Islam, she knew that Allah could summon her husband at will. The orders would not come directly from heaven, but from Allah's emissary, al-Bakr. If Zahid returned, it would be only upon the fulfillment of his obligation to God.

Surely there had to be other ways he could serve the Caliphate, she thought. He was a well-educated medical physicist, not a jihadist, at least not in her mind.

She tried to conceal the tears welling up in her eyes.

"Don't I always return home safely?" he asked, trying to comfort her.

"It's just a feeling," she confessed.

"Ah, a woman's intuition. Banish these thoughts from your mind."

It was Karin's turn to remain silent.

Zahid embraced her gently, kissing the top of her head. Minutes later, he rolled down the car window and gave a final wave before speeding off in the direction of Islamabad. His mind captured the moment like a photograph. It was an image he would cling to—not knowing when or if he would see his family again.

Traffic on the Lahore-Islamabad Motorway was light in the pre-dawn hours of December 1. Zahid's mind gradually shifted from thoughts of the family he was leaving behind to the immense tasks ahead. He was beginning to discern how the major events in his life formed a pattern that only God could have foreseen. It was preparation for holy Jihad—a nuclear Jihad. If he died fighting, it was for his children and for every other child of Islam.

The miles ticked by quickly while Zahid was caught up in thought. Soon Islamabad spread out before him. The city was divided into districts, each measuring two kilometers square and identified by a single letter and number. As he traversed the H-8 district, he passed Shifra International

Hospital, where he had trained in medical physics. The hospital's cancer clinic was a renowned center of excellence, and it offered a coveted residency for physicists and radiation oncologists who wanted exposure to the latest technology.

During his two years at Shifra, Zahid gained an appreciation for the tremendous destructive power of radiation. It was an invaluable education for an aspiring nuclear terrorist.

His interest in the power of the atom pre-dated his formal training. Recognizing his son's precocious grasp of physics, his father, a nuclear engineer, nurtured what was to become Zahid's calling. He provided his son with an endless supply of reading material. Among Zahid's favorites were *The Curve of Binding Energy* by John McPhee, *The Making of the Atomic Bomb* by Richard Rhodes, and *Hiroshima* by John Hershey. And although Zahid did not become an engineer like his father, his parents took immense pride in his chosen field of study.

Yet, it was not his innate talent for physics that made Zahid's parents most proud. As Islamists, they thanked Allah for their son's commitment to the restoration of a Holy Caliphate and for arming him with the knowledge to serve in the coming war against the West.

Zahid was armed with more than knowledge. His job provided ready access to cobalt-60, iridium-192, and cesium-137—material that could form the nucleus of a dirty bomb. Such a weapon was capable of rendering square blocks uninhabitable. Even so, its damage paled in comparison to that of a nuclear bomb.

And this is what ignited Zahid's passion. He was captivated by the exquisite force locked within the heart of the atom. It was an unfathomable amount of energy—the energy that powered the universe and its myriad stars—and it could be unleashed in the form of an uncontrolled chain reaction. In mere millionths of a second, twenty-six kilos of weapons-grade uranium could produce an explosive force equal to thousands of tons of TNT. He imagined what it must have been like to witness the wholesale destruction of Hiroshima and Nagasaki and wished that he could have been present for those cataclysmic events.

He could not turn back the hands of time, but he could be instrumental in re-creating such moments in history—moments when cities were incinerated and their inhabitants killed by the thousands. This time it would be an American city that was reduced to rubble. There would be an extraordinary beauty to it, as the American people were dealt their long overdue justice.

Zahid's mind snapped back to the present moment as he pulled into the driveway of the neat bay-and-gable house. He parked his car in the detached garage and followed a short stone path through a carefully cultivated flower bed until he reached the front door. Before he could knock, al-Bakr stepped out to greet him.

"You are always punctual, Zahid." Al-Bakr kissed the man on each cheek. "Yasir and Hassan are in the family room waiting for you."

As he entered the room, two men sprang from an over-stuffed couch to embrace him. Yasir Syed was the first to reach Zahid. He was a dark-skinned wiry man with sinewy muscles. Tough and intelligent, Yasir was one of al-Bakr's most trusted warriors.

Hassan Jutt followed. A virtual mountain of a man, Hassan weighed as much as Yasir and Zahid combined.

Adequately intelligent, his job was to protect al-Bakr at all costs. It was a calling that Hassan accepted with great pride.

"I am sorry to break up this reunion, but we don't have the luxury of time. I suggest we get started," al-Bakr began as he pulled up a chair facing the three men.

"Two great tasks await us: The procurement of a nuclear core and its safe transportation to the target. I will focus on the issue of procurement. Zahid, I will ask you to discuss shipment."

He waited for a nod of acknowledgement before proceeding.

"We have been counting on our friend, General Malik, to serve as the conduit to the nuclear material. He is a very arrogant man, too much so for his own good, but we will deal with that issue another time. What matters now is that Malik acquiesced to our request. He will facilitate the transfer of a twenty-six-kilogram uranium core."

"It was that simple?" Zahid was surprised.

"I didn't say it was simple. The general is as cunning as a fox and as dangerous as a viper. He required a bit of persuasion. But he eventually made the right choice."

Al-Bakr made eye contact with each of the three men, ensuring he had their full attention. "You will pay a visit to the POF. You will be dressed as Army officers and carry orders for the transport of a nuclear core. General Patel has promised a warm reception, courtesy of his son-in-law, Major Barr. Barr will guide you to the core, instruct you on its safe transportation, and then send you on your way.

"Before departing for Karachi, you will return to this house, pick me up, and drop off Hassan. Is that understood?"

"Yes, Sir," came the response in unison.

"Now, Zahid, tell us what happens once we arrive in Karachi."

"My job is to ensure that the core remains undetected during its 7,000-mile voyage to the West. The success of that journey will rely on several individuals who have been carefully selected. When we arrive in Karachi, you will meet the first of our contacts—a man named Shalil.

"Shalil's company is located a few hundred meters from the Karachi Container Terminal. His job is to conceal our package within a cargo container that will then be loaded onto the *Jasmine*—an older ship flying under Panamanian registry."

"Who is this man, Shalil?" al-Bakr questioned.

"He's in the shipping business . . . primarily low-level smuggling. According to Ahmed Dar, he's our best option."

Dar was a key player in the UIS network with operational responsibility for southern Pakistan. He was based in Karachi. Zahid knew that Dar's recommendation would be accepted without contest by al-Bakr.

"And the ship . . . why are you recommending the *Jasmine?*" al-Bakr asked.

"Its captain has a family whom he wishes to keep safe. The ship will make a two-day voyage to Nhava Sheva (Mumbai, India), where the cargo container will be transferred to the *Positano* for the final leg of its voyage," Zahid explained.

"And why the *Positano?*" al-Bakr inquired.

"The ship will be laden with containers full of scrap steel, which renders them virtually impervious to x-rays. If our container is inspected, the package, which is not much bigger than a softball, will simply disappear among the mass of metal. Once we're on board, it will be a twenty-two-day voyage from Mumbai to Halifax, Nova Scotia."

Al-Bakr questioned, "Why Halifax? Why not a port in New York?"

"Halifax is within striking distance of America's eastern seaboard, but less rigorous in its screening of cargo entering the port. We will still have to cross the border, but we will be assisted by our friends in America."

"Will the captains know what they are transporting?" Yasir asked Zahid.

"They will know that it is something very dangerous, and thus very valuable."

"And what will keep them from turning on us?" he pressed.

"Three heavily armed men who wouldn't hesitate to kill them."

Hassan interrupted, focusing his attention on al-Bakr. "I think it would be wise to have a fourth. What am I to do here? Sit in the kitchen all day and bake baklava like some woman?"

Al-Bakr stood and walked toward his faithful servant, who reflexively rose to his feet.

He placed his hands atop Hassan's massive shoulders. "Your sense of duty is admirable, but there is nothing to worry about. Zahid has taken appropriate precautions. As for why you must stay behind, there may be some cleaning up to do. Loose ends in the form of two generals who need to be buried with their secrets."

Hassan let out a small grunt signifying his agreement before sitting down.

Zahid resumed his briefing. "The captain of the *Jasmine* has a wife and two children living in Lahore. Ahmed Dar provided the man with several recent photographs taken of the children on their way to school. The message was received. From what we've been told, he's already lost one child."

"And what of the *Positano's* captain?" Hassan asked.

"He has a fondness for cash. He received $100,000 as an advance payment and the promise of an additional $400,000 once the container clears the port in Halifax. That's more money than he could save in a lifetime and enough to guarantee safe passage for our cargo."

Al-Bakr rose to his feet. "Tomorrow we will walk through every detail of the plan a final time. There can be no mistakes—no chance of failure. Go now and pray. Pray that Allah bestows his blessing upon us. Pray that he condemns the greatest enemy of Islam to a fiery death. And pray that the horror we create in one city foments terror across the vast American landscape."

CHAPTER FIVE

Washington, D.C.

THERE WAS LITTLE TO LIKE ABOUT ELLIOT FISHER. He was corpulent, disheveled, and downright nasty. Hart abhorred the man, but even Hart would concede that Fisher rarely called a meeting without having something important to lay on the table.

Fisher held a unique position in the National Security Agency—he was privy to the entirety of the agency's data collection and entrusted with the job of identifying significant patterns of activity at the highest level of analysis. That required a phenomenal level of cognitive horsepower and a blend of superlative quantitative and creative skills. In short, Fisher was brilliant. The problem was that he was too brilliant to tolerate the rest of the human race.

"You have our full attention," Marvin Kahn, Deputy Director for Operations at CIA, told Fisher by way of launching the discussion. "I assume you've discerned something of interest?"

"No. Actually, I haven't discerned anything."

Hart fidgeted uncomfortably in his chair, struggling to suppress his hostility toward Fisher. He said tersely,

"Perhaps you could enlighten us, Elliot, about why you called this meeting?"

Fisher bristled at the Commander's informality.

"Don't you see, Commander?"

"No, Elliot, I don't. So why don't you spell it out for me?"

Kahn was well aware of the enmity that existed between the two men and intervened before things could escalate. He said, "I think what the Commander is requesting is a bit more information, Mr. Fisher."

"It's too quiet. That's the problem." Fisher explained.

"What's too quiet?" Hart was fast losing his patience.

"The entire network. The level of chatter has diminished by two standard deviations over the past two weeks. I've never seen it dip like that before. There's always a flurry of activity before something hits."

"Are you suggesting that this time there may be a void rather than chatter before something bad happens?" Kahn asked.

"That's precisely what I've been trying to tell you since I sat down at this table."

"You know you're a smug little bastard, don't you?" Hart asked.

"No one has ever called me *little*, Commander. So I'll take that as a compliment. You have your anachronistic methods of deriving intelligence, and I have modern tools. I suggest you pay heed to what I'm telling you today. To borrow your crude vernacular, the shit is about to hit the fan."

With that, Fisher stood and abruptly walked out.

"No lectures," Hart advised Kahn, who was already pointing his finger and ready to tear into the Commander.

"God damn it, John! We all know he's a prick. Even he knows he's a prick. Can you just keep your thoughts to yourself long enough for the man to say his piece and leave?"

"Yes, Sir. I will not tell the little bastard that he's a little bastard again. I promise."

"Get out of here and try to find out what the hell is causing the crazies to suddenly go dark."

Hart spent the balance of the day trying to shine a light on a black hole. How in the hell was he supposed to illuminate a void in communications among crazy jihadists? Frustrated, he finally left the office at nine o'clock. He stopped by the gym for an hour before heading home. Dinner was courtesy of Stauffer's, the usual fare when Liz was in Atlanta. He caught thirty minutes of the news and then turned off the television. A minute later, his phone vibrated. It was Liz calling to say goodnight.

Hart answered. "Hi, I'm sorry, but I am not available to take your call. If you would please leave a message at the beep, I will call you back as soon as possible . . . beep."

"I love you, but you have the sophisticated humor of a ten-year-old," Liz responded.

"What do you expect? My emotional growth was stunted at an early age. In my mind, I'm still pre-pubescent."

"Oh, that's a good one. I'll remind you of that the next time you reach for my pants."

"How are you, darling?" Hart asked warmly.

"I'm fine. I think we're actually making headway on the Ebola vaccine. It goes into Phase I trials next week. That's always a little dicey."

"I hate to have you messing around with those hemorrhagic viruses."

"Well, at least this time I'm in a level IV bio-containment lab rather than fighting to contain such pathogens in a public outbreak," she said, referring to the bio-attack the previous year.

"Point taken."

"And how was your day, cowboy?" Her pet name referred to more than Hart's macho attitude. He'd grown up on a 640-acre cattle ranch just outside of Kalispell, Montana. The eldest of three boys, Hart's early education included driving cattle, mucking horse stalls, and shooting coyotes with his .22 rifle. Life doesn't get any better.

"My day? It was interesting."

"How so?"

"I learned that, in addition to being concerned when there's an abundance of chatter from the crazies, we should be worried when it's too quiet."

"Seriously? Who thinks of these things?"

"I'd better not share that over the phone, but the nicest word I can think of to describe him is *putz*."

"Oh, then I know who you're talking about. He's a royal pain in the ass, but he's the smartest human being on the GSA payroll."

"That's not saying very much, present company excluded."

"We both know he has a personality disorder. But he's right about ninety percent of the time. It's pretty tough to find fault with that kind of batting average. Have you thought about what it means if he's right?"

"I don't want go there."

"You sound anxious, Commander."

"Seals don't get anxious."

"Come on, John . . . drop the tough guy act. It's me. I know that under that uber macho exterior lives a vulnerable little boy."

"Oh please, Doctor. You sound like some kind of shrink. Last time I looked at your credentials, they proclaimed you an expert in virology, not psychoanalysis."

"Have it your way. What would you like to talk about— the weather?"

She knew how to push his buttons. Of course he felt anxious. It was functional. It helped to keep him alive in dangerous situations. There was nothing regressive about it.

"No. I'll answer your question. Yes, I feel anxious. When I know there are millions of people who would love nothing more than to destroy our country, I think anxiety is a wholly appropriate response. Maybe some people can shrug off things like that. Sorry, darling, but I'm not one of them."

"Why so defensive, Commander? I was just trying to get you to lower your guard. You need to trust me, John."

"I do trust you, Elizabeth."

"I'm not talking about state secrets. I'm talking about something you guard even more closely—your fears."

"Wow, and I thought this was going to be a pleasant little chat before bed. I didn't know we had a problem."

"Don't go there, John. I just want you to feel safe with me. I don't know that you've ever fully trusted anyone before."

"People let you down, Liz. It can be a pretty big fall."

"Who has let you down, John? I mean really."

"Maybe it's not who has let me down. Maybe it's who I have let down," Hart confessed. "I'll talk to you tomorrow, darling."

"Good night, John."

As he hung up the phone, a torrent of images flooded his mind . . . long-buried memories that dated back to childhood.

Growing up on a ranch had been idyllic for the first eleven years of John's life, but then things changed, and they would never again be the same.

On a warm July morning, surrounded by an endless blue sky, John and his youngest brother, Matthew, headed toward the cattle pond. His mother was busy with household chores and had promised to bake him a cherry pie as a reward for keeping an eye out for Matthew.

The boys meandered through the pasture, mindful where they stepped. When they reached the pond, John reached down and picked up a flat rock the size of his index finger.

With a sharp snap of his arm, John sent the rock skipping across the water. "One, two, three, four, five," he counted quickly as the rock danced across the surface before disappearing into the muddy brown water at the far edge of the pond.

"Let's see you beat that," he said as he handed his seven-year-old brother a rock.

Matthew did his best to emulate his older brother, but to no avail. The rock sank rather than skipped. John reached over and patted him on the shoulder.

"You just need some more practice. Let me get you some rocks. You can work on that throw of yours while I hunt prairie dogs." He pointed to his .22 caliber rifle with a 4X telescopic sight.

There was nothing cute about prairie dogs. Their deep burrows were like hidden traps awaiting a cow's hoof. John knew his father would be grateful for every critter he killed. One of their herd had broken a leg just the other day, forcing it to be put down.

Before setting off on his hunt, John assembled a pile of ten or fifteen rocks, admonishing Matthew to stay away from the water and off the rickety dock. He promised to return in fifteen minutes. He picked up his weapon and headed for the spot where he had last laid eyes on a varmint . . . just over a hill out of sight of the pond.

Luck must have been smiling on him that morning, for as he cleared the rise he could see the beady brown eyes of his enemy. He crouched low, moving a step at a time, until he was close enough to take the shot. Raising the rifle to eye-level, he moved the barrel until the critter was visible through the scope. He drew a deep breath and held it . . . then squeezed the trigger. The rifle made a sharp report as the prairie dog fell dead. Through the telescopic sight, he could see a small hole oozing blood below its ear. With his chin held high, John walked the fifty yards to collect his bounty.

Prairie dog in hand, John cleared the rise, giving him a full view of the pond, but Matthew was nowhere in sight. A wave of panic shot through his body as he dropped the carcass and ran toward the murky water shouting his brother's name. There was no response.

He leaped onto the dock and raced to its end, stopping himself just as he about to careen off the edge. Matthew lay face-down in the water.

"No!" he screamed, his voice reverberating off the embankment.

He jumped in, grabbed Matthew's arm, and pulled him to the edge of the pond, then onto the mud bank. Tears streamed down John's cheeks as he pounded his clenched fists on his little brother's chest, hoping to restore breath. But Matthew didn't move. In desperation, John leapt to his feet and made a mad dash to the house. He burst through the door. A flurry of words spilled from his mouth as he described the horror of what had happened. His mother stood, momentarily transfixed, then dropped a heavy, ceramic mixing bowl where she stood. It shattered on the floor.

More than his brother died that day. The joy that had once permeated every acre of land vanished forever. His mother never surrendered her grief. His father never forgave him—not only for the loss of Matthew, but also for the death of his wife's spirit. Though John did everything in his power to win back their affection, nothing was ever enough. Not excelling in sports, nor becoming an Eagle Scout, nor graduating first in his class. Not even a full-ride scholarship to Stanford.

That July morning, when the endless blue sky had seemed to herald a beautiful day ahead, became John Hart's defining moment.

Elliot Fisher sat in his office at NSA. With the lights turned off, only his silhouette was visible, thanks to a few watts of illumination thrown off by the diodes on his monitoring equipment. He liked it that way—listening to others while remaining invisible.

His attention was riveted on a conversation between a man and woman on encrypted cell phones. The only threat they represented was to Fisher himself. He was hoping to uncover a way to exploit the man's vulnerabilities. It was someone he despised, a Neanderthal—Commander John Hart.

Fisher's fixation was not limited to Hart. He also scrutinized every word Liz uttered. He wouldn't hesitate to get at the man through the woman. As he listened, he thumbed through both of their dossiers—background information he had illicitly cobbled together from classified sources. Hart's ghosts were there in black and white—including a copy of the police report following Matthew's death. He was certain that Liz's vulnerabilities were every bit as tantalizing as Hart's, but they remained far more opaque. By comparison to Hart, her childhood had been a fairy tale.

Liz Wilkins had grown up in Chapel Hill, North Carolina, the only child of a family physician married to an academician. Thomas Wilkins, her father, was part of the very fabric of the community—ushering in multiple generations, then caring for them throughout their lives. Her mother taught creative writing to graduate students at the University of North Carolina.

They lived just off Franklin Street, a few blocks from the arboretum. On weekends, her father took his young daughter on house calls. It was an invaluable lesson in the gift of life, as well as its fragility.

Liz flourished academically, but she was anything but bookish. She possessed the creative flair of her mother and the spunk to go with it. Liz's friends described her as deadly serious about studies and joyfully mischievous at other times.

Despite being raised a loyal Tar Heel, Liz accepted an academic scholarship to Duke. From the moment she set foot on the campus, her heart was set on pre-med. She fed her creative spirit with writing classes taught by the legendary poet, Helen Bevington.

Liz graduated summa cum laude, earning her a spot in medical school at Dartmouth. She went on to complete a residency in infectious disease at Johns Hopkins, as well as a Master's in epidemiology. She had the privilege of being mentored by D. A. Henderson, a man who had won the Presidential Medal of Freedom for his role in eradicating smallpox.

Meticulous, creative, and insightful, Liz soared through the ranks at the CDC, eventually being given responsibility for the Centers' Bio-Level IV Laboratory. The only thing missing in her life was a relationship . . . until John Hart entered the picture.

CHAPTER SIX

OUTFITTED IN BLACK FATIGUES AND COMBAT BOOTS, the three men stood shoulder to shoulder as they prepared for morning prayer. Leather holsters hung low on their hips, each harboring a military issue Sig Sauer P226. Black berets remained folded and tucked into their belts.

Raising their arms high above their heads, they proclaimed *Allah Akbar,* then prostrated themselves on prayer rugs fringed in gold. When finished with their recitations, the men bowed a final time to the east before rising. Their fate, the very fate of Islam, was now in the hands of God.

Their homage paid, the men moved toward the living room where al-Bakr was waiting to engage them. He motioned for them to be seated before launching into an aggressive interrogation.

"Zahid, what will you see as you approach the POF?"

"The street will divide with the left three lanes passing beneath an archway at the Jinnah Gate. We will continue to the main gate, where we will be greeted by an armed security detail."

"How many men will there be in the detail?" al-Bakr pressed.

"Two men, who will be wearing army khakis. They will have red berets."

"What will you say to the soldiers?" The pace of al-Bakr's questions was accelerating.

"Before saying anything, I will return their salute. Then I will hand them my orders for the transfer of a weapon."

"What else?"

"My ID—my Strategic Planning Division ID."

"Don't wait for them to ask for it," al-Bakr shot back.

"And then?"

"We will wait while they verify our orders and summon Major Barr to escort us. After that, we will be under his command."

"And once you've procured the nuclear material?"

"We will ensure we have the precise specifications for its diameter, mass, and composition before returning so we may furnish that information to our friends abroad."

"Hassan, what are your responsibilities?" al-Bakr asked.

"To ensure the team's safety. When we return to the house, I will stay and await your further orders."

"Yasir—your role?"

"To keep a close eye on the major and to do as instructed by Zahid."

"Good."

Satisfied, al-Bakr dismissed the men. Now began the hardest part of the journey—waiting for it to commence.

Eager to prove their mettle, the three jihadists boarded the van at 4:10 PM. Their destination was forty-five kilometers to the northwest in an area known as Wah Cantt.

Built in 1951 to address the military needs of a newly independent Pakistan, the POF had burgeoned into a sprawling complex devoted to death. More than a dozen factories spewed out an astonishing assortment of weapons that supplied munitions to not only the Pakistani army, but to the armed forces of more than forty nations, civilized and rogue. Two facilities, however, were absent from any map of the POF: a uranium enrichment facility built with Chinese assistance and a depot for nuclear weapons, which was their destination.

Passing under the Jinnah archway, the van stopped at the first check-point. Two sentries approached, each carrying an MPF5A2 sub-machine gun. It was an impressive weapon capable of churning out 800 rounds per minute—enough firepower to dissuade all but a small army. The POF had not always been so heavily fortified, not until a few unfortunate incidents involving suicide bombers had brought dramatic changes to its security. Heavily armed guards were only the most visible layer of protection. There were many more hidden safeguards that were evident only to the trained eye.

A brief flash of light atop one of the buildings caught Zahid's attention. Maybe it was nothing more than his eyes playing tricks on him—or maybe it was a glint of sunlight reflecting off the polished glass of a sniper's scope. At such a short distance, it would be child's play for an SSG Army sniper to bury a 7.62 millimeter bullet in the crown of Zahid's head. His skull would explode like a gourd being smashed against hard pavement—too fast for him to feel a thing.

One of the sentries halted five meters short of the vehicle, removed the automatic weapon from his shoulder, and leveled it at the van's windshield. The other man approached Zahid, who was carefully extracting the orders from his pocket.

The soldier snapped a salute the instant he spotted Zahid's captain's bars. He then motioned to his comrade to lower his weapon.

Zahid returned the salute, handing his orders and ID to the sentry. The man returned to the guardhouse and picked up the phone.

Zahid could see the man nodding furiously as though responding to a stern cascade of commands. He hung up the phone and shouted to the other sentry to clear a path for the vehicle.

"Park in the red zone," the man grunted, pointing to a small area just south of the guardhouse. "Major Barr will accompany you. He will be here shortly."

The soldier returned Zahid's documents, then raised the heavy metal gate allowing the van to enter.

A kilometer away, Barr was preparing to join the men. He felt no exhilaration, no adrenaline coursing through his veins. Rather, the officer was anxious and exhausted following a sleepless night and an interminably long day. Each minute was filled with recriminations. The thought of assisting terrorists in the acquisition of a nuclear device sickened him. He was about to become complicit in one of the greatest acts of mass murder in human history. Yet the alternative seemed worse.

Barr was a loyal soldier operating under orders—those of General Patel. How could he betray his father-in-law? The man was responsible for his rapid ascension to the rank of Major. Barr knew that if he toed the line, future promotions would follow. The rank of Colonel would soon be in reach.

But if he intervened—if he countermanded orders and tried to stop al-Bakr's men—he would likely die. If the jihadists didn't kill him, his father-in-law would. Even if he escaped such a cruel fate and the general was arrested, Barr's wife would never forgive him for turning on her father.

Five minutes. That's how much time he had before his actions would forever determine his future. He jumped into the jeep and headed for the red zone. When he lurched to a stop several feet from the van, he was no closer to a decision. With no resolution in sight, he climbed slowly out of the driver's seat and walked toward his destiny.

"Major." Zahid acknowledged the officer with a swift salute. "My orders, Sir."

"I'll ride with you. Follow the perimeter road to the left. You will stay on it past the factories. Keep going until the road ends."

"Yes, Sir," Zahid responded.

Before stepping into the van, Barr discreetly loosened the strap securing his pistol and removed the safety. His actions did not escape Yasir's scrutiny, who responded in kind.

Zahid was surprised by the scope of the installation. They drove past a uniform factory, a small arms plant, and a high explosives facility before clearing the western expanse of the complex. No more major buildings loomed on the horizon.

After a few minutes, Zahid could make out the faint outlines of a bunker. The structure came into focus just as the perimeter road ended. A gravel road continued—but first they needed to clear a security gate fortified with heavily armed guards.

"It's called the forbidden zone," Barr explained as he pointed past the gate.

"Why is that?" Zahid questioned.

"Uninvited guests may get in, but they sure as hell won't get out."

Four soldiers guarded the gate, including one straddling a jeep-mounted Chinese 12.7mm machine gun. It was formidable protection against a head-on attack by an enemy. But there were thousands of hectares of open land to either side that needed to be guarded.

"Your mind is very active, Captain. Are you wondering what prevents someone from circumventing our security?" Barr ventured.

"The thought did cross my mind."

"Do you see the small signs dotting the land to your left and right? If so, you will have your answer."

Zahid focused where the major had pointed. There were innumerable metal signs embedded in the ground. Though he could not discern their words of warning, he could make out the skull and crossbones.

"One of the products we manufacture here are land mines," Barr explained. "There are more than 5,000 of them in the forbidden zone."

Barr started to elaborate, but the approach of a tall slender soldier silenced him. As the man drew near, he saluted.

"Major, it is good to see you again, Sir."

"And you, Sergeant. Gesturing to Zahid, he added, "The captain here has our orders."

Zahid surrendered them, along with his ID.

"It will just be a moment," the soldier advised.

"Take your time Sergeant; we're not in any hurry." Turning to Zahid, he added, "I'm going to have a look, if you don't mind," as he reached for the door handle.

Yasir moved his hand closer to the grip on his pistol.

The sergeant returned moments later. He handed Zahid his orders and ID along with a small white card bearing a series of numbers. He proceeded to the side of the van where Barr was standing. As he approached the senior officer, he saluted crisply.

"Major, I believe the strap on your pistol is loose. You may wish to buckle it, Sir. I hope you don't mind my suggestion."

Without intention, the guard was giving Barr an opportunity to end the craziness. All the major had to do was reach for his pistol. Instead of securing it, he could dump the eleven-shot clip into the three men in the van. He had little doubt that hundreds of bullets would follow from the guards at the gate.

Barr froze.

Yasir began to slowly extract his pistol from its holster.

"Are you alright, Sir?"

"Yes, Sergeant. Thanks for the heads-up." Barr secured the strap on his holster and climbed back into the van.

Yasir replaced his pistol.

"A reminder, Major: Your men need to stay on the gravel or paved surfaces only. We had an accident last week. I'm sure you heard about it."

"I understand that one of our civilian contractors lost a leg."

"And then some," the man responded.

"We'll be careful," Barr assured the sergeant. "I believe these men would like to keep their legs and other body parts intact."

The sergeant waved them through. Their destination was 600 meters ahead. The underground bunker looked like a giant grave—a rectangular mass of earth rising five to six feet above the surface. It wasn't the visible portion of the bunker that interested the men, but rather the thirty to forty feet of underground storage hidden beneath the surface.

Two perimeter fences surrounded the bunker. Each topped out at just over four meters including the razor wire on top. The fences were separated by approximately ten feet of land—every inch of which was sowed with deadly landmines.

"From here on I suggest you stay in lock-step with me," Barr said as he climbed out of the vehicle and walked toward an intercom.

"State your business," a monotone voice demanded from the tinny speaker.

"Major Ali Barr, SPF, with transfer orders." Barr removed his mirrored sunglasses and peered into the video camera adjacent to the intercom. It would take a few seconds before the retinal scan confirmed his identity.

"Welcome back, Major." The voice on the other end took on a tone of familiarity.

"Thank you, Sergeant Kor."

"We'll see you momentarily, Sir."

Turning to Zahid, Barr pointed to a small loading dock. "Park it there."

As they made their way to the bunker's entrance, Barr asked Zahid for the white card he'd been given. Barr entered the seven-digit access code printed on it . . . numbers which had been randomly generated when their transfer orders had been verified. The electronic lock sprang open.

A single soldier was waiting to escort the men. The soldier saluted Barr before speaking. "Major, if you and your men would follow me, please. You know the protocol. An inventory control officer will meet us below."

The soldier then strode purposefully down two flights of metal stairs toward a cavernous subterranean warehouse.

The warehouse floor was separated by long wide aisles lined with metal storage lockers, each of which bore an electronic alphanumeric display. The security of their contents was ensured by a large black combination lock on each storage unit.

"May I see your orders, Major?" the officer responsible for inventory control asked in a firm but polite tone.

"Of course," Barr turned to Zahid, who handed the documents to the man.

The officer continued, "Major, I am afraid that I do not recognize your men. I thought I was familiar with all of the SPF soldiers handling transports out of the POF."

"You must have an eidetic memory," Barr joked.

"Actually I do, Sir." The officer responded with deadly seriousness.

Allah was giving Barr one more chance to prevent the carnage . . . to foil the plot before it succeeded.

"I don't believe I owe you an explanation, Lieutenant, but for what it is worth, these men were transferred from Gujrnwala two weeks ago. Do you have any more questions?"

"Not for the moment."

The lieutenant looked down at the fourteen-digit alphanumeric code contained in Zahid's orders, then moved rapidly toward a locker bearing the matching code.

Turning his back to conceal the combination, the man spun the large dial to the left, then right, then left before grabbing the handle on the locker and thrusting it open.

"Last step, Major. We need to verify the tag on the core," the officer explained as he pointed toward a metal box.

Zahid watched as the man removed the small heavy box from the locker. He opened it long enough to aim a handheld scanner at a thin piece of transparent film bearing a barcode. As he pulled the trigger, the top of the uranium sphere was bathed in ruby red luminescence from the scanner's laser.

He waited for the reassuring beep of recognition from the scanner. But no sound followed. His eyes darted from the sphere to Zahid. Zahid struggled to take a breath, his heart racing. He forced a smile at the man, a smug smile that politely communicated *fuck you*.

The officer was the final guardian at the gate—the lone soldier now capable of preventing the misappropriation of Pakistan's most precious asset. Without shifting his eyes, the man pulled the scanner's trigger a second time. It beeped, confirming the core's identity. He held Zahid in his gaze for a few more unnerving seconds before finally turning away.

The lieutenant latched the box securely before handing a requisition form to Barr for his signature.

"You are cleared, Major."

With those four words, the core of a fifteen-kiloton nuclear bomb began its long journey from a hidden bunker in the heart of Pakistan to the eastern seaboard of North America. The first hurdle had been cleared, but many more remained.

CHAPTER SEVEN

December 1
Islamabad to Karachi

CONTEMPT OOZED FROM EVERY PORE OF HIS BODY as al-Bakr emerged from the house to address his uninvited guest. "Major Barr, what an unexpected pleasure." He paused as he sized the man up and down. "I must confess that I am surprised to see you."

"My orders are to accompany the core until the end of its journey."

"Orders? From whom, pray tell? General Patel?"

"No Sir. General Patel's orders only pertained to the POF. It was General Malik who thought you would appreciate having a nuclear-trained officer at your disposal. He said you could consider it an insurance policy."

"Ah, so the general thinks we need insurance. How thoughtful of him, but I am afraid that you will be traveling thousands of miles from home for no purpose."

"Those are my orders."

"So be it." Al-Bakr gestured for him to move to the unoccupied bench in the back of the van where Hassan had been seated.

"We will be leaving shortly. Make yourself comfortable, Major. There's a toilet in the garage if you need it."—a not-so-subtle insult, since decorum demanded he offer Barr the comforts of his home.

Al-Bakr's eyes shifted to Zahid, whose head hung low like a dog anticipating a beating. Not a word was spoken until they were in the house and out of earshot.

"What in the hell is wrong with you?" al-Bakr barked.

"I had no choice. What was I supposed to do, kill him?"

"Someone is going to have to."

"Fine." Zahid removed the gun from his holster, his eyes hot with anger.

"Put that away. Not now . . . not here, but the man must not accompany us to America. I don't need any superfluous baggage on our trip," al-Bakr scolded.

"I understand. When it's time, I will take care of the problem." He returned the pistol to its holster, exhaling as if to cast away his ill temper.

"Give me the specifications for the core so I can contact our friends abroad," al-Bakr ordered, "then you can go babysit the major until we are ready to leave."

Though it felt harsh, Zahid knew it was a minor rebuke for a major fuck-up. He did as ordered.

Al-Bakr sent an encrypted text via satellite phone. It contained nothing more than a string of numbers: 7.68 . . . 26.12 . . . 90.

Karachi was twenty hours by road from the suburbs of Islamabad. It was 7:30 PM when Zahid climbed behind the wheel. Tired from not having slept the previous night, he feared the hypnotic lure of the long night's drive. The sun would not rise again for eleven hours.

"I suggest everyone get some rest. There's much work ahead," al-Bakr advised.

"Your break will come soon," he promised Zahid before closing his eyes and letting out a long, sonorous sigh.

As the others slept, Zahid fought to stay alert. Thirty-six hours without sleep was claiming a toll on him. He pulled two white pills from a small vial tucked in his pocket and downed them without water. *That should keep me going through the night,* he thought. Such practices were, of course, forbidden by the Quran, but the safe transportation of his crew and cargo outweighed all other concerns.

The van passed through a succession of towns beginning with Bhalwal, a rich agricultural area famous for its oranges. Zahid imagined how good a succulent orange dripping with juice would taste at this moment.

Next came the city of Chinoit, where the luminous glow of the full moon combined with lights atop minarets to illuminate the city's exquisite architecture. Spires rose out of the shadows, revealing ancient palaces as well as modern mosques. But there was no time to gawk. With little traffic, the city soon disappeared behind them as if in a dream.

After eight hours on the road, the van approached Multan. Zahid knew it as the City of Sufis, a town thought to date back more than 5,000 years. He began to daydream about life in the millennia before the Prophet walked the earth. But the images of Mohammed vanished in a heartbeat as he was jerked back by al-Bakr's voice.

"Take the Vehari Road exit. I'm sure you will find a petrol station. I trust that everyone could use a break," al-Bakr ordered his disciple.

Pulling into a Shell station, Major Barr and Yasir piled out of the van's side door. Zahid reached for his door handle, but al-Bakr put his hand on his shoulder, gently restraining him.

"Let them go. We will join them in a moment."

Zahid eased back into his seat.

"Zahid, you are my protégé, my most trusted warrior. I must have unwavering trust in you. Such trust is a gift that can be shattered in an instant and never regained. You do understand that?"

"I don't know what you are talking about."

"Don't compound the issue with a lie. You're far too wise for that." Al-Bakr's tone was intense.

Zahid looked straight at his mentor before lowering his head. It was the second time he'd been reprimanded in the span of less than a dozen hours. Without a word, he reached into his pocket and extracted the small glass vial containing a dozen white pills. He handed it to al-Bakr.

"I was merely trying to keep us safe," he confessed.

"I believe that's what you thought you were doing. We all have our vices, Zahid. If we don't control them, we are little more than animals. I trust we will never again need to speak of this matter."

It was not a question, but a clear message that such behavior would not be tolerated.

Al-Bakr stepped out of the van, dropped the vial of methamphetamine on the concrete, and crushed it beneath the heel of his shoe. Zahid knew he had reached the limit of al-Bakr's grace. There could be no more mistakes.

Karachi was still twelve hours to the south. The meth he had ingested would get him through the drive, but he knew a hard crash would follow. He counted on the reprieve promised by al-Bakr—sleep, precious sleep, before they embarked on their journey to America.

Major Barr sat silently in the back of the van, as if asleep, but his mind was on fire. He had hoped to leave a note in the bathroom—a call for help, but fear of discovery by his companions stopped him. He needed a new plan, a way to break free, before they arrived in Karachi.

CHAPTER EIGHT

THE TWIN TOWERS WERE A DEFINING FEATURE of the New York skyline when al-Bakr began recruiting his sleeper cell. His mission was simple: to find the brightest young minds in nuclear engineering from among thousands of loyal Islamists, then plant them strategically, ready to be harvested when needed.

After lying dormant for more than fifteen years, the cell was about to be awakened. Buried deep in America's heartland, its three members were now well entrenched in their adopted communities—occupying jobs in strategically selected organizations. All were naturalized citizens. Tariq Kuni was the cell's leader.

Tariq had grown up in the shadows of the Hindu-Kush mountain range in northwestern Pakistan. It was a place where the awesome power of God was manifest in peaks that stretched 25,000 feet toward the heavens.

It filled the young man with awe, forever instilling a reverence for the beauty of God's handiwork. But the mountains shaped more than his mind. His body was hardened by summers spent hiking vertical trails at altitudes where the oxygen thinned, turning his fingertips blue. He had learned many lessons from the mountains, not the least of which was the wisdom of patience when approaching a formidable task.

Such natural beauty was far from bountiful in his adopted home of Kansas. Here there were no mountains, barely even hills. Yet even the monotonous plains, which reached to the horizon, brought their own gift. Unobstructed skies flushed with color with the rising sun. Clouds burned with dazzling shades of yellow and crimson at sunset before giving up their color and fading to gray.

The morning of December 2 promised a beautiful day. A brilliant golden orb emerged from a low-hanging bank of clouds—the final remnant of a powerful storm that had swept through the small town of Burlington, Kansas the previous night.

Tariq welcomed the sun's warmth as it pierced his bedroom windows and dispelled the morning's chill. He stood in front of a mirror preparing for work. His short thick fingers struggled with the small buttons on the collar of his starched white shirt. Finally conquering the challenge, he cinched the knot on his conservative red tie until it was taut. He made a final check in the mirror and then moved toward the bedroom door.

There was an expected level of decorum for senior managers at the Tallgrass Prairie Nuclear Power Plant. While some of his colleagues challenged that tradition, Tariq adhered to protocol. The Pakistani never wanted to stand out, particularly as a foreigner in a xenophobic state.

It had not been easy for the single engineer to integrate into a homogenous town where diversity was measured by Protestant denominations, not colors of the skin. Here, virtually everyone was white. After fifteen years, Tariq had been marginally accepted. People no longer turned their backs on him in the grocery store or asked if he was *colored*.

Tariq took a final sip of coffee before setting the cup in the sink and moving toward the front door. Mid-stride, he stopped abruptly and listened as three rapid beeps emanated from his cell phone. The tone signaled the arrival of an encrypted message. Experience suggested that it would prove to be nothing more than a drill—a periodic reminder from abroad to remain vigilant. But that didn't stop Tariq from praying.

He prayed that the time had finally come when his years of lying in wait were over . . . when God would put his skills to use in battling the infidels. Donning his reading glasses, he reached for the phone. As the screen flashed to life, he saw a string of numbers: 7.68 . . . 26.12 . . . 90. He blinked in disbelief, but the image persisted.

The first number referred to the diameter of the nuclear core as measured in centimeters; the second figure was a precise measurement of its mass in kilograms. The final number represented the percentage of weapons-grade uranium composing the core. Together, these specifications would allow for the fabrication of the non-nuclear components to transform the core into a fully functioning nuclear weapon.

He transcribed the numbers onto a small piece of flash-paper, which he tucked into his wallet. A second alert then sounded, followed by a message containing five characters: 12–28, the date of the core's arrival in the United States. That gave Tariq less than a month to complete his mission.

He acknowledged receipt of the message with a simple code: 022177, his date of birth. Next he sent a short message to the two other members of the cell, Abdul Rana and Habib Faqir.

Within seconds of reading Tariq's text, Abdul and Habib both responded with a single word—Yes. According to plan, they would receive a call from Tariq later that evening in which he would impart instructions via a coded script.

Although Tariq abhorred being late, work would have to wait an additional fifteen minutes. He needed the time to submit an electronic order for fabrication of the bomb's housing. There were only a handful of machine shops in America that he trusted with the task, and Tariq had long ago selected one. The fabricators would be clueless as to the purpose of the tube they were manufacturing; they would know only that it was to be shipped to Burlington, Kansas, upon completion.

Abdul Rana was a quiet man who kept to himself. That made him a bit of an aberration in the beer-drinking, tailgating environment of Advanced Defense Works. It was, after all, a manufacturing plant where blue collar jobs outnumbered management five to one. But there was a deadly seriousness to the work done in suburban Kansas City, Missouri, and every employee knew it.

Advanced Defense Works was the principal source for many of the non-nuclear components of nuclear weapons— things like beryllium reflectors, tampers, neutron sources, and the other key ingredients needed to maintain the nation's nuclear stockpile. The plant was so critical to national defense that it once numbered among the former Soviet Union's highest priority targets in the event of nuclear war.

It was a fact of which the locals remained blissfully unaware . . . until a series of articles had appeared in recent years. Among them was a story that broke in the September 22, 2014 edition of the *New York Times*. It described "a sprawling new plant here in a former soybean field [that] makes the mechanical guts of America's atomic warheads. Bigger than the Pentagon, full of futuristic gear and thousands of workers . . . " the new plant replaced a former facility located at the Danforth Federal Complex a few miles away. Suddenly the plant's clandestine work was front and center.

A metallurgical engineer by training, Abdul started out on the factory line and worked his way up. It was a circuitous road to management, particularly for someone with a doctorate. But the extra time spent in the trenches earned him something invaluable—the respect of people destined to become his direct reports. These were plain-speaking, hard-working folks from the Show-Me state. People wise enough to be contemptuous of managers who had never gotten their hands dirty.

Abdul was viewed as a "lifer," someone who intended to spend his entire career at the plant. He certainly had a good start, with more than fifteen years behind him. Those years allowed him to amass not only a treasure trove of knowledge, but also an impressive collection of items critical to the construction of a nuclear bomb.

Habib Faqir completed the triumvirate. He was every bit Abdul's intellectual equal, but far more gregarious in personality. Employed by the Pantex Plant, Habib lived with his wife in Amarillo, Texas.

The Pantex Ordnance Plant had been built by the U.S. Army during World War II on 16,000 acres of Texas scrub. It was godforsaken country where the primary inhabitants were scorpions and armadillos . . . a perfect place to assemble, modify, and retrofit nuclear weapons.

The plant was home to 3,300 employees distributed across 650 buildings on 2,000 acres of the campus. Habib, an electrical engineer by training, served as the team leader responsible for the design and manufacture of sophisticated triggers used to detonate high-explosive lenses encasing the cores of nuclear bombs.

The precisely machined lenses were constructed of an explosive known as Octogen, which was bonded to a polymer before being shaped into uniformly dimpled polygons resembling modeling clay. The material fit snugly around the nuclear core. When triggered with perfect simultaneity, the explosive force from the lenses uniformly compressed a hollow sphere of uranium or plutonium into a super-critical mass. Billions of neutrons collided in the dense material, transforming the core into a super-heated cloud that expanded a thousand-fold in a few millionths of a second.

The key to a successful detonation lay in a tiny device known as a kytron. These ultra-fast switches allowed for the instantaneous firing of detonators distributed across the surface of the lenses. Other ingredients were needed, of course, but none were as tightly controlled as the lenses and kytrons.

Security was an ongoing challenge for the massive plant. Careful vetting of the staff, coupled with state-of-the-art surveillance technology, went a long way toward mitigating risk. Yet even the most sophisticated systems inevitably proved vulnerable to attack, something that Habib Faqir knew well.

Habib exploited those vulnerabilities without ever becoming too greedy, which allowed his methodical pilfering to go undetected. Over time, he amassed the high explosive lenses and detonators essential to the construction of a nuclear bomb.

"Running late this morning?" the guard asked as Tariq approached the security gate fronting the employee parking lot at Tallgrass Prairie Power Plant.

"My toilet backed up . . . oh my God . . . it was all over the floor. I couldn't just leave it," he responded.

"Shit happens, Tariq." The heavy-set guard waved him on before waddling back to his chair.

Sitting in the shadows of Strawn Cemetery, the Tallgrass Prairie Plant served as one of the premier power generation stations in the state. Its reactor complex produced more than 1,200 megawatts of electricity—enough to power 800,000 homes. After more than thirty years of operation, it continued to boast a spotless safety record . . . a fact that Tariq took pride in as one the company's lead engineers.

Most days, Tariq looked forward to work, but not this morning. Everything about the plant suddenly seemed terribly mundane when cast in the light of the tasks that lay ahead.

"What's one more day after fifteen years of waiting?" he asked himself.

But the anticipation of that evening's call proved an insurmountable distraction. Even mindless tasks took longer than usual as he struggled to focus. It was well after six o'clock when he finally left the plant. By the time he arrived home, fixed a light dinner, and cleaned the kitchen, it was 7:58 PM.

Cradling his cell phone in his hand, he waited. At eight o'clock PM precisely, he placed an encrypted conference call to Abdul and Habib.

"Good evening, my friends."

"Good evening," the men responded in unison.

"I am excited that our trip is just days away. I've spoken with our travel agent and confirmed the details. Before I give them to you, let me give you her number in case you have questions: 800-768-2612, extension 90."

"800-768-2612, extension 90," Abdul confirmed.

"Yes, that's it," Tariq responded.

"Let's plan on meeting here at noon on December 15. We need to be in the city by Christmas, which gives us a couple of weeks to get everything ready for the big celebration. Not all of our friends can make it by the 25th. A few won't be arriving until December 28. That means the real blow-out will be on New Year's Eve."

Tariq chose his words carefully, though the chances of the call being intercepted and deciphered were remote.

The wheels were firmly in motion. Tariq's rural home would serve as a manufacturing site where disparate pieces of a bomb would be carefully assembled before being delivered to the target. There would be little possibility of discovery on the isolated acreage. His closest neighbor lived more than a half-mile down the road. All that surrounded his house were fields planted with winter wheat and a few dozen dairy cows.

Before he retired to his bedroom, he extracted a small folded piece of paper from his wallet and held it inches from a candle on the kitchen table. His hand moved closer to the glowing flame until a sudden flash of light filled the room and the paper evaporated.

"And so, too, will New York be consumed by the wrathful fire of God," Tariq murmured to himself.

CHAPTER NINE

December 1-2
Karachi

BY THE TIME THEY REACHED THE OUTSKIRTS OF KARACHI, Zahid was coming down from his binge on speed and crashing hard. His eyes fluttered as he struggled to navigate through the massive city that sprawled like a metastasizing cancer across 3,500 square kilometers of land. He checked the GPS: Twenty minutes until arrival.

Ahmed Dar's home was located in the city's western quadrant, not far from Lea Market—a place made infamous by Taliban chief, Mullah Mohammed Omar, who took refuge there following the U.S invasion of Afghanistan. The fugitive had sold potatoes in the open air bazaar for three years without discovery. Karachi had a way of protecting such people.

Ahmed Dar was one of al-Bakr's earliest devotees—at the time, a highly spirited young man with a predilection for violence. Recognizing his protégé's potential, al-Bakr groomed Dar for a leadership position in the rapidly expanding United Islamic State. Two decades later, Dar now headed UIS operations in southern Pakistan.

Dar was in his element here. Whatever he needed was only a phone call away—prostitutes, arms dealers, assassins—whether for his personal penchants or for business. He loved the City of Light—the economic, educational, and political hub of Pakistan.

But to al-Bakr, Karachi was a dirty, crime-infested town that possessed little redeeming value. He marveled that anyone would choose to live here, including Ahmed Dar.

As Zahid struggled to keep his eyes on the road, the voice of the GPS unit sang out the words he'd been waiting to hear: آپ پہنچ چکے ہیں ("You have arrived"). It was 1:05 PM when he pulled into Dar's driveway and shut off the engine.

Unbuckling his seatbelt, Yasir reached from his seat in the back and tapped al-Bakr lightly on the shoulder. He pointed to a man peering out of the front window of the house.

"Don't worry," al-Bakr said. "Dar is a funny sort, but trustworthy beyond reproach. Just don't be fooled by his mirthful way. The man has the sting of a scorpion."

Ahmed Dar bounded out of the house and up to the van like a dog responding to its long absent master. He kowtowed obsequiously to al-Bakr until a stern look caused him to regain a measure of decorum.

"Will you forgive us, Ahmed, if the men retreat to the comfort of your beds? They are tired, and I need them to be fresh and alert this evening."

"Of course. I'm sure you must be exhausted from the drive," he said to his guests. "There are clean beds upstairs, and you will find towels by the shower."

Al-Bakr gestured for the men to take their leave.

The thought of a bed sounded like heaven to Zahid—an even greater pleasure than the seventy virgins promised upon his death as a martyr.

"Are you not tired as well?" Dar asked.

"Yes, but there are things we must discuss."

"Such as the extra man who keeps your company?"

"Unnecessary baggage," al-Bakr replied.

"And where did you acquire such baggage?"

"Zahid returned from the POF with him. The major is under orders from General Malik to accompany the core to America. Malik called it an insurance policy."

"Insurance for whom? I arranged transportation for three men, not four. I'll have to let Shalil know that the plans have changed."

"There will be no change in plans. We will take care of the matter this evening when we meet with Shalil. I am sure, for a small bonus, he will be more than happy to lighten our load."

Zahid was out cold the instant his head hit the pillow, and he didn't awaken until al-Bakr shook him back to consciousness seven hours later.

"It's time," al-Bakr told the men.

The men descended the stairs into the kitchen for a quick meal. Dar was busy ladling chicken biryani onto plates as al-Bakr introduced Major Barr.

"I don't believe we've met before, Major," Dar said, extending his hand.

"No, we have not," a troubled-looking Barr responded.

After dinner, the five men piled into the van and headed to Mariner's Fairway, a few blocks past the port. Their destination was a ramshackle building identifiable by a large weathered sign with the words *Shalil & Sons*.

As the van approached, a longshoreman with arms thicker than most men's thighs stepped out of a cinder-block building and into the night. He was cradling an AK-47. The five men exited the van, raised their arms to indicate that they were unarmed, then carefully approached Avid Shalil. When they closed to within five meters, the unmistakable click of a safety being removed broke the silence.

"That's close enough," the longshoreman called out.

"Do you always greet your clients with an assault rifle?" al-Bakr responded.

"Only when I'm in a good mood," the man answered.

"And when you are not?"

"I shoot first."

As his eyes adjusted to the darkness, Shalil recognized Ahmed Dar. Next to him was a small man wearing wire-rim glasses. Even in the darkness, he could see that the man was badly scarred. That's when it dawned on him: His gun was leveled at his client—al-Bakr. He lowered the gun, restored the safety, and tossed the AK-47 on the ground as if to distance himself from the threatening weapon.

"I am so sorry. One can never be too careful in Karachi. I hope you understand."

"Of course," al-Bakr said, accepting the apology and stepping forward to introduce himself. "I am Ibrahim Almasi al-Bakr."

"I recognized you," Shalil responded.

"It must be my handsome good looks."

"Of course," Shalil responded, relieved by al-Bakr's humor. "It was a Hellfire, I've been told."

"Occupational hazard, my friend. Now, perhaps you could show us how you plan to conceal our shipment."

The three men followed Shalil through the decaying building to its rear, where it opened onto a sprawling yard framed by a chain-link fence. Strewn across it were all manner of shipping containers.

Shalil approached the nearest one. Its yellow paint was blistered and peeling, revealing a deep layer of rust. The container measured twenty feet in length by ten feet in width. A metal door secured with a sliding bolt provided access at one end. Shalil pulled back the bolt and pried the door open, its hinges singing out in a high-pitched squeal. He flipped on a flashlight, illuminating the interior. It was filled to the top with scrap metal.

"As you instructed?" Shalil waited for confirmation.

"Yes," al-Bakr answered.

"Is that your cargo?" Shalil gestured toward a small container at Zahid's feet.

"Yes."

"You are paying a vast sum of money to transport something so small?"

"We are not paying you to think," al-Bakr responded.

"Forgive my intrusion. I will leave you to your work."

As Shalil walked back to the building, Zahid and Yasir set about carving out a space just big enough to accommodate the core among the scrap metal. The goal was to render it impervious to x-rays by sheltering it amid the dense steel. When he was finished, Zahid closed the container door and secured the bolt in position with a steel padlock.

"Do you think that will stop a thief?" al-Bakr asked.

"No, but it will discourage the curious. Shalil knows what will happen if the container is tampered with."

Shalil reappeared, summoned by the sound of the container being secured. He glanced at the padlock. "It looks like she's ready for shipment."

The cough of a diesel engine broke the still of the night, followed seconds later by the high-pitched creaks of a crane turning on its base. The men watched as a massive electro-magnet dangled above the container. With only a few feet to go, it snapped onto the container's metal top. It was then hoisted onto a flatbed truck for delivery to the port. It would be loaded onto the *Jasmine* in the early hours of the morning.

"There's one more matter that we must take care of before we leave," al-Bakr advised Shalil. As he was speaking, Ahmed Dar slid silently into position behind the major.

Like one of nature's great predators, Dar stood perfectly still. Soundless. His arm leveled at the back of Barr's head. In his hand was a sleek H&K 9mm pistol loaded with 150 grain, copper-jacketed hollow-point bullets. A black suppressor extended from its muzzle. The first shot would drop the major where he stood. A second would shut down all brain activity. Turning his eyes toward al-Bakr, Dar awaited permission to fire.

"Did you really think we were going to take you with us, Major?" Al-Bakr asked Barr.

Barr started to speak, but stopped, reaching for his service revolver. He snatched it from the holster, aiming it at the center of al-Bakr's chest.

Zahid and Shalil crouched ready to strike, but al-Bakr motioned them to stand down.

"Go ahead, Major," al-Bakr baited the man. "If you are going to shoot me, do it now."

Barr paused as if to mentally calculate his odds of surviving the encounter. He was outnumbered four to one. His hand holding the gun started to shake. With a sudden look of resolve, he pulled the trigger.

But it merely clicked. A horrified look crossed his face.

"You should be more aware, Major. This afternoon you slept like the dead." Al-Bakr extracted a handful of bullets from his pocket and dumped them on the ground.

Tired of the game, al-Bakr gave a quick nod to Ahmed Dar.

The major's body shuddered as the bullet found its mark, and crumpled to the ground. Dar hovered over him. Barr's eyes fluttered and his chest heaved. He was trying to say something. Bending down as if to hear the words, Dar pressed the barrel of his gun against the base of the major's skull and sent a second bullet rocketing through bone and nerve tissue. Barr convulsed a final time before lying motionless on the pavement.

"What should we do with the body?" al-Bakr asked Shalil.

"There's a 55-gallon drum of acid behind the building. Have your men dump it in there. Tell them not to get any of it on their clothes. I'll let the major stew for a few days. If there's anything left, I'll bury it."

Zahid and Dar carried the corpse to a black barrel. As they lifted the lid, a sulfurous smell permeated the air. Slowly they lowered the body into the oily liquid until the major's head was submerged. They returned the lid, pressing it firmly into position.

"It's always a pleasure doing business with you," Dar said as he handed Shalil a thick wad of American hundred dollar bills.

"And with you," Shalil responded.

"What happens when Major Barr fails to report in?" Dar asked al-Bakr on the drive home.

"His father-in-law, General Patel, will be furious. By then, we will be well on our way to America. As for Malik, the general will understand the necessity of Major Barr's sacrifice. He's smart enough to know that as the Caliphate rises, so does his stature. We will, of course, tell our followers of the instrumental role he and General Patel played in the destruction of the Great Satan. It costs us little to stroke Malik's huge ego. From Malik's perspective, what is one life when he stands to gain the adulation of millions?"

"But how will you appease Patel? He has to deal with his daughter's grief."

"The major will be eulogized as a hero who gave his life in service to Allah. Hopefully his wife will see the glory in such self-sacrifice."

The team had secured their cargo and dispensed with the extra baggage. The journey would begin in the morning, not a second too soon for al-Bakr, Yasir, and Zahid, who were counting down the days until they arrived on a distant shore.

The next morning, Ahmed Dar delivered the men to where the *Jasmine* was moored. He pointed to the solitary yellow container visible on the ship's deck. It sat surrounded by dozens of blue and red containers stacked five deep.

"Shalil made sure it would be easy to keep an eye on. You'll want to do the same on the next leg of your journey."

Satisfied that he had honored his obligations, Dar bade his guests goodbye and blessed their journey.

Al-Bakr labored up the ship's gantry where a dirty, heavily bearded man greeted him at the top. "Welcome aboard, gentlemen," the deep, raspy voice of the captain of the *Jasmine* called out.

He sized up the three passengers before addressing al-Bakr. "For you, it's our finest accommodations. I will show you to your berth." Then he spoke to Yasir and Zahid. "You bunk with the crew. It's a two-day trip. You'll be glad it's short."

With that, the captain gestured to the first mate to escort Yasir and Zahid to the belly of the ship, while he showed al-Bakr to a hammock strung in a dank closet not far from the captain's quarters.

"It's not long on comfort, but I trust that's not of great concern."

Holding up the Quran, al-Bakr replied, "I have my comfort, Captain."

CHAPTER TEN

December 4
Burlington, Kansas

TILSON REACHED INTO HIS DRAWER and extracted a small pair of reading glasses—cheaters he'd bought at Walmart. He slid the glasses up and down his nose until the words on the vacation requisition popped into focus. After a cursory glance, he set the form down and leaned back in his chair, his fingers laced behind his head.

"So you're finally taking some time off," he said to Tariq in his heavy Kansas twang.

"Yes, Sir. I haven't seen my family in years, Mr. Tilson. My mother is growing old. I should have visited her long ago. There are nieces and nephews whom I've never met."

"No point in beating yourself up, Tariq. What's important is that you are going now. Says here you'll be gone a couple of weeks."

"Yes, two weeks, plus the New Year's holiday."

"Is that enough time to go all the way to Pakistan?" Tilson asked.

"Thank you for your concern, Mr. Tilson, but I'm sure it will be adequate."

"If you need a few more days or a week, we can spare you. My God, all you ever do is work."

"There is much joy in work. One only needs to find it," Tariq avowed.

"You are one different son-of-a-bitch," Tilson offered in his language of endearment. "Hell, I wish I had a hundred of you. Most folks come to work on Monday with only one thought on their minds—how they're going to make it through until the weekend. But then, you're not most folks, are you, Tariq?"

"I guess not, Sir."

Mack Tilson felt damn lucky to have Tariq on the team. The man never missed a day, unlike his co-workers, who were often AWOL.

Unexcused absences were a problem at Tallgrass Prairie. They seemed to come in clusters—and always around hunting season. You didn't need to be a nuclear physicist to figure that one out. All you had to do was look at the parking lot full of pickup trucks with gun racks. These people were card-carrying NRA types whose diets consisted of venison, pheasant, quail, and any other creature that could be felled by bullet or bow.

But Tariq never showed an interest in hunting. Mack couldn't imagine the quiet Pakistani picking up a gun, let alone killing anything. He was too gentle. Plus, he wouldn't know a pheasant from a chicken.

Tilson reached for his pen to sign the vacation requisition. "You know, it's possible to give too much to your job. If you let it, this place will suck you dry."

An awkward moment of silence fell between the men.

"I meant that as a compliment," Mack clarified.

"So taken."

Tariq glanced at his watch. "If you'll forgive me, Mr. Tilson, I think I have just enough time to turn in my request to HR before the noon conference."

Tariq spent the balance of the day in a windowless conference room reviewing critical plant performance data. He flagged any significant deviations from benchmark for investigation. There was little tolerance for error by the Nuclear Regulatory Commission, and even less by Tariq.

The meeting adjourned promptly at 5 PM, and though Tariq rarely left before seven, tonight he would make an exception. He prayed that a surprise was waiting for him at home.

There was no traffic in Burlington, and only a single stoplight to momentarily slow his passage. Three miles past town, he turned off 172nd Street onto a gravel road leading to his property. Small pieces of limestone kicked up by his tires pinged against the car's undercarriage, while a fulminating cloud of white dust trailed behind him.

After a half-mile, he slowed to let the dust dissipate before turning off. A cluster of walnut trees adjacent to a bright red mailbox marked his property line. He passed through an iron gate and onto a long snaking driveway. It meandered through a thicket of poplars, sweet gums, and oaks before arriving at a clearing.

Tariq had planted more than 250 trees on the once barren property. The saplings had grown into sizable shade trees. Only in the dead of winter, when the trees had surrendered all their leaves, might a neighbor catch a glimpse of what transpired here.

As his land opened up before him, Tariq looked in the direction of the house. Thanks to a nearly full moon, he could make out three large wooden crates near the out-building. He parked his car just short of the boxes.

The crates were stamped with the name of the shipper: McKennon Machinery. Per Tariq's instructions, McKennon had air-freighted the cargo from Worcester, Massachusetts.

He tried lifting a corner of one of the boxes, but it barely budged. Since they were too heavy to carry, he shoved the boxes a few feet at a time across the rough concrete pad toward the out-building, working up quite a sweat in the process.

The windowless building was empty except for two large workbenches, a massive Craftsman toolbox, and a hodgepodge of power tools hanging from hooks on a pegboard. He grabbed a crowbar and pried the lid off each box. Meticulously packed inside were gleaming sections of metal tubing. When fully assembled, the pieces would form a cylinder, closed at both ends, that measured six feet in length and thirty inches in diameter. It would serve as the bomb's housing.

Tariq stared at the polished metal, its contours reflecting a distorted image of his face much like a funhouse mirror. He thought about the long chain of events leading up to this moment. Then his thoughts returned to the bomb.

It was based upon a design from the laboratory of A.Q. Khara, a metallurgist considered to be the father of Pakistan's nuclear program. Once a national hero, Khara's fall from grace was precipitous following a treacherous revelation: he had provided plans for nuclear weapons to an unholy trinity of rogue nations—Iran, Libya, and North Korea.

Charged with trading in state secrets, Khara confessed to the crime in 2004. His punishment was a slap on the wrist in the form of five years of house-arrest. During that time, Khara's nefarious activities ground to a stop. But in 2009, he reemerged as a player on the nuclear stage. This time, his clients were no longer rogue nations, but rather a Holy Caliphate destined to dominate the world.

Tariq replaced the lids on each of the three crates and pounded them in place with a rubber mallet. He exited the building and locked it. It would remain closed until December 15, when Habib and Abdul arrived.

Entering his house, he walked straight to the master bath, stripped off his clothes that were damp with sweat, and stepped into the steaming hot shower. As he let the water fall upon his head, he prayed that Allah would protect him until the weapon of Islam's salvation could be delivered to its target.

After toweling off, he threw on a robe and walked into the kitchen for a glass of water. He reached for the handle on the faucet, but froze in position, staring out the window. Two flood lights, mounted on either end of the out-building, pierced the darkness. They were on motion-activated switches.

An animal, he said to himself, though it was of little comfort as the lights clicked off and the building was again cloaked in darkness.

CHAPTER ELEVEN

December 4
Mumbai, India

AS THE SEA ROILED THIRTY FEET BELOW the captain's quarters, the small table separating al-Bakr and the captain of the *Jasmine* appeared to rise and fall with every swell. The quarters were tight . . . too tight. The smell of salt and sweat filled the air, robbing al-Bakr of what little remained of his appetite. But he had to eat or risk insulting his host.

The men dined on a Spartan meal of sardines and stale bread—the captain washing down the salty fish with a bottle of amber-colored rum. Al-Bakr abstained. After draining half the bottle, the man's tongue loosened.

"I hate this goddamn weather."

"I thought you would have grown use to it," al-Bakr remarked.

"Well, you thought wrong."

A long pause followed.

A scruffy looking cat intruded. It sauntered up to the captain and rubbed its face back and forth against his leg, leaving its scent and acquiring the scent of the captain.

An unfair exchange that the cat would regret, al-Bakr thought to himself.

Whether the cat was displaying affection or soliciting food was unclear, but the captain responded by pitching a sardine onto the wooden deck. Seizing the fish in its mouth, the cat trotted off to enjoy its bounty in private.

"It's better with rum," he called after the cat, lifting his bottle. Turning to al-Bakr, he said, "That cat and I have a lot in common. Two blokes stuck on this shithole with nothing better to eat than dried sardines."

"Tell me about your family," al-Bakr said, redirecting the conversation.

"You don't want to talk about my family."

"Please do me the honor of sharing your family with me, Captain."

"Okay." The sailor grimaced, nodded and then drained the remaining rum from his glass. He pushed back from the table, gaining a few inches of leg-room, folded his arms over his chest, and began to talk.

"My boy, Azra, was 17. He thought he was a man. You remember what it's like at that age, don't you?"

Al-Bakr nodded, "Yes, we think we are men when we still have the hearts and minds of young boys."

"Azra was bored to death. He craved excitement."

The captain paused to reach for another bottle. He removed the cap and thrust the bottle toward al-Bakr.

"Come on. God's not watching. Have a drink with me."

"Let's leave God out of it," al-Bakr stated.

"Have it your way."

"I believe you were telling me about your son . . . "

"I told Azra to join me. I promised him that there was plenty of adventure on the open sea. He laughed at the idea of excitement on a cargo ship."

"What did you say?"

"Say? I didn't say anything. I slapped him."

"And your boy, what did he do?"

"He walked out. A week later he returned to tell me he had joined Tekhirk-i-Taliban. That was the last time I spoke to him."

Tekhirk-i-Taliban was a terrorist organization composed of Sunni jihadists who occupied the semi-autonomous tribal region of Pakistan. Though the government of Pakistan remained its principal target, the group had attempted to strike the West—including a failed bombing of New York's Time Square. Known to be stunningly ruthless, TPP was an active target of the Pakistani Army, western military, and the CIA.

"One day I received a call telling me I had to claim Azra, or what was left of him. His training camp had been attacked the night before by the Americans. A squadron of F-15s unloaded their 750-pound incendiary bombs while everyone slept. I pray that my son never awoke to the horror. He was burned alive. I brought my boy home and buried him without allowing his mother or sisters to see the charred remains of his body.

"Are you glad you asked about my family?" The captain slammed his empty glass down on the table as a storm of emotion swept over his face.

"Your son died a martyr's death," al-Bakr responded.

"Sure," the captain replied. "*Paradise*, that's what they promised my boy."

"You will see him again someday," al-Bakr assured the man. "That may bring little comfort now, but trust and have faith in Allah."

Standing and swaying with the ship's motion, the captain moved to end the conversation. "I'd better get back to my duties."

"Why did you share your son's story with me?"

"Because you asked."

"I asked about your family. You chose to focus on your grief. Just as you choose to mask your pain with a bottle of rum."

"I don't know what you're getting at, but I don't like it. We have an agreement—I am to deliver three men and a container to Mumbai. That will happen in a day's time. Then I don't ever want to see you again."

"Do you ever envy your son?"

"Are you crazy?" the captain snorted.

"Your son found his excitement. And he found a path to God. That's more than most men ever accomplish in a lifetime. What about you, Captain . . . do you ever crave such excitement? And don't tell me there's plenty on the open seas. I'm talking about changing the world—making it into heaven on earth. Do you ever wish that Allah illuminated such a path for you?"

The captain stared at al-Bakr for a long time before finally settling back into his chair. He released a long breath and, with it, his anger.

"Maybe a long time ago. But what's the point in wanting what is beyond one's reach? I'm not a young man, and I'm not a warrior. I'm an old barnacle attached to a ship that should have been rendered into scrap long ago. I make my weekly passage to Mumbai. It's a living, a good one. I'm able to support my wife and daughters. That is the fate that God has bestowed upon this life."

"What if I offered you something more?" al-Bakr asked.

"Why would you do that?"

"Because it takes many souls to build a Caliphate. Some are recruited one by one. A man with your passion would be welcomed."

"Is that the offer?"

"I'm offering you the ability to strike back at the Americans who took your son. I'm offering you passage off of this freighter and freedom from the bottle. In short, I'm offering you a new life."

"*Paradise*, right?"

"Faith, then justice, and ultimately paradise. Mock it if you wish, but you will be deriding the very cause for which your son surrendered his life."

Al-Bakr paused to take stock of the man before continuing. "The path I have laid out is more difficult than you can imagine, but its rewards are commensurate with its challenges. Think about it. When we arrive in Mumbai, I will give you a way to contact us."

The sun was half across the sky when the *Jasmine* arrived in Mumbai. Al-Bakr watched as the crew pitched thick ropes to sailors waiting on the dock. In minutes, the ship was secured in its berth. Al-Bakr's attention then turned to the captain, who was fast approaching.

The captain betrayed no hint of the previous night's indulgences, despite the level of rum that had been circulating in his system.

"Your container is about to be off-loaded, then delivered to the *Positano*. I think it would be wise to have your men accompany it."

"Don't you trust the captain of the *Positano*?" al-Bakr asked.

"I trust very few men. I believe that is one of the secrets to a long life."

"On that we are agreed, my friend."

"Your ship sails for Halifax in two days. Why not stay aboard the *Jasmine* until then? You will be my guest. Where else can you find such lavish accommodations and home-cooked meals?"

Before he could respond, the captain added, "And there won't be any more liquor."

"Turning over a new leaf, Captain?"

"Something like that."

Al-Bakr put his hand on the man's shoulder. "Thank you for your generous offer. No one in his right mind would turn down an opportunity to bask in your lavish accommodations or be pampered by your rich food, but I must. I appreciate everything you have done."

"All I have done is ferry you from one port to another. As you suggested last night, perhaps there is more that I can do."

"Perhaps."

As he shook the captain's hand, al-Bakr deposited a small cell phone in the man's palm.

"The speed-dial is programmed with a number. Call it if you are serious about pursuing the opportunity we discussed. If not, drop the phone into the ocean."

Spotting Yasir and Zahid, he added, "I think I will heed your advice and speak to my men. Goodbye, Captain."

"You seem to have developed an affection for the captain," Zahid observed.

"Is there not wisdom in drawing in those who know our secrets? Would you prefer that I kill him?

"The man lives a Sisyphean existence—making his circuitous journey from Karachi to Mumbai with no higher purpose than to put food on the table for his wife and surviving children. What little joy he once had was stolen by the Americans when they killed his son in a bombing raid near Miran Shah.

"Last night, I saw an opening—a chance to not merely spare the man's life but to give it meaning. I would have dishonored Allah by failing to act on such an opportunity. Whether the captain accepts my invitation is wholly upon his heart."

Pointing to the yellow container, al-Bakr continued, "I want you to stay with the container until it is loaded on the *Positano*. I will meet you aboard the ship."

The captain watched as al-Bakr left his men behind and descended the gantry way. He followed the small man with his eyes until he could no longer separate him from the crowd that engulfed the dock. He returned to his quarters, opened a small hidden safe, and placed the phone inside. Closing the safe door, the captain turned his eyes upward. "Perhaps, my son, I will follow in your footsteps."

CHAPTER TWELVE

THE HEELS OF GENERAL PATEL'S BOOTS CLICKED with each step, like a metronome marking each second, as he paced the parquet floor of his office. Three days had passed since Major Barr and three members of the United Islamic State departed the POF with the core of a nuclear weapon. Yet despite explicit orders to report in upon his arrival in Karachi, not a word had been heard from the major. Patel was stunned by the silence.

He knew that it could mean only one thing—his support of al-Bakr had been repaid with the murder of a trusted comrade and beloved son-in-law. He never would have gotten involved with al-Bakr had it not been for the machinations of Malik. Furious, Patel demanded an immediate meeting with the general.

The drive from the POF to Malik's office served only to intensify Patel's anger. By the time he arrived, he was almost untethered.

Sensing Patel's fury, Malik ordered him to sit while he remained standing.

Patel sat.

"That murderous little bastard of yours," he seethed.

"Of mine? Do you think I control al-Bakr? Surely you've not grown delusional in your old age, General? But you have become insubordinate."

Patel jumped to his feet and glared at the man, enraged. "My daughter has been crying incessantly! Her children keep asking for their father. She doesn't know what to tell them. She doesn't know what to believe herself!"

"But surely Major Barr advised her that he might be gone for some time?" Malik responded.

"She asked him why he was packing a bag, and Ali told her. But he also told her that he would call her before he left. That was three days ago."

"I'm sorry that your daughter is suffering, but we cannot afford to let anger cloud our judgment," Malik advised.

Patel exhorted, "I'm going to take my finger and stub out that little bastard's other eye and then cut him up, piece by piece, with a knife."

"Come now, General. Major Barr knew the risks."

"Are you telling me I should accept the wanton murder of my son-in-law? That such a heinous act was necessary to the mission? I don't accept that, and neither should you."

Standing eye to eye with Patel, Malik put his hand on the general's shoulder. "We don't know what has happened to Ali. We don't know whether he is alive or dead."

"Of course we know. Don't play me for the fool. We've been friends far too long for that kind of petty deception."

"I'm sorry. The wound is fresh and the loss profound. It will be tragic if the major is indeed dead. If proven true, let's ensure that his death meant something—that his heroism does not go unrecognized."

Patel, exhausted of anger, seemed frail as he collapsed back into the chair.

"I just don't know what to say to my daughter."

"Say little, but comfort her greatly. She can know nothing of what has transpired until the day comes when our role in the destruction of the West is acknowledged and the forces under our command become protectors of the Caliphate, not confined to the borders of Pakistan."

Head held low, Patel nodded slowly in acknowledgment.

"We must be unified," Malik continued. "It is not merely the West that is our adversary, but also those loyal to Mughabi. His reign is about to end. Once the threat of U.S. intervention is gone, we will step forward and seize control."

As if on cue, the phone atop Malik's massive mahogany desk let out a shrill ring.

"I asked not to be disturbed," he shouted into the receiver.

"It's the president, Sir."

"Give me a moment, then put him through." Slamming down the receiver and turning to Patel, he said, "General, it's the president on the line. I plan to inform him of your presence, and he will undoubtedly request to be put on speakerphone."

As the call came through, Malik snatched up the receiver once again. "Mr. President, what an unexpected pleasure. I was just preparing to call you."

"Were you, General? And what did you plan to tell me?"

"General Patel is in my office. Apparently, there is a small amount of nuclear material that cannot be accounted for at the POF. We're not overly concerned, but we're taking the matter seriously, of course."

Malik could sense the anger building between Mughabi's punctuated breaths. "Put the call on speaker," the president ordered. I want both of you to hear what I am about to say."

Malik pushed a button, then set the receiver back in its cradle. "You are on speaker, Mr. President."

"I've learned that the missing uranium core was secured under orders to be transported from the POF to Gujranwala. The three men who executed those orders arrived at the Jinnah Gate dressed in standard issue black fatigues."

"Yes, Mr. President. We are operating under the same assumptions," Malik responded.

"Don't bullshit me, General. I've also learned that Major Barr assisted the men in the transfer, and that he accompanied them upon their departure."

"Are you suggesting that my son-in-law was somehow complicit in the disappearance of the core?" an outraged Patel demanded of the president.

"I'm not drawing any conclusions, General, not until I speak to Major Barr. Have him report to my office. My aide will expect him within the hour."

"I'm afraid that won't be possible, Sir," Malik responded.

"Why not?"

"We haven't been able to locate Major Barr for three days. That's why General Patel and I were conferring. We knew of his role in the weapons transfer on December 1, but there was no deviation from protocol during what transpired at the POF."

"Then where is the van, and, more importantly, where is the core?" Mughabi demanded. "How long did the two of you plan to wait before telling me?" The president was straining to contain his anger.

"We had hoped to be in a position to tell you more than just that Major Barr was missing, and with him one of our devices."

"Device? That's what you call the core of a fifteen-kiloton nuclear bomb capable of destroying a city? What a nice euphemism, General. You have twenty-four hours to locate the major and the *device*. Am I understood?"

"And what if we fail?" Malik asked without the slightest hint of backing down.

"I will call the American president, Jonathan Conner, and make him aware of what has happened. It's his worst nightmare—a loose nuke possibly destined for one of his cities. My guess is the Americans will demand to secure the remainder of our nuclear arsenal. If they are denied, they won't hesitate to invade our country with overwhelming force."

Pausing to let his message sink in, Mughabi continued, "I trust that they will have a long conversation with each of you."

"It's an empty threat, Mr. President," Malik spat out the words with contempt "Once our nuclear arsenal is removed from Pakistani control, do you think India will sit passively on the sidelines? No, I will tell you exactly what they will do. Despite a warning from America to stand down, they will seek an opportunity to repay us for the slaughter at Mumbai and a dozen other atrocities that they will quickly enumerate. We have kept India's bombs at bay through mutual assurance of each country's destruction. Remove that threat, and you remove the last impediment to Pakistan's safety and sovereignty."

"You think you are so clever, General. What do you believe will be accomplished by a nuclear attack on the West? Do you fail to see that the Americans' retaliation will be even swifter and more complete than anything India could muster? Are you that much of a fool, General?"

"I am going to ignore your insults for the moment, Mr. President, but it is not I who plays the fool. If the device is in the hands of terrorists . . . if it is intended for delivery to the West . . . if the terrorists are able to overcome all of the complexities required to build a bomb from the core . . . if they are able to deliver it to a major American city . . . then, and only then, do we have a problem."

Mughabi did not respond.

"Let's play this scenario out for a moment," Malik said in a more conciliatory tone. "A fifteen-kiloton bomb detonated in New York, Boston, or Washington, D.C. would shut down the entire country. Massive destruction would be created by the explosion, and the Americans would be waiting for the next shoe to drop."

"That's right, and they would unfurl their missiles in response," Mughabi shouted.

"At whom?" Malik asked. "At an enemy that they cannot see? Even if they assume it was UIS, what nation do they strike in retaliation for the deeds of an asymmetrical threat? UIS could have procured the bomb on the black market. It could be Russian in origin. Perhaps it was a plot engineered by Putin to look as though it had been executed by Middle Eastern jihadists. The truth is, it will take weeks or months to complete a forensic investigation. Only then will they be able identify that it was a Pakistani bomb."

"You'd better pray that we locate the core before we learn of a nuclear detonation on CNN!" Mughabi slammed down the receiver.

The *Positano* departed Mumbai on schedule, pulling away from the dock at 9 AM on December 6. The voyage to Halifax, Nova Scotia required twenty-two days at sea.

The ship, fully laden with twenty- and forty-foot containers, was traversing the Arabian Sea off the coast of Oman while, thousands of miles to the northwest in Manitoba, Canada, a woman was brewing a cup of tea. She, too, would soon be in motion and headed for Halifax.

CHAPTER THIRTEEN

December 8
Matheson Island
Manitoba, Canada

THE HIGH-PITCHED WHISTLE OF THE TEA KETTLE grew more insistent as Sarah Qaisrani, aka *Rachel Patel*, rose from the comfort of her reading chair and walked five paces to the wood-burning stove that heated her small log cabin. The woman looked more like a demure grandmother than a radical Islamist. She poured a cup of boiling water into a black mug emblazoned with the University of Missouri's logo—a remnant of her past life—then dropped in a bag of Darjeeling tea and let it steep.

Sarah lived alone on Matheson Island. It was a remote fishing village far removed from all but the faintest traces of civilization. She loved the gift of solitude that came with the territory and with the passing of her late husband.

Babur had been one of the terrorists who permeated the air within America's four busiest airports with a deadly biological agent. Recruited at the last minute to replace a defector, Babur had faithfully executed the man's mission by attacking the Dallas-Fort Worth airport. Unlike his co-conspirators in Atlanta, Los Angeles, and Chicago, however, Babur managed to evade capture, eventually travelling north to reunite with his wife.

Within hours of his arrival at the cabin, Babur was dead. Not from the virus or any wound received during the attack. His death had come at the hands of his wife. Sarah had injected him with a lethal dose of succinylcholine chloride.

It was a particularly ugly death, one in which Sarah took great relish. The official cause was listed as a heart attack.

People got under Sarah's skin. She tolerated them as long as they served a purpose, and Babur's purpose had expired. Their marriage had been one of utility. Sarah needed help with the family farm, and Babur's faculty position at the University of Missouri afforded him the time to provide that help.

She didn't love him. She never had. Love was an alien concept to Sarah, whose sole motivation was power over others. She honored the traditions of Islam and obeyed Sharia law . . . when it served her purpose.

With Babur gone, she was free to pursue her affair with al-Bakr. She would feed off of his power, hoping to one day supplant him as the leader of the United Islamic State.

Babur had not been the first victim of the black widow. Without a shred of remorse, Sarah had murdered her parents, though one had been declared an accident and the other a suicide. Her father fell under the blades of a combine on the farm. *Unimaginable* was the way the sheriff had described the man's body. Without the small tattoo of SEMPER FI that remained unscathed above her father's right breast, positive identification would have required DNA analysis.

Every deputy in the department had been touched to the core by the long, piercing wail that emerged from Sarah the day she had reported the death. When her job was done, she shuffled out of the morgue crying. Once out of sight, she unceremoniously wiped the tears from her face, smiled inwardly, and headed home for a cup of tea.

Eighteen months later, on a fateful day in October, Sarah called 911 after finding her mother dead. Her still grieving mother had swallowed a lethal cocktail of opioids and alcohol. It was not an easy suicide to fake. Yet the notion of Sarah's complicity never arose in anyone's mind.

Removing the tea bag, Sarah returned to her favorite oak rocker, which she had placed close enough to the stove to bask in its radiant heat. As she took a sip, there was a sharp knock at the door. There were only 117 people on Matheson Island, all of whom knew not to disturb the eccentric woman living in the old Stewart cabin.

Sarah walked to her writing desk and extracted a small pistol from the center drawer. Concealing it in the pocket of her oversized sweater, she opened the thick pine door. Recognizing the man as one of al-Bakr's couriers, Sarah took her finger off the trigger and greeted him.

The man had visited Sarah on several occasions—whenever important information needed to be exchanged with the assurance that no one was listening. Names, dates, and places related to the final assembly and delivery of the bomb to its target in New York were encoded using a complex algorithm and shuttled back and forth on flash drives. The correspondents were Sarah Qaisrani, al-Bakr, and Aswan Basra, who was the key to safely penetrating New York.

"As-salaam'alaykum," said the man.

"Wa 'alaykum salaam," she replied. "You've traveled far. Please come in."

"Thank you, but I'm only here to give you a message."

"Surely you are hungry. Allow me to fix you something to eat."

Sarah's reputation as a cold-blooded killer had spread through the ranks of UIS following Babur's death. Never referred to by name, she was known only as the *Arctic Fox*, a tribute to her cold surroundings and cunning nature. The courier knew the stories about the Arctic Fox were more than mere legend, and he was not about to set foot in her lair.

"Thank you, but no," he insisted.

"Then give me the message you have come to deliver," Sarah said abruptly, extending her hand to receive the flash drive.

"It is brief," the courier said. "There was no need for a memory device. The cargo has been secured. The teacher will arrive in Halifax on December 28th. He will meet you as discussed." The man bowed slightly at the waist while keeping his eyes on Sarah. "Ma'a as salaama."

"Allah yasalma," Sarah muttered in response as she closed the door.

"Three more weeks," she mused, as she contemplated the unfathomable destruction that would follow her reunion with al-Bakr.

She walked to the small bedroom in the rear of the cabin and removed a compact black suitcase from the closet. She planned to depart for New York City on the 18th. That would put her well ahead of the Christmas traffic. Though she knew she could make the drive in two days, she allocated three and hoped the weather would cooperate.

Sarah would be the guest of Awan Basra, the de facto leader of a terrorist cell initially formed by Sheik Gilani, a man implicated in the bombing of the World Trade Center. After Gilani was forced to flee to Pakistan, operational control of his network passed to Basra. The Brooklyn-based cell would provide the requisite infrastructure necessary to complete the final assembly of the nuclear bomb, then deliver and detonate it. It would also ensure safe passage out of the city for the Arctic Fox and al-Bakr prior to New York's annihilation.

CHAPTER FOURTEEN

December 8
Islamabad, Pakistan

Ayesha's frenetic world came to an abrupt halt as she put down the phone, stunned by the news shared by her father. Major Ali Barr, the husband of her life-long friend, Mizha Barr, was missing. Struggling to gather her thoughts, she walked to her nurse's desk.

"I need you to clear my schedule for the remainder of the day."

"But your one o'clock patient is here," the woman protested without even the courtesy of looking up at her superior.

"I trust you will take care of it. I'm sure she'll understand," Ayesha responded sharply.

Within minutes, she was on her way to Mizha's house. The mid-day traffic was unusually heavy. As she inched along the expressway, she asked Allah to embolden her with the right words to say under such difficult circumstances. Yet nothing she rehearsed felt adequate.

Ayesha and Mizha shared a long history. Their fathers had trained together, fought together, and risen through the ranks together. Along the way, their girls learned what it meant to be military brats: learning to cope with ever-changing environments, adapting to new schools, and accepting the sorrow that came with leaving friends behind. Such an itinerant lifestyle made it difficult to forge deep relationships; all the more reason that Ayesha and Mizha treasured their unshakeable bond.

But even forever friendships yield to the passage of time, distance, and the intervention of other forces. For Mizha, it was her marriage to a husband whom she adored; for Ayesha, it was an all-consuming calling to heal. Though the intensity of the friendship had faded, there was no falling out . . . just a gradual drifting apart as their lives carried them in different directions.

She knocked on Mizha's door, praying that she might bring comfort to her friend. No one answered. She knocked again, louder.

"What are you doing here?" Mizha asked as she opened the door, her bloodshot eyes brimming with tears.

"My father called to tell me that Ali is missing. I thought . . . "

"You thought what, Ayesha? That you would jump in and provide a comforting hand?"

Caught off-guard by her friend's sarcasm, it took Ayesha a moment to respond. "Something like that. I know it's been a long time since we spoke, Mizha, but I assumed everything was good between us. Have I have done something to offend you? If so, tell me so I can apologize and help you in your time of need."

"Can you apologize for the deeds of your father?"

"What you are talking about?" Ayesha asked as she stepped past her friend and into Mizha's home. As she entered, Ayesha continued, "I don't think your neighbors need to be privy to our conversation. Please tell me what you mean about my father."

"My husband was operating under orders from your father when he disappeared. He packed a bag and told me he would be gone for a long time."

"Did he tell you where he was going?"

"He refused to discuss it, but he promised to call me the following night."

"And?"

"I never heard from him."

"Mizha, I've come here as your friend, not as General Malik's daughter. I know nothing of his orders. Surely you understand that."

Mizha's resistance began to crumble. She ached for someone with whom to unburden her sorrows. Though she had many friends, no one understood her like Ayesha. Tentatively at first, she accepted her embrace. Seconds later, the dam holding back her emotions broke, and she sobbed until she was breathless. When she finally released her grip on Ayesha, Mizha wiped her tears dry.

"How can you help me, Ayesha? By your own admission, you know nothing more than that Ali is missing."

Though Ayesha lacked any tangible facts about the major's disappearance, she possessed an invaluable skill— one honed through her years of medical training and practice. Differential diagnosis was a way of solving problems that had application far beyond medicine. Her professors taught her that, if she listened carefully, the patient would provide most of the knowledge needed to make an appropriate diagnosis.

"What were Ali's responsibilities at the POF?"

"How can I tell you that when I am not allowed to know the details of his work?"

"But you do, Mizha. We have known each other since we were children. Have I ever betrayed your trust?"

"No, never."

"Then why would I begin now?"

"Because your father is at the center of this storm."

"You don't know that . . . only that Ali's orders were issued by my father, and now he is missing. I'm curious as to why your husband was acting under my father's orders, and not those of General Patel. Isn't your father his commanding officer?"

"Leave my father out of it, Ayesha."

"Of course, but let's look for more evidence before we convict anyone of a crime."

"In answer to your question, my husband was one of the officers responsible for the security of nuclear materials at the POF."

"That's a huge responsibility. What could possibly supersede it and require him to leave his post?"

"He only left the POF on rare occasions."

"What kinds of occasions?"

"It always involved the transfer of nuclear materials to new locations."

"Did such transfers require that he be gone for an extended period?"

"No, rarely more than twenty-four hours," Mizha said, shaking her head.

Ayesha's mind was already at work, assembling a cluster of seemingly random facts into potential patterns of cause and effect that might explain the major's disappearance.

That's when it hit her. A niggling thought that she couldn't dismiss. Was there a link between her father's meetings with al-Bakr, the jihadist's comments about an important emerging event, and the major's disappearance?

She could not clear her mind of the thought. Ayesha had arrived at a potential diagnosis, but one so devastating that she dared not share it with the patient.

A surge of nausea welled up in her gut.

"What's wrong?" Mizha asked of her friend, who was suddenly pale as a sheet.

Ayesha didn't answer. She bolted toward the bathroom, barely making it through the door before throwing up into the toilet.

She rinsed out her mouth, then wiped her face before returning to where Mizha was standing.

"I'm so sorry. I'm not feeling well. Forgive me, but I need to go. I'll call you later."

"Where are you going?"

"I'm going to speak to my father. If I learn anything, I will call you."

"Will you?" All traces of vulnerability were gone from Mizha's voice.

"Why do you ask this?"

"Because you are a daughter first, Ayesha, and a friend second. I don't expect you to betray the loyalty owed your father. Just don't deprive me of the right to hate him."

"Let's work to bring your husband back, not tear our friendship apart."

Ayesha gave her an unreciprocated hug and then headed for her car.

The awakening that had sickened Ayesha's stomach now impelled her to race across town in a rage. Her destination was Army Command Headquarters.

Flying past his aide, Ayesha burst into her father's office. Though he could see the anger exuding from her every pore, General Malik greeted his daughter with equanimity.

"My dear, what an unexpected gift to have you drop by unannounced."

"I just left Mizha Barr," Ayesha said in a low, menacing tone.

"That was kind of you. I hope she appreciated the gesture."

"You failed to tell me that her husband was acting under your orders when he disappeared," she continued, the volume of her voice rising.

"Lower your voice, Ayesha."

"Who do you think you are? I don't take orders from you," she snapped.

General Malik stepped closer to her. "Lower your voice, and then we can have a civil conversation."

She fought to contain the bile once again rising in her gut. After a tense moment, she sat. Her fists were balled, ready to strike, her face pinched tight.

"Major Barr was operating under my orders, though he reports through Colonel Kassar to General Patel. It doesn't matter. His orders were to transport a nuclear core from POF to our airbase at Gujranwala."

"But it does matter. Can't you see that?" Ayesha asked incredulously.

"What matters is that the transfer team was intercepted on their way to the POF by terrorists. The terrorists proceeded to the main gate, where they impersonated the army officers they had just killed. From what we can determine, Major Barr was forced to aid them in their theft of a nuclear core. He departed with them and has not been seen since. Unfortunately, it does not bode well for your friend's husband."

Ayesha let her head sink into her hands as she sat across from her father.

"If you share that information with anyone, including Mizha Patel, I will have you arrested and locked in a cell," the general promised his daughter.

Ayesha knew he wasn't bluffing. She also knew that he was sharing only a part of the story.

"And you, of course, have no knowledge of who the terrorists might be?"

"Of course not. Now you are talking nonsense."

"Am I?"

"My patience is wearing thin, Ayesha." Malik stood to dismiss her, but Ayesha refused to budge.

"And I suppose that Major Barr's disappearance has no relationship to the numerous meetings between you and one of my patients?"

"You are talking crazy. It must be the stress of your mother's death. I'm going to have my aide call for a doctor."

"If I'm crazy, then tell me: What was the important matter that al-Bakr insisted on discussing with you? And what of the critical role he said you would play in reestablishing the Holy Caliphate?"

"Do not speak another word," General Malik said, carefully enunciating every syllable.

"Or what, father? Will you have me disappear, too?"

"You are privy to many things, but others should be left alone, Ayesha. Major Barr is an officer. He understands that all missions carry risks. He also understands the sacrifices that are sometimes required for a greater good. Do not probe any further. Comfort your friend, but share nothing of what I have told you. It is not your job. If it is anyone's, it belongs to her father."

"So now you are implicating General Patel?" Ayesha was incredulous at her father's audacity.

"Our conversation stops now." Pointing to the door, he ordered, "Go, and remember what I have said. Take it to heart, my dear daughter, and do not test your father's resolve. It would not be wise."

CHAPTER FIFTEEN

December 14
Amarillo, Texas
Kansas City, Missouri
Burlington, Kansas

HABIB METHODICALLY PACKED EACH PIECE of the cache he had amassed during his tenure at Pantex into a large plastic bin. The high explosive lenses, detonators, and triggers would be riding shotgun during the seven-and-a-half-hour drive to Kansas, and he didn't want them to be jostled. When he was finished, he snapped on the lid and then turned toward his wife, Maria, who had watched him without uttering a word.

Her husband was a soldier of God, a fact that she had come to accept—as much as any wife can accept such things. She had always known that the time would come when Habib would be summoned by Allah to serve a greater cause. Still she had prayed for another day, a week, a month with the man whom she had grown to love. With no family within a thousand miles of Amarillo, Habib was all she had. God had left her childless, despite a constant refrain of intercessory prayers.

"We have a few hours." Habib's tone was subdued, but loving. He encircled her waist and pulled her gently toward him. As their bodies met, he kissed her . . . softly at first. He caressed Maria's cheeks, stroking them with the tips of his fingers. Then, one by one, he undid the buttons of her blouse. As she unhooked her bra, he reached with both hands to embrace the fullness of her breasts. She stared into his rich brown eyes as she let her skirt drop to the floor. She reached for his belt and tugged until it was freed.

"My beautiful bride," he murmured to the only woman he had ever known.

She smiled, but her eyes betrayed her sadness. "Whatever beauty God graced me with faded long ago. If I am beautiful, it is in your eyes, Habib, and I am thankful for your blinders."

After making love, they lay together in silence until Habib spoke: "Pray for me, Maria. Pray that I fulfill my obligation to Allah."

"Of course I will pray for it. And I will pray that Allah returns you safely to me."

She caressed his hair until he fell asleep, his arms embracing her. She lay awake for hours, tucked in against the warmth of his body, wishing she could somehow preserve the feelings of that night.

Maria finally fell asleep moments before the disharmonic pulse of Habib's alarm shattered the calm of their bedroom. It was 4 AM. There would be no long goodbyes. He kissed his wife once on the forehead before bolting out of bed. By 4:30, he was on the road to Kansas.

Traffic on I-40 was light. He headed east on the interstate until he came to Oklahoma City, then north on I-35 until he reached the exit for Highway 75. From there, it was a straight shot to Burlington. Door to door, it was 500 miles.

As Habib approached the Kansas border, Abdul Rana was doing some last minute packing in the basement of his home in Kansas City. Under the greenish glare of bare fluorescent bulbs, he secured a set of beryllium reflectors in bubble wrap and then placed the brittle material in a heavily padded box.

In a separate container, he placed a neutron initiator, a small component composed of a miniaturized particle accelerator and a pellet of deuterium hydride. The neutron initiator ensured an adequate supply of sub-atomic particles to jump-start a full-fledged nuclear reaction.

His final contribution was a precisely honed tamper of tungsten. Less than an inch thick, the tamper weighed a hefty eighty kilograms. It had been fabricated based upon the precise dimensions of the uranium core, coupled with the measurements of the beryllium reflectors— a formidable task with the facilities under twenty-four-hour video surveillance and super-tight inventory controls. On top of it would be placed a ten-centimeter-thick layer of high-explosive lenses weighing seventy kilograms.

Relieved that those challenges were behind him, Abdul stowed the material in the cargo hold of his 2003 Toyota 4Runner. Since he lived alone, there were no goodbyes to be said. He threw a small suitcase in the backseat and headed to Burlington.

The men arrived at Tariq's home within minutes of one another. This was the first time the three men had shared each other's company since shortly after arriving in America. Two weeks of ceaseless labor lay ahead of them. They would depart for New York in less than ten days and arrive with the device on Christmas. Three days later, they would rendezvous with al-Bakr.

But Tariq knew that, first, they needed a few hours to rekindle their bond. He invited them into the kitchen where he had spent hours preparing a feast for this occasion. He handed Abdul and Habib plates and told them to cover every inch with their favorite foods and then join him at the table.

As they reminisced about their fatherland, Tariq felt a sense of melancholy. The middle-aged men sitting across from him looked so different from his memories of the young men who had been dispatched to this far-away land to do God's bidding. Their jet black beards were now streaked with gray, and lean waists had yielded to age and American diets. Yet one thing had not changed—their resolve to succeed regardless of the cost.

After lunch, Tariq showed them around his property, working his way toward the out-building. As he approached the site where they would work, he stopped abruptly and pointed to a set of tire tracks in the mud.

"I found these a few days ago. It's probably nothing . . . just someone looking for a place to sleep . . . maybe a hunter. That happens around here. People don't call them break-ins because it's rare for anything to be stolen. Of course, sometimes food or liquor gets borrowed."

"You don't seem too worried," Abdul observed.

"Aware, yes; worried, no," Tariq responded.

"And what if the hunter is hunting us?" Habib asked.

Tariq thought about the moment in the kitchen when the exterior floodlights had been activated by some type of motion.

"There is a 9mm pistol in the top drawer of each of your nightstands. The clips hold eleven bullets. The guns are not suppressed. There's no one around to hear the noise. If you need something more, there's an AR-15 in the closet. Any other questions?"

CHAPTER SIXTEEN

TOM O'HARA HAD BEEN WALKING A BEAT in south Philly for years. He was a cop's cop . . . the kind of guy you wanted covering your back. During his nineteen years on the force, O'Hara had been offered numerous promotions, all of which involved a quiet desk job far removed from the urban madness unique to the City of Brotherly Love. He had accepted one of them years ago, but it hadn't lasted. The siren call of the streets had lured him back.

"The streets get into your blood," he would explain to people, including his wife, who couldn't understand why he took such risks. She knew she wasn't going to change Tom—he was an O'Hara, from a long line of cops who were both respected and feared.

It was a crisp and clear Saturday morning when O'Hara approached an SUV that was illegally double-parked at 5th and Chestnut. The sidewalks were lined with people waiting for Independence Hall to open. He weaved his way through the bystanders toward the street.

When he was a few yards away from the car, he made a cranking motion with his hand, signaling the driver to roll down his window. There was no response.

O'Hara stepped forward cautiously, the fingers of his right hand gripping the handle of his service revolver. With his left fist, he rapped on the window.

The driver slowly turned his head and faced the officer. He was smiling as he raised his left hand to window height. It wasn't a gun he was holding, but rather the switch for a detonator. Before O'Hara could react, the man pushed the red plunger.

Milliseconds later, the SUV was catapulted into the air, the charred hulk of metal falling to earth with a terrible screech. Blocks away, at Penn's Landing, the ground shook and windows burst from the bomb's pressure. Tom O'Hara's dismembered body lay a dozen yards from the epicenter. As the smoke cleared, the deadly aftermath of the explosion was revealed: twenty-seven bodies lay motionless . . . dead on the street. Another sixty people were injured, many grievously. Thirteen of them would die in the coming hours.

First responders were overwhelmed by the carnage, as were the trauma services at Thomas Jefferson University Hospital and a half-dozen other medical centers. Patients were triaged based upon the severity of their injuries; those with life-threatening wounds were taken to the closest facilities able to handle high acuity patients.

Numerous law enforcement agencies, including metro police, Counter Terrorism Units, and the FBI arrived on the heels of the EMTs. The area was cordoned off to protect evidence, as well as to ensure there were no more devices or active combatants. Even though a forensic analysis would be required before any definitive conclusions could be reached, analysts on the scene were already surmising that the Toyota Landcruiser had been packed with as much as forty kilos of Semtex and then laden with nails, ball-bearings, and other forms of shrapnel.

Prohibited from intervening in domestic matters, CIA officials watched live-feeds from surveillance cameras in the area. The video was supplied by the FBI's Philadelphia office in response to the request of Marvin Kahn, Deputy Director of Operations at CIA. Seated next to Kahn observing the calamity was Commander Hart.

"God damn bastards," Kahn began, "We've not seen an attack of this magnitude in years. I trust you've seen their audacious message, Commander."

"No, Sir, I haven't been privy to it yet."

"UIS claimed responsibility via videotape." Reading from a transcript, Kahn continued. "'Today we strip you of your freedom. You will live in fear as you have forced us to live in fear.'"

"Have we validated UIS's claim of responsibility?" Hart asked.

"The video was posted thirty seconds before the detonation." Kahn replied. "I assume that's confirmation enough.

"Commander, we need to be more than passive observers. We need to be ferreting out the individuals who put this plan in motion. That means providing whatever support is deemed beneficial by the Bureau and others. Regardless of the number of resources required, we need answers quickly."

"Perhaps we should consider all of our options, Sir."

"I've never seen you back away from a fight, Commander. Why in the hell wouldn't we pursue these bastards until we've rounded them up or, better yet, terminated them?"

"What if it's a diversion?"

"Diversion? Do you want to tell Sergeant O'Hara's wife that her husband was killed in a diversion? Come on, John, what are you thinking?"

"What if the intent is to consume our counter-terrorism resources while something much larger is being planned?" Hart asked.

"Larger . . . you mean twenty-seven dead and sixty wounded is an insufficient body count to warrant emergent intervention?"

Unruffled by the DDO's rebuttal, Hart continued, "By comparison to their biological attack, this is a minor incident. I'm not diminishing the human toll, simply asking why UIS would regress. Why go from a weapon of mass destruction that killed 85,000 to a car-bomb?"

"I'm listening," Kahn responded.

"If we divert our key resources to investigate this crime, we expose our flank. UIS can then strike with a vengeance. I would contribute resources in name only and rely on the locals in Philly to do their job."

"And if you're wrong, Commander?"

"If I'm wrong, then this may prove to be the first in a wave of suicide bombers to hit our country. Hundreds could die. But if I'm right, you can multiply that death toll a thousand-fold."

CHAPTER SEVENTEEN

December 16
Somewhere in the Atlantic Ocean

AL-BAKR NOTICED THE SAILOR the moment he boarded the *Positano*. Every exposed inch of the sailor's skin revealed the crude work of a cheap tattoo artist. His muscles bulged under ill-fitting clothes that had been patched front and back. He was unshaven, and based upon the stench that trailed him, unbathed. Most importantly, he was eyeing everyone who came on board.

Al-Bakr recognized the man—not literally, of course. Bullies were a ubiquitous scourge, whether on a school playground or the deck of an ocean-faring ship. Other people's pain was their pleasure. The challenge came in avoiding engagement with them. Bullies latched onto their prey like a lamprey onto a shark. And this man was looking for his mark.

Al-Bakr planned to give the sailor a wide berth and pray for an uneventful voyage. For a while, it appeared that his strategy was working.

The *Positano* was halfway to Halifax when the sailor's taunts began.

"You're a strange looking little shit. What happened to your face? Looks like a dog's been gnawing on it." The man leaned into al-Bakr's face as he hurled insults.

Al-Bakr ignored the man, spreading out his prayer rug on the deck in the direction of the rising sun. As he knelt in preparation for his recitations, he felt a large boot lodge against his back. He strained to rise, but the man held him in check.

"What are you doing? Can't you see that I am praying?"

The man dug his heel into the base of al-Bakr's spine before finally lifting his boot. "Keep your fucking religion off my deck," he said, then spat inches from al-Bakr's face.

How ironic, al-Bakr thought. He was prepared to battle the greatest superpower the world had ever seen, yet all of his planning could be derailed by the errant actions of this pathetic excuse for a human being. Though angry enough to kill the man, he chose instead to ignore him. It was trouble they didn't need—not in the middle of a lawless ocean.

Unaware of what had just happened, Zahid approached al-Bakr. He was out of breath from ascending several flights of stairs.

"I just received a message by satellite. It's done. The Americans are consumed with what happened in Philadelphia."

"Do you have a death toll?" al-Bakr asked.

"Twenty-seven as of now, sixty more injured. The death toll will definitely climb."

"Good. One more piece that has fallen into place," he said, patting Zahid approvingly on the shoulder. "It should keep them busy for a while, and their eyes far from the ports."

The next morning, hoping to avoid his new-found nemesis, al-Bakr prayed below deck before emerging into the brilliant light of the sunrise. As he walked the circumference of the ship, stretching his sea-weary legs, the man seemed to materialize out of nowhere. He stepped directly into al-Bakr's path.

"What's in the container?" the man demanded.

"What container?"

"The yellow container that your men watch so closely."

"Scrap metal," came al-Bakr's terse response.

"Men don't put a heavy lock on a box of scrap metal. Open it."

"I can't."

The man cocked his fist, then feigned a punch at al-Bakr's face. He didn't blink. Strapped parallel to al-Bakr's calf was a ten-inch serrated blade—his insurance policy when not accompanied by a bodyguard. With a single swift movement, he could draw the knife, sever the man's carotid artery, and watch him bleed out on the deck. The thought pleased al-Bakr, but it would be messy.

"I don't have the key. It's with Yasir. I'll go get him."

"No. You will tell no one. Bring the key tomorrow morning."

"And if I choose not to?"

The man closed the distance between them until the soles of his boots rested on top of al-Bakr's thin shoes. The sailor pressed down with all of his weight, hoping to elicit a wince of pain, but al-Bakr remained expressionless.

"You will have to swim to Halifax. Do you understand?"

"Yes, I understand."

The man took a half-step back, then shoved al-Bakr out of the way and walked past him.

Realizing that he could no longer ignore the problem, al-Bakr waited until the man had disappeared from view before navigating his way to the captain's quarters. The door was open.

"I'm sorry to disturb you, Captain, but we have a problem."

"We?"

"Yes, *we*, Captain. I believe there is a large sum of money awaiting you upon our safe arrival in Halifax. Would you like for me to continue?"

The man removed his reading glasses and looked up from his nautical navigation chart. Al-Bakr explained what had happened on deck. The aging captain shook his head.

"He's a prick. Nothing but problems. I should have dealt with him long ago."

"Perhaps you would allow me to relieve you of this problem," al-Bakr suggested.

Sizing up the diminutive man in front of him, the captain cautioned, "I think you may be biting off more than you can chew. That man is like a mad dog. He will tear you apart if he is provoked. I've seen him do it to men twice your size."

"Let me worry about that, Captain."

"Do as you wish," the captain said, returning his gaze to the charts.

Before al-Bakr could leave, the captain stopped him. "I'm going to expect payment as promised, whether you are on board when we reach Halifax or not."

On the final morning of the sailor's life, his intended victim had begun his ritual walk around the deck. As al-Bakr rounded the stern, the sailor appeared.

"Have you brought the key?"

"Yes." Al-Bakr gestured toward the starboard side of the ship where the faded yellow container rested flush with the deck.

"Give it to me," the man demanded as he pushed al-Bakr toward the door of the container.

Al-Bakr surrendered the key.

The man opened the heavy padlock and let it drop onto the deck. As he swung open the door, two men leaped from within the metal box, grabbing the stunned sailor's arms in vice-like grips.

"Let me introduce you," al-Bakr began with quiet authority. "On your left is Yasir and on your right is Zahid. They are going to give you a swimming lesson."

The man twisted violently but was unable to break their hold. Yasir and Zahid dragged the man to the leeward side of the ship while al-Bakr replaced the padlock.

"You can't do this!" the man shouted, his voice infused with fear. "The captain will have you arrested the minute we reach port."

"The captain has already thanked me for taking care of his problem."

The sailor thrashed harder. Soon his back was against the ship's rail.

"Even a mad dog knows when not to attack."

As al-Bakr spoke his final words, Yasir and Zahid heaved the man overboard. His body flailed as it fell thirty feet to the dark, foaming ocean below. He wouldn't last long in the forty-degree water.

The man's screams drew an unwelcome crowd. A group of sailors encircled the three men.

Al-Bakr spoke, turning the full circumference of the circle so as to look into each man's eyes. "We boarded your ship in peace, and we plan to depart in peace. That man was worse than the vilest animal. You served with him. You know that I speak the truth. We have relieved you and your captain of a burden. Now, we trust that nothing more will disturb our passage to Halifax."

Al-Bakr could feel the circle of men tightening around them like a noose around his neck. In minutes, the sailors would set upon them with a fury.

A deafening burst of gunfire rang out, causing everyone to dive for the deck. The captain looked down on the crowd, an AK-47 in his hands.

"Take another step toward our guests and I'll spill your blood all over the ship," he growled.

"But they killed Mustaffa!" a man cried out.

"Thank Allah that they have rid us of that scum. I am the law on this ship. These men acted with my permission. Now go about your business and don't test my resolve."

The sailors dispersed like ants scurrying from a disturbed nest. Even so, the threat of retaliation would occupy al-Bakr's mind until the voyage ended and they docked safely in Halifax.

CHAPTER EIGHTEEN

December 18-20
Islamabad
Langley AFB

TWENTY-ONE DAYS HAD ELAPSED since terrorists had infiltrated the POF and absconded with a nuclear core. President Mughabi was exhausted. Yet, despite his earlier threats to notify American president Jonathan Conner, the president remained mute—unwilling to break the silence surrounding the disappearance of a nuclear core. He knew that if the Americans caught a whiff of a loose nuke, they would be crawling all over his country. He wasn't about to sacrifice Pakistan's sovereignty to the U.S. and its safety to India.

Beyond Mughabi, Malik, and Patel, only two people knew the details surrounding the core's disappearance, and one of them had vanished. With Barr out of the picture, that left Colonel Salman Kassar—a man all three trusted implicitly.

Like his compatriots, Kassar had risen quickly through the ranks of Pakistan's military. As second in command at the POF, the colonel was responsible for all nuclear devices housed proximate to the POF, including those at Kamra Airbase. Major Barr was his direct report.

Kassar was extraordinarily competent, but he was also a man of great appetites—for power, for women, and for prestige. His hunger had cost him an earlier promotion to general. This time, his promotion was in the bag.

Niya Jamali, one of the nation's most respected journalists, hosted a weekly news program on Pakistan Television Corporation. She had met Salman Kassar while interviewing the colonel in the aftermath of a suicide bomb attack on the POF. Not wanting to appear unseemly, he waited a week before inviting Niya for coffee. "Just to say thank you," he told her. It wasn't long before they were meeting often.

Niya emerged from the lavish marble bathroom in the Imperial Guest House wearing a short black silk robe that barely covered the top of her thighs. It was a gift from her lover. She seductively tugged at the robe's belt until the knot unfurled, then let the shimmering garment slide from her shoulders. She watched the excitement mount in Kassar's eyes.

Wearing nothing but a sheer bra and panties, she approached him until she was just beyond his reach. He rose from the pillows and stretched his arms out, awaiting her embrace.

She extended her long thin fingers toward him and then withdrew her hand at the last instant.

"Why do you tease me so, my darling?" the colonel asked, grasping in hopes of snaring the goddess.

"Because I want this dance to last."

But Kassar couldn't wait. He threw back the covers and lunged toward Niya. Wrapping her tightly in his arms, he carried her to bed and laid her across the satin sheets. She reached down and took hold of him, tugging rhythmically. Kassar moaned in delight.

"Enough, enough," he cried out . . . frantic to penetrate her.

"Don't you want to play some more? Maybe a kiss or two?"

But Kassar was no longer listening. He was on top of her, eager for the rush he would feel once within her warm, wet body.

In seconds, it was over—long before Niya had any prayer of climaxing. Kassar seemed oblivious to her needs. She had learned to expect little more from the narcissistic colonel.

His hunger for adulation was what attracted Niya to her target. If she administered the right strokes, it would unleash his tongue and secrets would pour out—or so she hoped.

Kassar lit a cigarette and offered one to Niya. She shook her head and snuggled up against his body, feigning contentment.

"I hope you enjoyed that, my love," she said, momentarily raising her head to look into his eyes. "Would you like more?"

"My dear, you have far too much energy for your aging lover. I'm quite content," he said as he drew deeply on the foul smelling Turkish cigarette, then exhaled in a flourish of smoke. It was a confident gesture, the kind men exhibit after completing a conquest.

Stroking the gray hair on his chest with her finger, Niya asked, "When can I see you again? I hate it that we are not together. You know that."

"Be grateful for what you have, Niya, and don't wish for what is beyond your reach. Things are very hectic at work right now."

"But you are a colonel . . . are you not in charge of your own destiny?"

"Soon to be a general," he corrected her.

Niya sat up abruptly. "What are you talking about? You've not said a word about this to me."

"Niya, you are a journalist, someone whose job is to uncover things of great interest."

"In this room, I am your lover . . . nothing more . . . nothing less. I trust you with my reputation, and I honor you with my silence," she responded.

"If you ever breach my confidence, the repercussions will be profound—for both of us. You do understand that?"

"Yes, darling. So tell me about your exciting news."

"I did an important favor for a very powerful man."

"And that favor . . . ?"

"No, my dear, that I cannot tell you."

Niya reached down and took him in her hand. "Please?" she pleaded softly while fondling him.

"Let's just say that the Americans will soon suffer the same degree of pain they have long inflicted on others."

"Don't be so cryptic," she cooed.

"No, I've already said too much. Wait until the New Year; then you will understand."

Kassar smiled as he stubbed out his cigarette, then rose from the bed. He pulled on his trousers, buttoned his shirt, and then carefully arranged the jacket of his uniform. Staring at himself in the mirror, he squared up his hat. He turned side to side, ensuring that nothing was out of order, then faced Niya.

"You will forgive me if I dash."

"Of course, but when will I see you again?"

"My wife and the children will be visiting her parents on the 25th. We can spend the night together, if you'd like." Without waiting for her response, he tipped his hat and walked out the door.

Niya jumped out of bed, headed for the bathroom. She grabbed a washcloth and bar of soap and then scrubbed herself in an effort to remove every trace of the man she so despised. After waiting fifteen minutes to ensure the colonel would not return, she removed a satellite phone from a pocket in the bottom of her bag. In seconds, she was connected to her handler at Langley.

Carl Johnson was a piece of work, but he was also one of the Agency's best when it came to running agents.

"Did he whisper sweet nothings in your ear?" he asked Niya.

"Be glad you are seven thousand miles away, Carl, or I would claw out your eyes," she responded, only half in jest. "The man is disgusting, and I should win an Academy Award for my performance each time I bed him."

"You've won the undying appreciation of your adopted country."

"Yeah, right. I've heard that from the DDO plenty of times, always when we're discussing my salary."

"You didn't call in to complain, Niya. What's going on?" Johnson knew that their time on the phone was limited.

"I don't know exactly, but I sense that something big is coming down."

"What did Kassar tell you?"

"He said that America would soon suffer the same pain that it has long inflicted on other nations."

"That's really specific."

"Don't be a smart-ass, Carl."

"Okay. Any clue as to what he meant?"

"Only an oblique reference to New Year's . . . it sounded like a pivotal date."

"Why didn't you probe further?"

Niya knew that only someone safely ensconced within the confines of headquarters would ask such an inane question.

"Remember, Carl, I am his adoring lover. Not his inquisitor."

"What's your confidence level, Niya?"

"High. The son-of-a-bitch was puffed up like a rooster as he bragged to me of his impending promotion and the deeds leading up to it."

"Mr. Kahn will want to hear this directly from you," Johnson said, referring to the DDO.

"I understand. You know how to reach me."

"Be careful, Niya. Kassar may realize the gravity of the mistake he made by sharing this information."

"No, he doesn't think with his head . . . not the one atop his shoulders. He's too busy planning our next rendezvous."

"And when would that be?"

"On Christmas Day."

She didn't wait for Carl's response before terminating the call and replacing the phone in the hidden compartment in her bag.

CHAPTER NINETEEN

December 20
Langley AFB
Islamabad

CARL JOHNSON KNEW NOT TO INTERRUPT the DDO unless the matter was urgent. Marvin Kahn glared at Johnson as he pulled him out of a meeting with Jason Harding, Deputy Director for the CIA's analytic division.

"I trust it's important, Carl."

"Yes, Sir. Well, I believe so, Sir." He always became a bit flummoxed when speaking to the DDO.

"Let's not keep Deputy Director Harding waiting any longer than necessary," the DDO warned, his tone a bit less caustic.

"Niya Jamali reported in twenty minutes ago. She has been with Colonel Kassar. Based upon some comments made by the colonel, Niya believes that something significant may be in play."

"What in God's name does that mean?" Kahn's tone was once again impatient.

"She believes that some action may be taken against the United States before the New Year."

"Well that's real insightful," Kahn's contempt was growing by the minute. "Get her on the phone, now."

Niya was en route to the television station when she sensed the almost imperceptible vibration of her sat-phone. Picking it up, she heard Carl Johnson's voice.

"You are on speaker, Niya. I am in with Mr. Kahn."

"Good evening, Ms. Jamali. It must be late there?"

"Yes, Sir. Quite late."

"Mr. Johnson has briefed me, but I would like to hear it from you: What transpired in your meeting with the colonel?"

Meeting—is that was she had just endured? Niya asked herself, swallowing hard before responding.

"The colonel is anticipating a promotion to general. He said that it was the result of a favor he had performed for a very important man."

"Is that your news, Ms. Jamali?" Kahn questioned.

"Sir, the colonel went on to say that Americans were about to suffer the same pain they had inflicted on others. Though he did not provide any details, he told me that things would become clear at the New Year. "

"I see. Thank you, Ms. Jamali."

"Thank you, Mr. Kahn."

Johnson terminated the call.

"Do you believe this warrants a special meeting with the president?" Johnson asked his boss.

"Our president seems to think that I over-react. So, no, it will wait until morning. There is someone I do want to be briefed, however. I need for you to stay, Carl. I'm going to ask Dottie to track down Commander Hart."

CHAPTER TWENTY

Port of Karachi

THE NIGHT WAS COOL AND BLACK. High clouds obscured the stars, and a slight wind was blowing in from the north. The *Jasmine* rocked gently in its mooring. The rhythmic motion went unnoticed by the captain, who lay obsessing in his bunk. Like a continuous loop tape, his last conversation with al-Bakr kept replaying in his head. If he had been a man of faith, he would have prayed for sleep. Instead, he lay there, bedeviled by his thoughts.

"I'm offering you the ability to strike back at the Americans who took your son. I'm offering you passage off of this freighter, and freedom from the bottle. In short, I'm offering you a new life."

It was a promise too good to be true. But did he have the courage to open that door . . . to walk a path without the certainty of where it led? His son had had the guts to pursue a dream, and look at where it had gotten him.

When sleep finally overtook him, it brought little relief. Anxious dreams came and went, leaving him to toss and turn in their wake.

As morning's first light dawned on the horizon, the captain was engaged by a phantom. It was a dream he had experienced repeatedly since his son's death . . . a dream in which Azra was cloaked in a white shroud unscathed by burns. The boy smiled, as if to reassure his father that he was alright, but said nothing.

That's when the dream always ended, but not this morning. As his father approached, the boy held up an outstretched palm—in it was a cell phone. The captain was jolted from his slumber. He lurched from his bed, sweat dripping from his forehead.

Before rational thought could intrude, he moved toward the safe and spun the combination dial. As it clicked open, he reached in and extracted the phone. Powering it up, he was relieved to see that it still held a small charge. He pushed the speed dial number as instructed, and a ringtone followed. It was 6:30 AM.

He heard the phone connect, but no one answered.

"Hello? Hello?"

There was no response.

"This is the Captain of the *Jasmine*," he continued, feeling awkward and vulnerable.

Seconds ticked by. Finally, a man spoke.

"I need you to listen carefully, Captain; I am going to say this only once." The voice paused before continuing. "1102 Bethel, December 23, 1600 hours. Wear a red jacket and a black stocking cap."

The captain's lips moved silently as he repeated the information under his breath, hoping to encode it permanently in his memory.

"Repeat what I have told you," the voice instructed.

When the captain complied, a final instruction followed. "Now walk to your ship's railing and drop the phone in the water."

"But what if I need to contact you?"

His question was ignored, followed instead by a final admonishment: "The day of our meeting, I will wait ten minutes, no more. If you have not arrived, I will leave. We will not speak again."

The phone went dead.

A third person remained on the line. He was seated in a cubicle at Fort Meade, Maryland, and he had listened to the entire conversation. He waited a second before pressing a key on his computer, terminating the recording at fifty-two seconds. Before contacting his supervisor, the man cued up a voiceprint from Ahmed Dar. When compared to his new audio file, it was a perfect match.

"Sir, we've got a hit on Ahmed Dar."

"You're certain it was Dar?"

"It matches his voiceprint and it's coming from a cell phone believed to be in his possession."

"I'll be right there," the man replied, as he walked out of his office and into the sea of workstations filled with analysts busily monitoring communications around the world. He plugged his headphones into a jack on the front of the analyst's computer.

"Play it for me," the supervisor instructed.

And then, "Play it again, please."

"Who is this captain of the *Jasmine*?" he asked, after listening intently to the full recording.

"We're still working on that, Sir."

"You need to work faster," his supervisor ordered. "I want everything that is discoverable about the captain downloaded onto a flash drive within the hour. The admiral will want to be fully informed before reaching out to the DDO."

"If I may ask, Sir, what makes you believe the admiral will engage the Agency?"

"Because someone needs to intercept more than just a phone call."

A ghost within the NSA was already at work trying to identify the captain. Elliot Fisher knew that information was power, and he wasn't about to be overshadowed by a lowly analyst working in a cube farm.

CHAPTER TWENTY-ONE

December 20
CIA Headquarters

"The DDO needs to speak with you ASAP, Commander," Dottie informed Hart after reaching him by cell.

"Fine, put him through."

"He wants you on-site."

"I'm twenty minutes away. Tell Mr. Kahn that I'll see him shortly."

Kahn wasn't in the habit of yanking Hart's chain . . . not unless it was for a damn good reason. As he turned onto the GW Memorial Parkway, Hart floored his vintage 850CI black BMW, stoking the V12 that lurked under its hood. It was Hart's one true indulgence—feeding his need for speed. Hitting ninety mph in a forty-five mph zone, he backed it down a notch. No point in being picked up on his way to work. It required too much explaining.

A scant twelve minutes later, the commander was striding down a long hallway toward the DDO's private conference room.

"He and Carl Johnson are waiting for you . . . " Dottie said, as Hart breezed by her.

He gave a cursory knock before entering. Kahn and Johnson sat opposite one another at the center of the oval table.

"Have a seat, Commander, we're going to be here for a while," Kahn instructed.

"Yes, Sir," Hart responded.

"It looks like you might have been right, Commander."

"About what, Sir?"

"The car bombing in Philly. Mr. Johnson has some information supporting your assertion that something more serious may loom on the horizon. Go ahead, Carl. Bring the commander up to speed."

Johnson was all business as he downloaded the gist of what he had learned from the covert operative in Pakistan.

"What do you make of it, Commander?" Kahn asked.

"How long have you been running Niya, Carl?"

"Five years."

"And how reliable would you rate her intel?"

"I'd stake my life on it."

Hart stood up and walked over to a white-board.

"May I?" he asked Kahn before beginning to outline the key elements from Niya's report.

"We know that Kassar is responsible for the storage, safety, and transportation of nukes at the POF, as well as Kamra. That means that anyone acting under his authority has direct access to nuclear material." With a red marker, Hart wrote the word *nuke* on the board.

"Kassar is pretty far up the food chain. I can only think of two people in his orbit that have the ability to request a favor and then reward it with such a promotion: General Patel, to whom he reports, and General Malik." Hart added their names to the board.

"Patel is a good soldier, but Malik has him under his thumb. According to our sources, it's been that way since they first served together as lieutenants in the disputed Kashmir region. So I'm betting that the favor is at the behest of Malik. And what do we know about Malik?"

Johnson spoke, "We know that he's in bed with UIS. And we know that he played a role in last year's biological attack."

Hart wrote *UIS* in huge letters on the board.

"Kassar said that America 'will suffer greatly.' I believe we have some inkling as to what the words *suffering greatly* mean to an organization that killed tens of thousands with a virus intended to kill millions." He added the words to the whiteboard.

"Finally, we have an approximate date for the event." He wrote *January 1.*

"Commander, you're concluding that UIS has procured a nuclear weapon . . . and that weapon will be used against the United States no later than New Year's. Is that what you are saying?"

"Yes."

"Is there room for less draconian interpretations?" Kahn asked.

"Is there a fault in my logic, Sir?"

"No."

"Then I believe my interpretation is reasonable."

"There's more, Commander." Marvin Kahn picked up a folder and slid it across the width of the table toward Hart. "Go ahead and open it," he instructed.

Inside was a grainy satellite photo of a woman getting into a large vehicle. Several more images followed, each providing a wider angle to provide perspective. The vehicle was departing a cabin adjacent to a frozen lake. Hart knew it was too early in the season for lakes in Minnesota and the Dakotas to be frozen over, so it had to be farther north. No smoke was emanating from the chimney. And there was no propane tank to suggest a source of heat other than a wood-burning stove. Therefore, whoever was leaving did not plan to return any time soon.

"Canada?" he asked Kahn.

"Very good, Commander. Now, tell me if you recognize her."

Hart was searching his memory, but coming up short. There was no way to recognize the woman in a photograph taken from a satellite orbiting 350 miles above the earth, but there was something about the car and the location.

"Sarah Qaisrani?"

Kahn turned toward Carl Johnson. "The man has more memory than a Cray supercomputer."

Hart smiled briefly before asking, "Where is she?"

"You know that we've had her under surveillance since the event," Kahn began.

"Yes, Sir."

"We hoped she would eventually lead us to al-Bakr."

"Is there a reason why I haven't been briefed on Qaisrani's activities before today?"

"There was nothing to share, Commander. Since the bio-attack, Sarah Qaisrani has been a model citizen of Canada, and she's never ventured more than a few miles from home. She's had one repeat visitor. Our guess is that he's a courier. We've not intervened to date."

"And now?"

Kahn clicked a remote and a flat-screen television displayed the image of a map. A red dot could be seen in the center of the map. It was moving east.

"That's a live tracking of the vehicle's movement." He pressed the remote a second time, and a swath of color highlighted an area from Philadelphia south to slightly north of New York City. "Based on her current trajectory, our best guess is that she will arrive in New York in a few days."

"There's one more image, Commander." This one was razor sharp, taken from a low altitude drone at close proximity. It showed Qaisrani conversing with a man on her doorstep.

"This is the man we suspect to be a courier, He showed up a few weeks ago. The man drove all the way to Matheson Island only to stay five minutes. He didn't even enter the house," Kahn reported.

"So he delivered a message and was wise enough to avoid any extended contact with the Arctic Fox," Hart ventured.

"That seems to be a reasonable interpretation."

"Did we pick him up?"

"No, we tracked his return to a small town outside of Columbia, Missouri. We'll keep an eye on him for now."

"Gentlemen, are you connecting these two events—the movement of Sarah Qaisrani with the pillow talk of a narcissistic colonel half a world away? What do the escapades of Colonel Kassar, as reported by Niya, have to do with the Arctic Fox?"

"We were hoping you might answer that question," Kahn answered.

"I like to solve puzzles, Mr. Kahn, but it's tough when you only have half the pieces."

"Indulge me, Commander. How might these pieces fit?"

"Yes, Sir. Qaisrani has been holed up in a godforsaken piece of Canadian tundra trying to stay off our radar screen. Suddenly she leaves the security of her cabin and heads to a major East Coast city, presumably New York, shortly before New Year's. Her actions are triggered by a messenger delivering unknown news."

"And?" Kahn wanted to skip to the bottom line.

"Worst case scenario? She is going to rendezvous with al-Bakr, who carries with him some type of nuclear device intended to light up New York as part of the New Year's celebration. Now that would give Kathie Lee something to talk about."

Kahn ignored the flippant remark. "Are you confident enough, Commander, to share that interpretation with President Conner?"

"Yes, Sir."

"Good. We're scheduled to brief the president and his advisors at 6:30 AM."

"Sir, I suggest we detain the messenger. I'd like to speak to him."

"I'll have him picked up."

As Kahn moved to wrap up the meeting, Dottie stuck her head into the room.

"Excuse me, Mr. Kahn, but I have Vice-Admiral Wilson on a video link. He's asked to speak with you. He understands that Commander Hart and Mr. Johnson are present. "

"Put him through," Kahn instructed.

Seconds later, the bald head of the Director of the NSA filled the sixty-inch screen at one end of the conference room.

CHAPTER TWENTY-TWO

CIA Headquarters

"ADMIRAL, TO WHAT DO WE OWE THE PLEASURE?" Kahn inquired.

Pleasure was not the best of words to describe how the DDO felt about the admiral. A level of competitive tension always existed between leaders of sister organizations, despite the necessity of collaboration. It was at its worst during budget season, when agencies competed for federal dollars. Greater budgets meant greater power, which fueled the animus. Fortunately, most senior intelligence service execs were politically adroit enough to keep their feelings in check.

"Gentlemen, thank you for letting me intrude on your meeting," Wilson said by way of greeting.

"Actually, we were just finishing up, Admiral, so your timing is good. I trust this is not a social call."

"No, Mr. Kahn, it is not. We picked up a communication a few hours ago from Karachi. Two men were talking cryptically about a meeting. You are quite familiar with one of the men—Ahmed Dar."

"And the other?" Kahn asked.

"The other man is the captain of a ship named the *Jasmine*, which is docked in the Port of Karachi. It's an old rust-bucket flying under Panamanian registry. We know that a meeting has been set up between Dar and the captain, but not why."

"Is there anything else you picked up?" Kahn asked.

"It's clear from their conversation that the two men have never met. You'll see it in the transcript, which I am having sent to you as we speak."

"What are you suggesting, Admiral?" Kahn asked.

"It will be the first time since the bio-attack that we can predict Dar's whereabouts on a given date. Appropriate management of Mr. Dar has been sanctioned. So I suggest we capitalize on this opportunity."

"And what of the captain of the *Jasmine*?" Hart asked.

"I don't think that's material. Dar is our target," the admiral responded.

"With all due respect, Admiral, I beg to differ. For Dar to risk a meeting with someone he doesn't know, let alone trust, suggests a level of importance that we shouldn't ignore . . . or perhaps a direct order from al-Bakr."

"Alright, Commander, what would you do?"

"I would put one of our field agents in Dar's place—allowing the agent to complete the meeting with the captain as scheduled. Since the captain has never laid eyes on Dar, the deception should be easy to pull off. We may learn something in the process."

"And what do you hope to learn, Commander?"

"For starters, whether the captain has had any contact with a badly deformed man wearing wire-frame glasses, and if that man was transporting any type of cargo."

"Isn't that a bit of a stretch, gentlemen?"

"No, Admiral, not based upon what I've learned tonight," Kahn replied. "There seems to be mounting evidence of a potential plot against the United States involving weapons of mass destruction. It's too early to say more than that, but the *Jasmine* may be involved."

"We should be working hand in hand, Mr. Kahn."

"Agreed Admiral, we should." Kahn terminated the call.

"What a smug son of a bitch." Kahn spoke what Hart was thinking.

"Yes, Sir," the Commander responded. "It looks like I'm headed to Karachi, Mr. Kahn."

"No. I'm holding you in reserve, Commander. Let the field agents handle it. I need you here. We've got less than eleven hours to assemble a buttoned-down plan for the president. Hopefully that includes getting a little sleep, too."

The men hunkered down until shortly before 2 AM, completing their detailed situational analysis based upon the existing intelligence. A series of recommendations followed the analysis, including the termination of Ahmed Dar and the interception of the man with whom he was to meet. It would be up to the president to approve the Agency's proposed course of action.

CHAPTER TWENTY-THREE

December 21
The White House

Sixty years before Jonathan Conner was sworn in as the forty-sixth president of the United States, John F. Kennedy was hard at work building his legacy. He faced a plethora of challenges—from the growing threat posed by the Soviet Union to internal issues, such as racial inequality—capable of ripping apart the very fabric of American society. But Kennedy was undaunted. He never blinked. No challenge was too big or too small . . . even those dealing with the White House bowling alley. Commissioned by Harry S. Truman, it provided the former haberdasher with a way of managing the heat while remaining in the kitchen—a reprieve from important decisions . . . such as dropping the atomic bomb.

But Kennedy had no need for bowling. What he desperately wanted was a nexus for communications related to national security, a place where evolving geopolitical situations could be discussed in earnest. So he instructed his National Security Advisor, McGeorge Bundy, to create a 24/7 connection with the nation's vital defense assets. When completed, it became known as the *Situation Room*.

Bundy's original design expanded over fifty years into a 5,000-square-foot complex of secure meeting rooms equipped with the latest technology. The main conference room seated twelve at its table, with room for an additional eighteen on the perimeter. There were six flat-screen monitors mounted on the walls, controlled by a staff that included thirty national security specialists.

"Welcome, gentlemen. I believe you know everyone in the room," President Conner said as he swept his arm across the Situation Room. A half-dozen faces gazed up from the table at Hart and Kahn, each man and woman undoubtedly wondering what prompted the CIA to schedule an emergency meeting.

"Let's get to work, gentlemen," the president said, his shirt-sleeves already rolled half-way up his forearms. "The floor is yours, Mr. Kahn. Please proceed."

"Thank you, Mr. President. Ladies and gentlemen, there are three events that we wish to discuss with you—events that may be harbingers of dark days ahead unless we are able to intervene. The first concerns a deeply placed asset in Pakistan—a female agent who has developed an intimate relationship with a Pakistani colonel named Salman Kassar." As Kahn spoke, a life-size image of Kassar appeared on the screen.

"Colonel Kassar reports to General Ash Patel." With a press of the remote, Kahn replaced Kassar's image with that of Patel.

"As you will recall, General Patel is the Chairman of the Pakistan Ordnance Factories, which supply armaments to nations across the world. Along with an adjoining air force base at Kamra, the POF also serves as a repository for a significant portion of Pakistan's nuclear arsenal. Colonel Kassar's job is to safeguard those nukes."

"Where is this taking us, Mr. Kahn?" Conner asked impatiently.

"We've long suspected that General Patel has ties to UIS, along with his army buddy, General Malik. Yesterday we received a satellite communication from our asset following a recent encounter she had with the colonel. It appears that Colonel Kassar, acting at the behest of Generals Patel and Malik, may have contributed materially to UIS's ability to foment terror."

As the former governor of New Mexico, President Jonathan Conner was imbued with a heightened sensitivity to nuclear issues. His state had been home to the world's first nuclear detonation at a test site in Alamogordo. Today, it housed Sandia National Laboratory—a vital center for atomic research.

"Tell me, in plain English, what you're getting at, Mr. Kahn," Conner instructed.

"We believe that senior Pakistani Army officers, in collusion with UIS leadership, have provided terrorists with nuclear materials."

The tone in the conference shifted abruptly. President Conner waited until a measure of decorum returned before speaking.

"I trust you have impeccable evidence upon which to predicate such a damaging conclusion?"

"We have evidence that points in a direction, Mr. President." Kahn responded.

"You are saying that it's inconclusive?"

"What I'm saying, Sir, is that it is sufficiently credible to warrant this group's attention."

"It sounds like you are asking us to consider substantive action based upon pillow talk shared by a CIA seductress."

"That's not how I would characterize our asset, Mr. President, nor would I diminish the significance of what she learned at great risk."

"I'm sorry. I should not have been disparaging of our agent. Please continue," President Conner urged.

"The colonel is a vain man and could not resist sharing news of his impending promotion to the rank of general with his lover. He volunteered that the promotion was recompense for providing a major favor to an important man. Based upon his position, that means he sought to curry favor with Patel or Malik."

"And it's your assertion that such favor equates with the transfer of nuclear material to a terrorist organization . . . do I have that right, Mr. Kahn?" Conner asked. "Couldn't it be something a bit more mundane?"

"Colonel Kassar stated that 'America would soon suffer greatly.' He even went so far as to specify the date by which the suffering would occur—New Year's. When these messages are considered in totality, it's not difficult to arrive at a catastrophic scenario involving the theft of nuclear weapons."

"That's it . . . no more detail?" The Secretary of Homeland Security protested.

"With all due respect, Mr. Secretary, if our asset pressed the colonel for details, it would surely raise his suspicions. She has done everything possible without betraying her position."

"You began this briefing by talking about three matters, Mr. Kahn. You've shared one. Let us hear the remaining two," the president instructed.

Kahn advanced to the next slide, which contained an aerial reconnaissance photo of a woman standing by the door of an SUV. There appeared to be snow on the ground, and the woman was wearing a heavy coat.

"This woman is Sarah Qaisrani. We've had her under surveillance since locating her after the biological attack last year. As we agreed during a briefing at that time, we did not take her into custody, hoping she would lead us to al-Bakr."

"You are presuming al-Bakr is alive," Conner interjected.

"As I recall, Mr. President, you supported such an assumption."

Conner nodded his head in acquiescence.

"Sarah Qaisrani, aka the *Arctic Fox*, has left her cabin in Canada and is headed east . . . presumably to New York. We don't think these matters are coincidental. Our bet is that she plans to rendezvous with al-Bakr and his recently acquired nuclear device."

"That's a hell of a leap," the Director of Homeland Security interjected.

"Yes, Sir, it is, and I hope I'm wrong. But if I'm right . . . "

"If you are right, we're facing unimaginable devastation," Conner said quietly.

Kahn continued. "The third and final thread concerns communication between the captain of a ship in the Port of Karachi and Ahmed Dar, one of al-Bakr's trusted lieutenants. Dar has arranged a meeting with the captain of a vessel known as the *Jasmine*. It is possible that the ship's captain was somehow complicit in transporting al-Bakr and his stolen cargo out of Pakistan."

"With all due respect, Mr. Kahn, that sounds as though you're filling in the blanks with conjecture," the president observed.

"That's my job, Sir."

"It's also your job to either verify or invalidate your conclusions based upon data so that we may take informed and appropriate action."

Conner's tone at times verged on being prosecutorial, a result of his professional pedigree. He had graduated first in his law school class at the University of Texas and then had gone on to clerk with U.S. Supreme Court Justice Sandra Day O'Connor.

"Yes, Sir. To that end, I've asked Commander Hart to share our recommendations with you."

Kahn was relieved to hand off to Hart. There was always tension between the DDO and the president. Conner had questioned many of Kahn's prior threat assessments, refusing to take action without clear evidence. Hart, on the other hand, enjoyed Conner's full confidence. Conner knew that, without Hart, there would be no United States. An unholy caliphate would rule a world whose population had been decimated by a virtually unstoppable virus. The debt of gratitude owed Hart was immeasurable, a fact that the commander never leveraged to his advantage.

"Commander, tell us what you and Mr. Kahn are recommending."

"Sir, like Mr. Kahn, I believe that these threads are woven together and that a major attack may be imminent."

Conner lifted his elbows from the table and sat back in his chair, hands folded in contemplation.

"There are four courses of action we wish to pursue, Mr. President. The first involves Colonel Kassar. We wish to arrange for his extraction."

Tom Harden, the Attorney General, sprang to attention. "Are you suggesting that the president authorize the kidnapping of a foreign national, Commander?"

"Stand down, Tom," Conner ordered.

"But Mr. President . . ." the AG knew his protestations were in vain.

"You were saying, Commander."

"The colonel will have a short visit to one of our sites in Thailand, and then I will speak with him in London. I don't think we need to get into the specifics, but there are methods to encourage his cooperation."

"You know how I feel about enhanced interrogation, Commander."

"Yes, Sir. It's a topic on which our views differ, but I don't anticipate the need for any form of enhanced interrogation where the colonel is concerned."

"And your second recommendation, Commander?"

"We will work closely with the Bureau and local law enforcement agencies up and down the coast to monitor Sarah Qaisrani's movements. The Bureau will also take the lead in assembling dossiers on known UIS sympathizers in Boston, New York, Washington, and Philadelphia. Once they are completed, the photos of persons of interest will be circulated to hotels, rental car agencies, bus and airline terminals, and, of course, law enforcement.

"Third, we will close the loop on the captain of the *Jasmine* and Ahmed Dar. I don't know what intelligence may be gleaned, but my intuition tells me it will be something important. At the very least, we will eliminate the ongoing threat posed by Mr. Dar."

Conner implicitly granted permission by failing to raise any further objections.

"You mentioned four interdictions, Commander. I've counted only three."

"The fourth involves going out on limb, Mr. President."

Tom Harden, the AG, tried to stifle a laugh. As though they weren't already being hung out to dry.

"I believe we should attempt to co-op Ayesha Naru, the general's daughter," Hart said.

"What makes you believe that she is involved in this scheme?"

Tom Harden had to jump in. "Another hunch, Commander?"

"I wouldn't call it that, Sir. We know that Dr. Naru allows her father to conduct clandestine meetings in her clinic," Hart responded.

"That's a far cry from participating in the theft of a nuclear weapon destined for our borders. Still, I'll grant you that she may be complicit in some small way. But explain to me why she would turn on her father—betray him," Conner asked.

"We believe that she is quite conflicted. She spends her days trying to repair the damage inflicted on children by war. I can tell you from experience that the images of maimed babies don't fade quickly from one's memory. I cannot imagine that she would stand idly by as her father participated in the wholesale murder of civilians, many of them children, no matter how much she despises the United States."

"Why do you say that she despises us, Commander?"

"A year ago, her mother died under suspicious circumstances in a car accident. It was assumed that her father was the intended target and that the accident was the work of the Agency."

"Was it?" asked the president.

Kahn reacted. "No, Mr. President, we had nothing to do with it. We believe the 'accident' was perpetrated by ISI acting upon the orders of President Mughabi."

"Why would Mughabi order his commanding general's death?"

"Presumably it was in repayment for General Malik's treachery during the bio-event," Kahn speculated.

"If Ayesha Malik holds us culpable, surely she won't talk to you, Commander," Conner responded.

"I won't be the one to approach her, Sir. We're positioning someone to play that role . . . someone whom she is coming to trust."

"Is there more, Commander?"

"There is one other person who may be responsible for her mother's death."

"And who might that be?"

"General Malik, Sir."

"You are suggesting that he would kill his own wife, the mother of his daughter, and frame the CIA?"

"Yes, Sir. It is a possibility."

Hart looked toward Kahn, whose body language sent a strong message not to reveal any further details. To do so would risk unmasking Kahn's cover-up.

"Would you care to elaborate, Commander Hart?" the president asked.

"No, Sir, that's all I have to share at this time."

"Comments?" Conner asked of the assembled group.

Herb Copeland, Director of Homeland Security, was the first to speak. "On the surface, I think it all sounds ludicrous. You'll forgive me for being so blunt, Gentlemen. But it's no more ludicrous than a biological attack would have sounded a few years ago. The commander has earned my trust. His intuition is sufficient cause for me to recommend raising the level of alert at our borders and ports."

"Sir, if I may?" Hart waited for the president's approval before continuing.

"We are searching for something small enough to be carried in a backpack. The core is approximately seven centimeters in diameter and weighs twenty-six kilos. It is the proverbial needle in the haystack. U.S. Customs and Border Protection personnel inspect a hundred thousand shipments each day. It's not much of a reach to suggest that something might slip through, despite our efforts."

"That's why we have equipment to screen for radiation, Commander, particularly neutron emissions," Copeland reminded Hart.

"With all due respect, Sir, it's difficult to pick up the radiation signature of a uranium core, particularly if it incorporates shielding. If it were plutonium, I would be in full agreement with you. The bottom line is that our scanners can be fooled."

Senator Mark Rigbee, Chairman of the Senate Intelligence Committee, came at Hart hard, "Commander, you have no reliable evidence that al-Bakr is in possession of a nuclear core, let alone that he plans to smuggle it into the United States. Hell, we don't even know if the bastard is alive. Yet you have convinced yourself that al-Bakr is armed with a virtually undetectable uranium core en route to our shores. Aren't you getting a bit carried away?"

"Al-Bakr has had years to study our border security. His organization employs nuclear engineers, physicists, and a host of other professionals schooled in how to evade our counter-measures. Senator Rigbee, al-Bakr would not randomly choose to smuggle in a U-235 core—one that weighed three times that of a core fabricated from plutonium. He would knowingly pick uranium because he knew it could be rendered virtually undetectable."

Conner jumped in. "Let's assume for a moment that you are right, Commander. You've failed to mention retaliatory measures against Pakistan—even if only to secure its remaining nukes and neutralize the threat they represent to our nation and our allies."

"Mr. President, I believe there will be plenty of time for retaliation against Pakistan, as we deem fit, including appropriation of their entire nuclear arsenal. If we move on that today, we may inadvertently trigger two actions. The perpetrators of the nuclear theft will become aware that we have uncovered their plot and may accelerate the timetable for detonating the device. If there is a plot in place, we need every possible minute to stop it. Furthermore, any action that removes Pakistan's nuclear umbrella makes it vulnerable to attack by India."

"But we can intervene with India and explain the importance of standing down," Conner insisted.

"Can we, Mr. President? I know the hatred incited by the viciousness of the attack on Mumbai by Pakistani terrorists. India is itching for a fight and would love nothing better than to reclaim the Kashmir region. I don't think we want to throw fuel on that fire."

"What about reaching out to President Mughabi?" Conner asked.

"Sir, I trust that President Mughabi is aware of the disappearance of the weapon and probably assumes that Kassar, Patel, and Malik played a part in it. He's a shrewd man, as you know well, and has probably weighed his options . . . much as we are doing. Mughabi, with the counsel of his advisors, will decide that the threat of an attack by India outweighs any potential benefit gained by discussing the loss of nuclear material with our government."

Conner knew it was time for him to render a verdict. "We've known for decades that we would eventually face this challenge, and now it has been laid upon our doorstep. Do as you must, gentlemen."

Conner stood. The meeting was over.

As the group exited, Conner pulled Hart aside. "Commander, I'm counting on you to get us through this mess."

"Yes, Sir. That's what I do," Hart said with determination.

"Is there anything you need from me, Commander?"

"There's one small thing, Sir. With your permission, I would like to read Liz into this matter."

"Why? Don't get me wrong, I have great respect for Dr. Wilkins, but I fail to see how an expert in infectious diseases can assist in a potential nuclear holocaust."

"You witnessed the role Liz played in stopping a global pandemic, Mr. President. Dr. Wilkin's discernment and critical thinking skills are superb, and they are in no way limited to the field of medicine. She could be invaluable as we seek to respond to whatever lies ahead."

"No disagreement, Commander, but if she were my fiancée, I'd put her on the first plane as far away from here as possible . . . and I sure as hell wouldn't let her return until well after the New Year. But I can see by the look on your face, Commander, that's not going to happen."

"No, Sir."

"Based upon Dr. Wilkins' familiarity with our health care infrastructure and its ability to respond to a catastrophic situation, I'll instruct the Secretary of HHS to designate Liz as the Principal Federal Officer. That will make her responsible for managing interagency coordination should an event arise. I will also speak with the Secretary of DHS to ensure that Liz plays a role in the implementation of the National Response Plan . . . which, by the way, is an area where you will be called on to serve as well, Commander . . . should it come to that."

"Let's hope we can stop things well in advance of needing such initiatives, Sir."

"Agreed. There's one more thing, Commander."

"Sir?"

"You spoke of a uranium core. A core isn't a bomb. I'll grant you it's the most critical and difficult component to procure, but we both know the complexity of achieving a nuclear blast. How would al-Bakr transform a core into a weapon of mass destruction, and do so over a matter of weeks, not years?"

"I'm working on that, Sir."

CHAPTER TWENTY-FOUR

December 21
Washington/Georgetown

TWICE A YEAR, THE POWERFUL ENERGY COURSING through Washington, D.C. was momentarily quelled. It happened in April, when the cherry blossoms bloomed, and at Christmas. Even entrenched Washingtonians slowed their frenzied pace in deference to the holidays. It was as if a wisp of humanity momentarily replaced the partisan bickering that normally divided the city.

Christmas was fast approaching, and Liz was thrilled to have two weeks off from her job at the CDC. Though she spent most weekends with Hart, they always felt rushed. Friday nights vanished in a blur of exhaustion on the heels of nonstop work-weeks. Once she was rested, Saturdays spent with John were blissful, but they passed far too quickly. Then Sunday came, and with it the anxiety of being separated once again. All the more reason Liz was determined to make the most of each day ahead.

But aspirations weren't assurances, she realized, as John walked through the door. Something was wrong.

She hadn't seen him in nearly twenty-four hours—not since he sped off to meet with Marvin Kahn. He'd called late, awakening her from a deep sleep, only to tell her that he wasn't coming home. With a 6:30 AM meeting looming on the horizon, there was little point in returning to the apartment. He would just camp out at the office and hope to see Liz by early afternoon.

"You'd make a hell of a poker player," Liz said, reaching for his coat before he could dump it unceremoniously on the couch.

"I don't know what you are talking about."

"You know damn well what I'm talking about, cowboy. So 'fess up, what's happening that's got you in such a funk?"

"I've got to leave for a few days."

"That doesn't sound too awful. I'll survive. Is there more? Did something happen last night?"

"We need to call off the trip to New York."

His words hit her like a roundhouse punch. It brought on a sinking feeling—like the one she experienced after first learning of the pandemic.

"Call it off?" she asked incredulously.

"Postpone it."

"Why on earth would we do that? Don't tell me that you've got to leave the country on some damn mission."

"That's not it, Liz."

"Then what is it, John?"

"Let's move this conversation into my office."

It was the most secure spot in the condo. The extra bedroom had been converted into Hart's home office with the help of a CIA contractor. In addition to being soundproof, the windows were coated with a unique film manufactured in

Martinsville, Virginia. Though only a few thousandths of an inch thick, it blocked all electromagnetic signals from entering or exiting the space, thus creating a secure environment.

"Give me a break. It's not like there are laser listening devices trained on our windows with foreign agents hanging on every word. Sometimes I think you overplay all this cloak and dagger stuff."

"That's because you don't live in my world."

"I lived in your world for months, remember, when we were fighting together to stave off a pandemic that killed thousands? For what it's worth, I was damn glad to get back to my own reality."

"Point taken."

Hart smiled, but was unyielding as he gestured toward the office.

"Fine," Liz responded, "I'll play along with your little charade."

Hart proceeded, undaunted by Liz's attitude. "I requested the president's permission to read you in to the briefing."

"President Conner? What are you talking about? I thought you were at the Agency all this time."

"I was in a meeting with the DDO and Carl Johnson. We spent half the night formulating a plan to present to President Conner and his key advisors at daybreak—a plan that is in direct response to a potential existential threat against our nation."

Liz's body jerked involuntarily. She'd ridden out Armageddon once already, which was enough for a lifetime. She struggled to comprehend how another cataclysm could arise on its heels.

"I'm listening," she murmured.

Hart explained what had transpired over the past twenty-four hours, giving her ample time to appreciate the magnitude and veracity of the threat.

"So, as I said a minute ago, we need to talk about rescheduling New York."

"The hell we do," Liz said with a resolve that stopped Hart short. "We're not capitulating to terrorists. Screw these crazy people. Whatever the risk, it's no greater than what we've already been through. Plus, you don't know for certain that a nuclear weapon is headed for the U.S., let alone that New York is the intended target."

"Sorry, Liz, but it's not going to happen. I'm not risking your life," Hart said, trying to regain control.

"It's not your life to risk. I make my own choices. I count on you to respect that. Are we clear, Commander?"

"I thought I might lose this battle. Yes, Doctor. It's clear.

"I've spoken with the president about a role for you as things continue to unfold. He's going to speak with the Secretaries of HHS and DHS, but I think you can count on an upcoming appointment as Principal Federal Officer."

"Why did you just put me through that, John, only to then tell me that I was quarterbacking part of the action?"

"Because I love you and want you as far away from harm as humanly possible. Fault me if you like, but it's as simple as that. I do have to leave for a few days . . . London, nothing too exotic."

"I think you should take me with you," Liz suggested.

"No can do, darling, but I promise I won't be gone long."

CHAPTER TWENTY-FIVE

The Port of Karachi

ENORMOUS PALM TREES LINED THE DOCKS at the Port of Karachi. Straight and tall, they stood like a garrison of sentries called to attention. Each tree was the width of two men at its base and had been anchored at the dock for more than fifty years. They conveyed a touch of sophistication to an otherwise seamy waterfront.

A man dressed in the uniform of a port inspector rested in the long shadow of one of the trees. It provided him with an unobstructed view of the *Jasmine*, yet he was far enough away to avoid attention. He wanted his visit to be a surprise—an unwelcome one.

He glanced at his watch. It was 3:45 PM—fifteen minutes before the scheduled meeting between the captain and Ahmed Dar. If the captain planned to be on time, he needed to leave now.

As if on cue, the captain appeared wearing a red coat and black stocking cap. He moved toward the gantry, where the inspector intercepted him.

"I need to speak to you, Captain."

Pointing to his badge, he added, "I am here to inspect your vessel, with your permission, of course."

The captain stared at the badge, then up at the man. "You've picked a hell of a time. I'm on my way to a meeting."

"We both know that there's never a good time for an inspection. It won't take long—an hour at the most."

The captain reached into his pocket and removed his wallet.

"If you would do me the kindness of waiting until tomorrow morning, I'd be most grateful." He deposited a crisp, U.S. hundred dollar bill in the inspector's palm.

"Surely you're not trying to bribe an officer of the Port Authority, Captain?"

The captain snorted, then withdrew the remaining bills. He folded them in half, grabbed the inspector's wrist, and slapped the money into his hand.

"I'm not trying to do anything but get you the hell out of my way. I've told you that you can inspect my ship tomorrow."

"Very well. Shall we say 8 AM?"

Side-stepping the man, the captain scowled. "Fine. Eight AM."

As he cleared the docks, the captain tugged at the chain on his pocket-watch. It was 3:58 PM.

A kilometer away, at 1102 Bethel, a man was loitering in front of a dank-looking Middle Eastern restaurant. The potent smell of garlic permeated the air, filling his nostrils as he paced back and forth in his red jacket and black stocking cap. Hidden from view, Ahmed Dar had been observing the man for ten minutes. Confident that no one had followed him, Dar crossed the street just as a solitary bell tolled 4 PM.

"So good to see you," he greeted the presumed captain as if he was an old friend, slipping his arm across the man's back and steering him toward an alley. "Why don't we continue our conversation in a more private place?"

Once freed from the afternoon crowd, Dar spoke openly. "So, you've decided to accept our invitation."

"It's hard to accept an invitation without knowing who has issued it, wouldn't you agree?"

"Forgive my rudeness. My name is Ahmed Dar. I am here at the request of al-Bakr."

Having confirmed the identity of his target, the agent extracted a .380 caliber pistol from under his jacket and pointed the barrel inches from Dar's face.

"I know who you are, Ahmed, and I have a few questions for you."

Though caught off-guard, Dar didn't flinch. "I suggest you remove that gun from my face."

"Tell me the names of the men who were on board the *Jasmine*."

"They were just sailors. Who else would be on a cargo vessel?" Dar responded dismissively.

The butt of the gun crashed against Dar's nose, causing a dark river of blood to flow down his shirt.

"One more time," the man said as he pulled back the hammer on the pistol. "I want to know who was on that ship and what they were transporting."

"Fuck you."

The words were barely out of his mouth when the first bullet tore through Dar's left eye, leaving a dark, empty socket. Two shots followed in rapid succession. As Dar collapsed onto the street, the man grabbed his arms and pulled his lifeless body toward a dumpster.

Careful to avoid the gray bits of brain seeping through the bullet holes, he hefted Dar's body onto his shoulder and deposited it atop the trash. He stripped off his jacket and cap, quickly throwing the disguise over the body, and slammed the dumpster lid closed.

He returned to 1102 Bethel and waited.

The captain appeared at 4:08, wearing a red coat and black stocking cap as instructed. The agent approached him at 4:09.

"You cut it quite close, Captain. Another minute and I would have been gone," the agent said.

"I'm sorry," he blurted. "An inspector decided to pay an unscheduled visit to my ship. It took a few minutes to get rid of him."

"Why don't we find a place where we can talk privately," the agent suggested. "There's a park not far from here."

Minutes later, the two men skirted the perimeter of a neighboring park until they came to a quiet refuge with three wooden benches. They sat, and the agent wasted no time seeking to discover what the captain knew.

"So, you've met our mentor?"

"If you are speaking of the small man with the badly disfigured face, yes, I have met your mentor."

"Did he share with you his destination?"

"Yes, but why are you asking me that?" the captain asked.

The field agent began to back-pedal.

"I simply wanted to fill in any missing pieces."

Twenty-five years of dealing with the refuse that washes up at ports of call had equipped the captain with an antenna for trouble. He stood up. "I think I'll be going now."

"But you just arrived," the man protested.

Without a word, the captain stood to leave. As he turned his back on the agent, he felt something round and hard pressing against his spine.

"Turn around very slowly, Captain," the man instructed.

The gun was now pointed at his abdomen.

"The first shot won't kill you but you'll wish it had. I'll take my time with next two. Now sit your ass down on that bench and don't move a muscle."

With his left hand, the man removed a cell phone from his pocket. He pressed the camera app and a photo appeared. He turned the screen toward the captain and watched as a look of horror registered on his face. The captain stared at the bloody image of a freshly murdered man.

"That's the man you were supposed to meet," the agent explained. "We had a few words before you arrived."

As he spoke, the captain noticed that another man had crested a small rise and was heading toward their bench.

"We're leaving now, Captain," the first man explained, locking onto one of the captain's arms, while the other man followed close behind.

"Where are you taking me?"

"On a little adventure. Do you like planes?" the man asked.

"Hate 'em."

"That's too bad. You'll be on one for about nine hours. Let's go."

The agent started walking north. While one hand steered the captain toward the park's exit, the other hand clenched the pistol hidden under his jacket. As they approached the street, a minivan flashed its lights twice.

The agent could feel the captain straining, as if ready to bolt. Pulling back his jacket just enough to reveal the suppressed semi-automatic pistol, he communicated the futility of trying to escape. The captain's arms went slack.

"That's better," the agent said as he pressed down on the captain's head and shoved him into the rear of the minivan.

As he landed in the backseat, the captain felt the sharp prick of a needle. It was the last thing he would remember until coming to in Thailand.

CHAPTER TWENTY-SIX

A Site Outside of London
Islamabad

HART'S DESTINATION WAS A TWO-HOUR DRIVE southeast of London near Kent, a stone's throw from the lavish gardens at Sissinghurst. Built in the early 1800s from stone and mortar, Turnbridge Manor looked more like a castle than a home. But unlike other palatial structures that were cold and cavernous, the interior of the manor exuded warmth. Elaborate moldings carved from cherry and rosewood framed rooms where multi-colored tapestries and vintage paintings adorned the walls. Hart felt carried back in time to nineteenth-century England, a bygone era of chivalry and gentility that disappeared following the Great War.

Despite local lore, there was no dungeon in the manor. There were, however, plenty of spooks. The south wing housed MI-5 and MI-6, while the CIA occupied the north wing. It was a cozy arrangement designed to facilitate collaboration between the allies' counter-terrorism units.

Though it was not equipped with leg irons, the facility did have a lower level. It offered accommodations for up to six guests—each in their own soundproof isolation cell. Though the Brits claimed great compunction regarding the use of advanced interrogation, they ensured that each cell could be continuously bathed in blinding light and blaring music.

There was a special room reserved for those guests who proved resistant to gentlemanly persuasion. It had all the accoutrements necessary to encourage cooperation—from a pharmacopeia of mind-altering drugs to electrical shock devices. Everything was calibrated so as not to leave a trace . . . no bruises, no burns . . . just profound psychological trauma.

Hart, mindful of his promise to the president, trusted that a civil approach would be all that was required to elicit the cooperation of his guests, the first of whom had just arrived—chaperoned by Niya Jamali.

When not between the sheets with Colonel Kassar, Niya Jamali had been busy scheming how to win the trust of a woman she'd never met. The first step was to sell her station manager on the idea of producing a poignant exposé documenting the horrors of war as seen through the eyes of physicians. The second step was to ensure that topping her list of interviewees was a young doctor known for her dedication to the childhood victims of war. It had gone swimmingly.

"I'm so grateful that you chose to accept my invitation to be interviewed," Niya began as she sat in the doctor's office admiring the numerous framed accolades to her work.

"It is I who should be grateful," Ayesha Naru exclaimed. "You are giving me an opportunity to talk about a subject near to my heart, and to touch a thousand other hearts in the process."

"If you're ready, we'll begin. Just relax and pretend you're having a quiet conversation with an old friend, and, of course, pretend that there are no cameras, studio lights, or backdrops," Niya teased.

Ayesha didn't need any coaching. She was a natural—poised, confident, and charismatic, all traits that made her magical on camera. The interview went on for just over an hour. Niya explained that it would be edited down to a handful of sound bites that could be interspersed with video footage.

As they wrapped up the session, Niya asked, "Would you grant me one more favor?"

"And what would that be?" Ayesha asked.

"I'd love to take you to dinner. It's my way of saying thanks for being so generous with your time today."

"I would be delighted," came Ayesha's quick response.

They settled on a restaurant not far from the hospital, a quiet, cozy place where strangers became friends, and friends became lovers. Requesting a booth in the far corner of the restaurant, Niya began cautiously.

"I feel as though I have known you for a long time, Dr. Naru."

"Please, call me Ayesha."

"Tell me, what is it like to grow up the daughter of one of the most powerful men in our country?"

"I thought we were here to discuss the children and how we can help them," Ayesha said.

"We are . . . I didn't mean to intrude. Forgive me."

"You didn't intrude. It's just that when you grow up in the shadow of someone as formidable as my father, you crave moments when you can step out and feel as though you have substance of your own."

"Indeed." Niya smiled warmly and reached across and gave Ayesha's hand a small squeeze.

"Is your mission to heal the wounded or to open people's eyes to the atrocities in which thousands of innocent children perish?"

"I've dedicated my life to repairing the injured. It's much harder to play a role in the elimination of conflict. That appears to be the domain of diplomats, not doctors."

"What if you could extend your role . . . help stop the carnage before hospitals and clinics were filled with the maimed and dying? Would you do it?" Niya probed.

"That's a difficult question, since my world is limited to the narrow confines of my practice. I can't envision how such a role would materialize."

"Play along with me, Doctor. I'm curious as to how far your conviction might take you."

"That's the kind of game only a skilled journalist would play."

"I meant no offense," Niya assured her guest.

"No, but it is meant to test my integrity," Ayesha responded.

"Really? How so?"

"If my convictions are as magnanimous as I claim, then the answer to your question should be an unequivocal *yes*. And if not, my words are hollow like a clanging bell. So, how do you propose to test me, Niya?"

"I thought we were here for dinner," Niya responded.

This time Ayesha's reached across and squeezed Niya's hand. "Are all journalists as clever as you? Go ahead; our food won't be here for a while. Test me," Ayesha said confidently.

"Are you sure? You promise not to get upset with me?"

"I promise."

After pretending to ponder, Niya refocused on her dinner-mate. "Okay, I've got it, and it's going to strike pretty close to home."

"All the better. It is a test, after all," Ayesha said, undaunted.

"What if you learned that your father was involved in a plot to detonate a nuclear bomb in an American city— let's pretend it's New York." Niya carefully monitored the woman's face for anger, but there was none. There was, however, a look of horror.

"Why would he do that?" Ayesha asked, her voice rising in fear.

"I should have come up with something less dramatic. Let me try again."

"No, it's okay. I agreed to the game. Please continue," Ayesha insisted.

"You're sure?"

"Yes."

Okay. Let's assume that the bomb is capable of killing a million people—two hundred thousand of whom are children. What would you do, Ayesha?"

"That's an unsolvable problem, Niya. I have no answer for you."

"Why is it unsolvable? What if you possessed the ability to help avert the attack? Would you do it?"

"An act of treachery committed against my father? Is that what you are asking?"

"No . . ."

"But it is, Niya. You are asking if I would turn against my father to save the children."

"I am asking if you would be faithful to your conviction and act to save the children."

Suddenly feeling a bit faint, Ayesha asked, "Can we please talk about something else? I'm afraid you've overwhelmed me. Let's talk about something light—tell me about your home, your garden, how you love to spend time when you're not working."

"Of course, I'd love to," Niya responded with a cheerful look, though she resolved to return to the subject before dinner ended.

By the end of the evening, a bond of trust was being forged between the two women. There were few people that Ayesha took into her confidence, but she sensed that Niya could be one.

"I want to answer your question, Niya."

"What question is that, Ayesha?"

"What you asked me earlier about my father, and what I would do in the situation you described."

"I thought we decided not to press that issue."

"Yes, you graciously put it to the side, but now I feel as though it deserves an answer. Indulge me, if you will."

"Of course, Ayesha. Whatever you like."

"I love my father. Some people believe he's a monster. And some people believe that of the people whom he aids. I know him to be a good man whose actions follow principles that he holds within his heart."

"I'm sure you're right," Niya interjected.

"Please let me finish. This is not easy for me. My father sees the world in black and white. There are sacrifices he is willing to make that I am not. The scenario you have suggested is repugnant to me. If I believed my father to be complicit in such a plan, I would do everything in my power to stop him.

"I think you should tell me the truth, Niya," Ayesha suggested. "That was no mere invented game. You need to tell me what you know and how you came to know it."

"Such truth would put us both at great risk."

"Have we not already crossed that line?" Ayesha asked, taking Niya's hand.

"Let's take a walk," Niya suggested. "I think it best that our voices be silenced by the wind rather than shared within the small confines of the restaurant."

"Agreed."

The two women strolled down the sidewalk, arms linked, until the pavement ended.

"The scenario that I mentioned is a real one. Your father is believed to be involved. Do not ask me how I know this. That's not what matters at the moment. Just tell me if you meant what you said a moment ago."

"Of course I meant what I said." Ayesha was adamant. "But that doesn't mean that I can help. Even if your scenario is true, who am I to prevent such terror?"

"You are the holder of certain secrets—information that could prove very powerful in the right hands. Information that might stop an attack."

"And what would happen to my father?"

"I don't know."

"That's not an acceptable answer."

"It is a truthful answer. In my world, things are negotiable, Ayesha."

"Who are you suggesting I speak with, Niya? My father's tentacles reach far and wide. There are few powerful people within Pakistan with whom he is not, in some way, connected."

"Come with me to London. There's a plane waiting for us. I can have you back at the clinic in two days. If you call in sick, no one is going to question your absence. Tell them it's a stomach bug and you don't want to risk infecting your patients."

Ayesha hesitated.

"Who are you?" she asked, as she looked intensely into Niya's eyes.

"You know who I am. I'm Niya Jamali, a broadcast journalist with PTC."

CHAPTER TWENTY-SEVEN

DESPITE THE LONG FLIGHT, Ayesha was surprisingly alert when the private jet touched down at London's Heathrow airport. She noted every detail of the trip—from the plush cabin of the G550 that ferried her non-stop from Islamabad to the time required to reach Turnbridge Manor.

She followed Niya up a short set of stone steps leading to the front door. Before her companion could knock, the door swung open, revealing an unusually tall, muscular man with brilliantly blue eyes. "I'm John Hart," the commander said, extending his hand.

"Is that your real name?"

Hart laughed, "I'm afraid so.

"Where are we, Mr. Hart, and for whom do you work?"

"Doctor, one question at time, if you don't mind. You are at a house not far from Kent."

"Do you live here?"

"No, I'm just borrowing it for a few days."

"And for whom do you work, Mr. Hart?"

"Actually, it's Commander Hart, U.S. Navy."

"Niya told me a frightening story involving a nuclear bomb. I find it hard to believe but was sufficiently intrigued to listen. Now I am here. But for what?"

"Won't you come in?"

Niya and Hart escorted Ayesha to a conference room in the lower level, where she took a seat opposite Hart as instructed. Niya moved toward the door.

"Aren't you staying?" Ayesha asked, her tone a little fearful.

"No, you are in good hands," Niya assured her as she closed the door.

Though Ayesha tried to remain poised, her tightly interlocked fingers, combined with the nervous tapping of her foot, betrayed a high level of anxiety.

Hart got straight to the point. "We believe that the core of a fifteen-kiloton nuclear bomb has been stolen from the POF. We believe that the act was perpetrated by UIS and facilitated by people on the inside."

"People?"

"Two generals in particular: General Patel and your father."

"And your proof for such an outrageous accusation?"

"I don't believe you agreed to come here at substantial personal risk to deny these allegations. We are days away from a catastrophic event. Even if you choose to help us, chances are it will be too late. But it's my job to never give up. That's why we are talking, Dr. Naru, in the hope that your innate decency wins out."

"Don't speak to me of decency, Commander. It's your bombs that maim and kill our children."

"Yes, there is a horrible and undeniable tragedy to war, and the United States plays its part in such conflicts. But never with the intention of harming children or civilians," Hart responded.

"The morally pure United States . . . the country that was behind my mother's accident." Her words were bathed in contempt. "You killed her to punish my father for his purported role in the biological attack on your country. There was never any blood on my mother's hands, yet you felt justified in taking her life."

"We had nothing to do with your mother's death." Hart's eyes bored into her. He waited a moment before speaking again. "Our moral compass is far from perfect, but we don't deliberately kill innocent women and children. You can choose to believe that or not."

"And I choose not, Commander. So what now? Do you detain me? Or do you subject me to the treatment dispensed to so many of my countrymen in your dark sites?"

"I hate to disappoint you, but there's no water-boarding in your future. There may be something far more painful, however."

Ayesha winced as her foot tapped incessantly.

Hart reached for a folder to his right. Lifting it just enough to keep its contents hidden from her, he extracted the top page.

"Do you recognize this woman?" he asked as he pushed the paper across the table toward Ayesha.

"Of course I recognize her," she said somberly.

Ayesha began to read the information on the page—vital statistics about her mother, from birth to death.

"What is this?" she demanded.

"The first page of your mother's dossier," Hart explained.

"So my mother was the intended target of the CIA . . . that's what you are proving? Why tell me what I already know, Commander?"

Hart turned the file toward Ayesha, and gently guided it into her hands.

"Your mother worked for us."

"Go to hell."

"Why would we kill one of our own, Dr. Naru?"

"My mother would no more work for you than she would betray my father."

"I'm afraid she did both."

Ayesha lunged, screaming at the Commander. Hart snared her in his arms and then shoved her back into the chair.

"I'm going to kill you!" she seethed.

"I'm sure there's nothing that would give you more pleasure, Doctor." He stood, preparing to leave. "Read the contents of the folder. I'll be back in two hours. Perhaps we can have a civil conversation then."

Niya, waiting for Hart in another room, had watched the interrogation via a video monitor.

"That was lovely," Niya ventured.

"She'll come around," Hart assured her.

"What makes you believe that?"

"The undeniable facts. Ayesha has a puzzle to solve. We just showed her how the pieces fit. It may not yield a pretty picture, but it answers all of her questions."

"You seem so sure of yourself, Commander."

"Not always, Niya, but about this . . . yes."

Hart turned to the analyst at the video console.

"I'd like to see the last five minutes, please."

"Yes, Sir." The man began rolling the video.

"Back a bit further . . . to when I handed her the first page of the dossier."

As the video played, Hart pointed out cues to Niya, starting with the frequency with which Ayesha's foot tapped the floor. Next came an almost imperceptible twitch in her left eye.

"It's not her words that determine my confidence, Niya. It's her body language . . . the way she responds to being confronted with certain facts. She's a civilian, not a hardened agent. Her feelings couldn't be more transparent. You'll see in a few hours . . . it's not going to take much for her to break."

"Be gentle on her, Commander."

"Is that an order?"

"No, Sir. I didn't mean to be out of line."

"Whatever feelings you have for Dr. Naru, Niya, I suggest you temper them. Is that understood?"

"Yes, Sir, it's understood."

Hart waited an extra hour before returning—plenty of time to let Ayesha stew. As he walked into the interrogation room, he found the doctor huddled in a fetal position on the floor. He walked slowly toward her, touching her gently on the shoulder.

"Get your fucking hands off of me!" she snarled with the ferocity of a wounded animal.

"Get your fucking ass back in that chair," the Commander responded, lifting her off the floor and thrusting her into the chair.

"You are directing your anger at the wrong person, Doctor. I didn't recruit your mother. And I sure as hell didn't put an end to her life."

"Who did, Commander? Are you implying that it was President Mughabi or the ISI acting on his behalf?"

"I think you know who is responsible for your mother's death."

Ayesha drew her knees up to her chest and buried her face in her arms, sobbing uncontrollably. Hart sat motionless, waiting for a break in the tide. After ten minutes, her breathing slowed. She raised her head and stared at the Commander.

"Did my mother spy on my father?"

"Not in the beginning. Only after your father was implicated in the biological attack on the U.S."

"And you believe that he would actually have her killed for doing so?"

"Don't you?" The commander's voice was gentle, not harsh.

"How did this happen? How did my mother become a pawn of the CIA?"

"Your mother was no one's pawn. Not ever. She was an extraordinarily bright woman who came from a family with sufficient means to send her to school abroad. As you know, she went from an undergraduate program at Yale to earning her Master's from the Kennedy School at Harvard. It was during her time at Yale that she was introduced to the Agency."

"*Introduced?* Is that the euphemism for recruiting foreign nationals to become spies?"

"No one coerced your mother. She saw what was happening in her country. When the government of Ali Bhutto was overthrown by General Zia-ul-Haq, a movement toward the Islamization of Pakistan began. Your mother knew she had to act. She believed that the only way to prevent the eventual destabilization and radicalization of Pakistan was through Western intervention. That's why she chose to work for us—to keep the country she knew and loved from becoming the next Afghanistan."

"That's absurd. My mother would never commit treason. She would never betray her husband."

"Is it treason to act in your country's best interest? Is it treason to prevent a man from aiding others in genocide? No, your mother was never treacherous. Noble, yes. Treacherous, never."

Ayesha, still holding her knees to her chest, rocked slowly in the chair. In a barely audible voice, she said, "What is it you want of me?"

Hart had her.

"I need you to help us avert the murder of countless children."

Ayesha was silent, thinking of her mother and recalling her conversation with Mizha Barr, the major's wife. It all made sense—horrible, undeniable sense.

"I'm going to give you a few minutes alone to think," Hart advised her before again leaving the room.

When he returned twenty minutes later, there was a visible change in the doctor's demeanor. Almost as if purging herself of a dreadful secret, Ayesha began to speak.

"The core of the weapon you are seeking was stolen by UIS with the help of my father, General Patel, Colonel Kassar, and ultimately, Major Barr."

"How do you know this?"

Ayesha ignored Hart's question, revealing details at her own tempo.

"I believe that everything my father has done has been at the behest of Ibrahim Almasi al-Bakr. If you find al-Bakr, you will find the weapon."

"Al-Bakr was killed in a drone attack, along with Beibut Valikhanov and Ahmed Al Hameed—the key perpetrators of the biological attack on America," Hart responded.

"We both know better, Commander. Al-Bakr is my patient and has been since that fateful night when your Hellfire missile failed to kill him."

"What makes you believe that al-Bakr is the linchpin in this attack?"

"Al-Bakr met with my father twice in the weeks leading up to the disappearance of the nuclear material. Though the conversations took place in my clinic, I was not privy to them. There was one comment, however, directed to me.

"Al-Bakr told me that, someday, I would be very proud of the role my father had played. I didn't understand it at the time. When I asked my father what al-Bakr had asked of him, he told me 'a great favor.' That is all I know, and far more than I should have shared with you."

"Your mother would be very proud of you, Ayesha. I'm sure that's cold comfort at the moment, but someday I believe it will mean a great deal to you."

"Cold comfort, indeed, Commander. Now, what happens to me?"

"That's a good question, Doctor. If we return you to the clinic, we run the risk that you will alert your father. If al-Bakr learns that we are closing in, he will accelerate the detonation of the weapon."

"If my father becomes aware that I shared information with the CIA, he will personally put a bullet in my head. Surely you are smart enough to know that, Commander."

Hart knew she spoke the truth. "Niya will return with you to Islamabad. Consider her your shadow—not materially by your side, but inescapably close. Am I clear?"

"Yes, Commander Hart, you are quite clear."

A knock broke the awkward silence as Niya appeared at the door of the conference room.

"The plane is waiting, Ayesha. We need to go now."

Hart's work was not done. Before he could return to the States, there was one more actor in the intense, unfolding drama awaiting Hart's interrogation: Colonel Salman Kassar.

As Kassar awoke from a drug-induced stupor, Hart hovered over the Colonel. He slapped the man on each cheek, trying to rouse him. Finally Kassar raised his hand to guard his face.

"Enough, enough," he pleaded, squinting at his captor as he struggled to open his eyes. "Where am I?" he demanded, his voice becoming steadier.

"You are my guest," Hart replied.

"And who the hell are you?" Kassar growled. "Do you know who I am? Do you have any idea of what is going to happen to you?" the Colonel asked Hart.

"I know you are an unfaithful prick, Colonel," Hart began. "And I know you went on a binge in Thailand."

"I don't know what you are talking about." His eyes were already moving toward an image taking shape on a far wall.

Hart held up a remote, pointed it toward the LCD projector, and launched the lurid slideshow. The first photo showed the colonel, buck naked, on top of a prostitute, her legs splayed wide. Next, another prostitute, this one male, appeared to be spooning with the colonel. Finally, the threesome was locked together in a most unnatural pose.

"Don't worry, Colonel, I've been told that only the first stone hurts," Hart said, alluding to the Quranic punishment for infidelity and sodomy.

"What do you want?"

"I want to see the look on your wife and children's faces when these photos are posted on social media. Do you have a Facebook page, Colonel?

"And I want to watch the public reaction to the story of a wayward colonel, responsible for nuclear weapons, who went in search of twisted sex at a time when he was scheduled to be on duty. It could air on PTC as early as tomorrow. At least that's what Niya Jamali tells me."

"That fucking bitch!" Kassar said as he realized who had betrayed him.

Hart's tone shifted abruptly. "What did you mean when you told Niya that Americans were about to suffer greatly?"

"Give me a cigarette," the man demanded with a hint of condescension.

A dreadful thud followed as Hart's clenched fist struck Kassar's face. The force of the blow knocked him out of the chair and into a wall. The Commander lifted Kassar with one arm and threw him back into the chair. Blood was running from a deep cut under the Colonel's right eye. With blinding speed, Hart struck him with the other hand.

The blow landed flush with his left eye. Kassar lurched back, fading in and out of consciousness.

"No, you're staying right here with me," Hart said as he began shaking the man to keep him from blacking out.

His hands now covered with Kassar's blood, Hart paused to let the colonel consider his position.

"Well, Colonel? Are you ready for round two?"

All Hart got was a hateful, contemptuous stare.

"I'll take that as an answer." Rather than strike the man, Hart reached into his pocket and pulled out a large knife. With the flick of his wrist, the razor-sharp blade locked into position.

"Give me your hand," Hart demanded.

Kassar's eyes darted wildly. He lurched back, but not soon enough to prevent Hart from grabbing his wrist and slamming it down on the table. Hart raised the knife above his shoulder, seconds away from driving the blade through the back of Kassar's hand, when the man screamed out.

"Stop! I'll tell you what you want to know!"

Hart froze in position, his knife ready to carve up the bastard. Ever so slowly he folded the knife, returning it to his pocket. He let go of the colonel's wrist.

"If you fuck with me for even a second, I'll bury this blade so deep in your chest that you'll feel it coming out your back. Do you understand me, Colonel?"

The Colonel nodded furiously.

"What did you mean when you told Niya that Americans were about to suffer greatly?"

"UIS is in possession of the core for a fifteen-kiloton weapon. It was taken from storage at the POF."

"What type of core?"

"Weapons grade uranium, 90 percent pure."

"Why not plutonium? It would be half the weight."

"They didn't want plutonium—too easy to detect with a scanner."

"Where did they take the core after its removal from the POF?"

"I don't know."

Hart pulled the knife from his pocket.

"I swear to you, I don't know," Kassar pleaded. "I believe it was on a ship bound for America."

"Who took the weapon, Colonel?" Hart pressed.

"If I tell you that, I am dead man. He will hunt me down and cut my throat."

"And if you don't tell me, Colonel, I will do the job for him," Hart assured Kassar.

After a long pause, Kassar continued, "Al-Bakr. He has two of his most trusted men with him."

"What is the target?"

"New York."

"When?"

"New Year's Eve."

"Be more precise."

"Midnight."

"Get him out of here," Hart told a man guarding the door.

"Where are you taking me?"

"Don't worry, Colonel. We're sending you home."

"I don't believe you. You wouldn't dare let me go."

"You won't say anything. If Generals Malik or Patel discover that your lover is a CIA agent, you will disappear. And if the photos of you become public, you will wish you had disappeared. Actually, Colonel, I believe this is the beginning of a long and beautiful relationship."

Hart put his hand on the drooping shoulder of the colonel and smiled. "Now go back and do your job like nothing happened," he snapped.

"And how do I explain this beating?" Kassar demanded as the commander was halfway out the door.

"Tell people you got in a fight with your wife and she won."

"One more thing, Colonel. If anything happens to Niya, you are a dead man. Do you understand me?"

"Yes."

Hart spoke to a man waiting in the hall.

"Clean him up. I want Kassar back in Islamabad before the prick is missed."

CHAPTER TWENTY-EIGHT

December 21
Safe House
Brooklyn, NY

Sarah Qaisrani marveled at the clumsiness of the men surveilling her. She was barely out of her driveway when she noted the beige Ford Explorer attempting to remain just out of eye-shot. "Surely you can do better than that," she thought with a smile.

Her uninvited escort made for a good game, something to keep her sharp on the long drive from Matheson Island to New York. Some people might have been annoyed, but not Sarah. She took it as a compliment that the government was hell-bent on keeping an eye on her. The key to winning the game was not to let the watchers know that she knew she was being watched.

After a couple days of playing dumb, it was time for Sarah to get serious about vanishing from the radar screen. The New York City Police Department's Counter Terrorism Unit was now tracking her, having received a hand-off from the State Highway Patrol shortly before her SUV cleared the Lincoln Tunnel. Their instructions: Observe from a distance, but do not interfere with the Arctic Fox.

More than a dozen pairs of eyes were locked on Sarah as she parked her SUV in a lot adjacent to Penn Station. She removed a backpack from the rear hatch before moving toward the entrance. A female agent, dressed in skin-tight jeans and a skimpy top, followed her into the vast expanse of the terminal. The agent lagged just far enough behind not to lose her trail. When Sarah stepped into a bathroom, the agent advanced. She closed the distance to the women's room but did not enter. Instead, she leaned provocatively against a wall, took out a nail file, and went to work on her two-inch crimson nails while waiting for Sarah to emerge.

Four minutes later, Sarah, wearing a gray wig, a pale blue flannel shirt, jeans, a corduroy jacket, and a heavy wool scarf, slipped out the bathroom door and made a beeline for the trains. She boarded one headed for Harlem, seemingly unaware of the swarm of agents following close behind. She found a seat between an elderly woman who was busy crocheting and a man sitting head-down wearing bright red headphones.

Forty minutes later, as the doors of the train opened, she jumped out onto the platform and broke into a run. In seconds, she was sprawled out on the ground, cuffed and then yanked to her feet. A female officer stepped forward and stripped the wig from the woman's head, revealing close-cropped red hair. The woman they had followed was not Qaisrani.

She radioed into command, describing her captive. Command ordered the one remaining agent in Penn Station to approach the bathroom in search of Qaisrani.

Clasping her .357 magnum, a finger on the trigger, she threw open the door, her gun leveled.

The bathroom was empty. She fell to her knees and peered under the stalls. There was something on the floor in the farthest stall. It was a backpack . . . the same backpack that Sarah had been carrying a mere half hour ago. Ripping it open, the agent dumped out its contents. A pale blue flannel shirt, jeans, a corduroy jacket, and a heavy wool scarf lay in a heap. She called in to the unit commander. Her voice was laced with panic.

"She had a double. The real Qaisrani must have changed into other clothes. She left behind a backpack with her old clothes and a cheap lipstick."

"What color?" the man demanded.

"How the hell do I know," the officer responded while popping the cap off the gold and burgundy case. "It's hot pink. Are you happy now?"

"It's something." The incident commander made an all-call to his officers. "We're looking for a female, five feet, four inches, wearing hot pink lipstick. She's probably wearing an outfit to match—something that doesn't shout Islamic jihadist. Get down to the tracks—now. Maybe we can still find her."

Without a word, the officer dropped the lipstick onto the pile of clothes and dashed out the door. A staircase led down to the trains, but which one? There were still hundreds upon hundreds of people making their way home via Penn Station, and Sarah probably had a substantial lead.

It was to no avail. Sarah Qaisrani was on the Seventh Avenue Express headed toward Sterling Street in Brooklyn. Her final destination was the Prospect Avenue station in the Kensington neighborhood. She sat far back on the torn subway seat, smacking her gum, her legs parted, not crossed. Her bleached blonde wig and heavy iridescent eye shadow gave her the look of either a prostitute or a lonely Jersey housewife.

When she reached the station, Sarah moved quickly toward the exit. Stepping out of the flow of fast moving bodies, she stopped abruptly at the bathroom closest to the stairs. A tall, exotic-looking woman was brushing her hair at the sink. Without a word, the woman picked up a satchel and handed it to Sarah, who headed for the farthest stall.

Ensconced in the stall, Sarah removed her make-up—all of it—then flushed the towelettes laden with foundation and eye shadow. She traded her low-cut blouse, short skirt, and thigh-high boots for the clothes of a conservative Muslim. Finally, she wrapped her head in a scarf before exiting the stall. As she walked slowly past the woman at the sink, she was handed a set of car keys.

"Lot C, space 115. It's a burgundy Camry."

The woman did not follow Sarah. She remained behind, collecting all of Sarah's discarded clothes and stuffing them into a canvas bag. She ensured that no trace of Sarah Qaisrani would ever be found.

The car was easy to spot, as were the directions tucked under the floor mat. Before leaving the lot, Sarah took a deep breath and let it out slowly. She'd made it. There was no longer a sense of urgency. No one was following her. Sarah Qaisrani had disappeared as planned.

She programmed the GPS for 310 E. Eighth Street—a narrow three-story house that had once belonged to Sheik Mubarak Gilani, a radical cleric who claimed to be a direct descendant of the prophet Mohammed. Sarah admired

Gilani, who proselytized that violence was the only means to a pure Islamic state—one destined to dominate the world. His followers became known as Muslims of America and forged strong ties with terrorist organizations including Jamatt al Fuqra and UIS.

A permanent fixture on the State Department's reports on terrorism, Gilani was finally taken into custody for his presumed complicity in the kidnapping and murder of noted journalist Daniel Pearl. Pearl was abducted in January 2002 shortly before arriving at the Village Restaurant in downtown Karachi, where he was scheduled to interview the Sheik. Nine days later, a video was posted on the internet by his captors. It showed Pearl's throat being slit and his head severed. Gilani was arrested upon returning to the states.

However, with a paucity of evidence proving the Sheik's involvement in the particularly heinous crime, authorities were forced to release him. He was admonished not to leave the city. Realizing he was under the threat of subsequent prosecution, the Sheik skipped town—only to resurface in Lahore, Pakistan. Numerous friends welcomed him home, including Ibrahim Almasi al-Bakr.

The Department of Justice seized Gilani's house and put it up for auction. It was during the worst recession ever to hit America when the housing market had collapsed almost overnight. Despite the adverse economic climate, the Sheik's house was quickly snatched up by a professor of linguistics at Brooklyn College. The day the transaction closed, all surveillance of the property was terminated.

The feds had done their due diligence on the professor and his wife. Clean as a whistle. They had failed to uncover the academician's ties to Gilani—ties that went back decades. The modest house became a destination for an amazing cadre of terrorists, but none as deadly as those soon to inhabit it.

Sarah slowed the car to a crawl as the GPS unit reported, "You have arrived." She parked the Camry on the street in front of the house, glanced in all directions to ensure that she was alone, then proceeded to the front door. Before she could ring the bell, a man threw it open, stepped onto the porch and greeted her with a hug, then guided her into the home. Closing the door, his tone became all business.

"Did you encounter any problems?"

"No, everything went as planned," Sarah assured him.

"Are you sure? How do you know that you weren't followed? Think for a moment. This is very important."

"Of course, I'm sure." Her was tone clipped, showing her annoyance at the man's continued questioning.

"If you don't mind, I'm tired. I would like to retire to my room. In the morning, I will expect a briefing on every detail of the plan," Sarah stated, leaving no question as to who was in command.

"Of course. My apologies. Al-Bakr is very protective and expects us to take impeccable care of you."

"I don't need anyone to take care me, Mr. Basra. Until tomorrow morning, then."

Basra knew he was dealing with a pit viper, and any misstep could result in a lethal bite. If Sarah didn't kill him, al-Bakr most certainly would. So before retiring, he rehearsed the briefing he would give to the Arctic Fox in the morning . . . word by word.

CHAPTER TWENTY-NINE

SARAH SLEPT POORLY, HAVING BEEN AWAKENED by a vivid dream of her husband, Babur. It was the day of the bio-attack, and she was sitting in the cabin staring out a window as Babur pulled into the driveway. He had completed his mission—unleashing a deadly virus at the DFW airport—before escaping north.

Sarah greeted Babur with the warmth of a wife grateful that her husband had survived the war. She put a plate of warm muffins in front of him before putting the needle of a syringe in his back. It was filled with a lethal drug that raced through Babur's bloodstream, shutting down the nerves that controlled his muscles. Within minutes, his respiratory system would be paralyzed, and he would asphyxiate.

But unlike the swift death that had occurred in real life, in the dream, Babur did not die. Instead, he looked pleadingly into Sarah's eyes and asked *why?*

She awoke at 3 AM shaken by the specter of her dead husband. She finally fell back to sleep at 4:30, but the dream returned . . . the phantasm refusing to be vanquished. By 5:30, Sarah had had enough. She pulled back the covers, climbed out of bed, and got dressed.

Careful not to wake anyone, Sarah descended the stairs barefoot, holding her sandals in one hand. As she walked into the kitchen, she was surprised to discover that Awan Basra was awake and already finishing what she presumed to be his first cup of coffee.

"You're up early," she said in way of a greeting.

"I didn't sleep well. Hopefully, you were blessed by a good night's sleep," he said with genuine warmth.

Sarah only smiled.

"I'm eager to learn about the plans. When can we begin?" she asked.

"Right now, if you'd like." Gesturing to the living room, he asked, "Is there anything that I may get you before we begin?"

"I'll have tea when we're finished."

Once they were comfortably seated, Basra began. "The package will arrive in Halifax in six days—on the 28th. It will be off-loaded onto a semi-truck for transportation south. Before being released, it must receive a certificate of inspection."

"What type of inspection? A physical inspection of the contents?"

"No, a radiographic examination. It's not as intense as the procedures now in place at the U.S. border, but it has the potential to identify certain types of hidden threats."

"And does al-Bakr understand this risk?"

"He does, and he knows that we've done everything possible to mitigate the threat of discovery—including the use of scrap metal to obfuscate the core. The probability of detection is extremely low."

"Mr. Basra, I count on certainty, not probability. I want to be certain that nothing is detected . . . just as I want to be confident that the three men accompanying it will receive safe passage." She continued, "Are you a betting man, Mr. Basra?"

"No, I am not."

"Well, you are betting your life on the safe passage of the core and my colleagues. Do we have an understanding?"

"Yes, Mrs. Qaisrani, we have an understanding." With a slight tremble to his voice, he asked her permission to continue.

"Once the shipping container is safely loaded onto the semi, your colleagues will ride in the truck's cab with the driver. He's a Somalian by birth, but he's been in the States for twenty years. He came here for college—earned a degree at Cornell in nuclear engineering. Not bad for someone who grew up in abject poverty."

"I appreciate his academic pedigree, but it means little to me without absolute allegiance to our cause."

"He's among the most trusted members of our organization. He's proven himself time and again. You can count on him to reach the border unhindered."

"And when he reaches the border?"

"The truck will enter the United States at Calais, Maine. Each man will be carrying a U.S. passport. As I mentioned, we expect a heightened degree of scrutiny at U.S. Customs. They employ the latest technology to ferret out radioactive material . . . that means x-ray radiography, as well as gamma and neutron detection. These instruments are not easily fooled."

"You are making me less comfortable by the minute, Mr. Basra. Is that your intent, or is it a reflection of weaknesses in your planning?"

"Neither, I pray. I was about to explain that the man responsible for analyzing the output from these detection devices is one of us."

"How did you manage to infiltrate U.S Customs and Border Patrol?" Sarah questioned.

"The man's predecessor became quite ill one evening after eating at a Middle Eastern restaurant. The doctors never determined the nature of the poor man's ailment, but it left his body ravaged. Because he was unable to return to work, the agent's position became open. We made certain that a perfect candidate was front and center when the interviews began. Fortunately, he was hired.

"So the good news is that, no matter what appears on the scans, the container will be cleared and false radiographs submitted," Basra promised.

"And what happens after clearing customs and immigration in Calais?"

"The semi will rendezvous with a van on the outskirts of Bangor, Maine. The core will be removed from the shipping container and will be transferred to the van. The driver of the semi will continue south, eventually dumping his load at a refinery in New Jersey. The van will return to New York City."

"And who will be in the van?"

"Why you, of course, Mrs. Qaisrani. You and I will complete the rendezvous with al-Bakr . . . no one else."

"Is the van ready?"

"No, but it will be shortly. My men are finishing their work on the shielding. It was not easy to retrofit a van with 1,500 pounds of lead. The suspension had to be re-built to handle the weight of the sarcophagus."

"Instruct your men that they have twenty-four hours to finish the job; then I want to see it. More importantly, I want to see it tested," Sarah said firmly.

"As you wish," Basra said, while cursing the bitch under his breath.

CHAPTER THIRTY

New York

THREE HOURS HAD ELAPSED since Hart had left Turnbridge Manor and boarded the private jet for the States. He waited until the captain throttled back the Gulfstream's twin Rolls Royce engines before picking up an encrypted satellite phone and calling Tom Levin.

Levin was a maverick, something Hart admired. A graduate of Harvard Law, he never practiced. Instead, he accepted a position as an investigator in NYPD's Division of Internal Affairs. It was a thankless job, but Levin performed it impeccably. His tenacity, fearlessness, and sense of justice earned him the respect of cops throughout the department, even those he investigated.

After five years in Internal Affairs, he was offered his choice of assignments. Most men would have taken something cushy, but not the nebbish-looking man from the Bronx. Levin still had something to prove. So he opted for the most demanding position in the department—building a massive, new counter-terrorism operation.

That's how Hart had met him three years before at a conference in New York. Hart stood a full foot taller and

75 pounds brawnier than Levin; the men could have been taken for different species. But beyond their physical differences, they shared a remarkable collection of traits: They were both brilliant, driven, and self-sacrificing.

"Good morning, Tom, it's John."

"Good morning, Commander. I was expecting your call."

Despite Hart's insistence that Levin drop the formality, the cop wouldn't hear of it. He always addressed Hart as "Commander."

"Sorry to be running late . . . my interviews took me longer than expected," Hart said as if he'd been speaking to job candidates.

"I hope they weren't disappointing."

"On the contrary, I learned a great deal. Want to get down to business?" Hart asked, "Are you in a secure location?"

"Yes, Commander."

"Good, then I'll begin. We have amassed enough credible evidence to suggest that a nuclear strike against New York City is imminent."

"When?" Levin asked abruptly.

"Midnight, December 31. My guess would be Times Square—that would provide the maximum number of victims concentrated within a definable area," Hart ventured.

"What do we know about the perps?" Levin still maintained the language of a cop.

"The fingerprints of UIS are all over this one. It appears to be the brainchild of al-Bakr, aided by a number of jihadists, including the woman you are following, Sarah Qaisrani."

"Were following, Commander," Levin corrected him.

Hart felt his blood pressure surge and his temper rise. But he knew there would be no value in lashing out at Levin.

"Tell me what happened."

"I'm not sure. My best guess is that she had a body double waiting in the bathroom in Penn Station. My people fell for the masquerade. While they were busy pursuing the decoy, Qaisrani was radically altering her appearance. She was able to slip past our remaining agent on-site. We have no idea where in the city she is at this moment."

"That's not good news, Tom."

"No, Sir. I'm meeting with my team following this call. We'll find her. You have my word on it."

"Before the stroke of midnight on December 31, I trust."

"Yes, Sir. Now, if I may ask, how did they get the bomb?"

"They didn't. They got a nuclear core courtesy of a few high ranking officers in the Pakistani Army. That little son-of-a-bitch knows it's a lot easier to smuggle in something the size of a grapefruit than a bomb the size of refrigerator." Hart paused briefly. "Aside from the fact that he's one messed-up son of a bitch, al-Bakr probably planned this attack with precision. He doesn't want to fail twice."

"It's not that simple, is it, Commander? I mean . . . to build a nuclear bomb?"

"I read an article years ago in *Washington Monthly* that quoted the former chief weapons designer at Los Alamos. Ted Taylor claimed he could build a bomb in his kitchen sink that could destroy half of Manhattan. Apparently, once you've got the core and few other key components, it's plug and play, Tom."

"Come on, Commander, where would they get the high explosive lenses, the neutron initiator, even the housing?" Levin asked.

"I thought you didn't know anything about nukes. Those are big words for a former Internal Affairs officer. What do you know about neutron sources and high explosive lenses?" Hart asked.

"I guess we've both been doing our homework, Commander."

"For now, we need to assume that they have the needed materials in hand and that the bomb will soon be in the final stages of assembly," Hart advised. "I need you to keep me apprised of what's happening in the investigation. One last thing. Liz and I will be in New York after Christmas—staying through the first of the year. I'll send you my travel dates via encrypted text."

"Excuse me, Commander? You are bringing your fiancée to New York for New Year's?"

"She likes a little excitement, Tom."

"I trust that was joke."

"A poor one, I'm afraid. Liz will be in the city with me. She's part of the team. The President has asked the Secretary of HHS to designate her as the Principal Federal Officer. If we have to deal with mass casualties, she'll be invaluable. Remember, she helped save our asses during the pandemic."

"I'm concerned that Dr. Wilkins not become a casualty herself."

"I appreciate your concern, Tom, and I share it."

"Yes, Sir."

Hanging up the phone, Levin moved to a conference room where a portion of his staff was waiting.

"Ladies and gentlemen, our failure to maintain a tail on a fifty-five-year-old woman who was squarely in our gunsights may have cost the people of New York immeasurably. I say that not to belittle you, but to inform you of the severity of our situation. We now believe that Sarah Qaisrani is in New York to rendezvous with Ibrahim Almasi al-Bakr. We further assume that he is in possession of nuclear material.

"Let me be specific," Levin continued without acknowledging the sea of hands that rose in response to his opening remarks. "There is credible evidence that al-Bakr plans to smuggle in a uranium core for a fifteen-kiloton nuclear bomb. The planned date of detonation is midnight on New Year's Eve, and his presumed target is Times Square."

The group visibly stirred, and numerous side-conversations ensued. Levin shut them down. "You'll have plenty of time later to talk among yourselves. For now, I need you to listen.

"No one in this room was alive when Truman made the decision to drop a bomb on Hiroshima. Even so, every one of you can conjure up images of the devastation wrought by that event. It was a fifteen-kiloton bomb that killed more than 100,000 people. We believe that a similar event, occurring on New Year's Eve in New York, will kill upwards of a million. No one in this city would be untouched by the massive loss of life."

Levin wasn't finished. He wanted his troops fired up and looking in every hole and crevice across the vast city for people connected to al-Bakr.

"The devastation will spread beyond New York. Cities downwind will be hit with potentially lethal fallout. An event of this magnitude could destabilize our country, at which point the crazies have won. We have a job to do and little time in which to do it. If we fail, it will be our last job. If we succeed, the American people will never be aware of the sacrifices made by each of you in an effort to stop this impending calamity. You will be the silent heroes that saved the city. Before I go on, are there questions?"

Anita Gorman, a young lieutenant on the force, rose to her feet. "Assuming you are right, Sir, what are you proposing we do to stop the attack with little more than a week before the New Year?"

"Once the core is fitted into a housing with the necessary components to complete the weapon, the bomb ceases to be a small device. In fact, we assume that it will be five to seven feet in length and weigh hundreds of pounds. It's not like we are trying to stop a jihadist carrying a suitcase nuke up 44th Street with plans to deposit it in Times Square just as the ball is falling. No, this one is going to be in some type of vehicle that has been pre-planted in anticipation of New Year's."

"And what are we doing to locate that vehicle?" the woman persisted.

"Our immediate priority is to assemble a list of all public parking facilities within six blocks of Times Square. That's the distance at which fifty percent of the people would be killed instantly by the blast. There will be thousands of cars in that vicinity . . . all of which need to be scanned. It's not going to be easy. Frankly, I don't know if it's possible."

"That doesn't sound very optimistic, Sir."

"I'm just being honest. In fact, each of you needs to think long and hard about whether to stay in the city or get the hell out of here. Many of you have families, and you will want them to be out of harm's way."

Another young woman said, "Sir, I believe I speak for the group when I say that we are here to protect and serve, not to run. Our families understand our obligations. We have to trust that this will turn out well."

A man asked, "Beyond looking for a radiologic needle in the haystack, what else can we do?"

"We can find al-Bakr and Qaisrani. Their photos are circulating, as are the photos of suspected UIS supporters. We've got to hope we get a hit. If we make it through Christmas, we'll have six more days to find the bomb before a cloud rises above this city. I pray we use them well."

CHAPTER THIRTY-ONE

December 23
Brooklyn, New York
Al's Auto Shop

With a few deft strokes of a brush and just the right mix of colored powders, Sarah's face was transformed into that of a much younger woman. She covered her head with a hijab and went downstairs to meet Awan Basra.

"I barely recognize you," he exclaimed as she approached.

"The make-up provides a bit of cover on the street. But it does nothing to stop their visual identification software from scoring a hit. It's hard to hide from video cameras and detection algorithms," she responded, deflecting what she knew was meant to be a compliment.

"Whatever you say." Basra gave her as second look, more licentious, as the woman climbed into his red 2005 Buick LeSabre.

"What are you looking at?" she asked, annoyed. "Just drive." She shooed away the nuisance with her hand.

Al's Auto Repair was less than a mile from the safe house. *Al* was short for Ali. The Americanized name was better for business.

Ali Jadoon greeted them as they entered the garage. "Welcome. Awan told me that you wish to see our progress," the gregarious mechanic said to the stoic Sarah Qaisrani.

"Yes. And I wish to see it tested."

"Of course, of course. It's in a separate building."

Sarah and Basra followed the mechanic past the carcasses of vehicles that had died from rust and exhaustion to a small garage toward the rear of the property. Entering through a locked door on the side, Ali flipped on the lights. Parked in front of Sarah was a white panel van. It was completely undifferentiated from a thousand others that traversed the streets of New York every day.

"We finished it early this morning. I'll have Jamal show you," he said motioning to a man who had followed them in.

"As-salaam'alaykum." Jamal greeted the guests before moving to the rear of the van. He opened the hinged doors to reveal a myriad of electrical tools and supplies clinging to racks on either side of the interior.

"We are transporting a bomb, not supplying an electrician," Sarah said caustically to Basra. "How can you say that you are finished?"

"First, we are rendering the bomb undetectable. Then we are transporting it," Basra said calmly. "These men are fine craftsmen. As you look upon the van, you will see only what they wish you to see."

"Look carefully at the cargo compartment," Jamal instructed, but Sarah saw nothing.

"I don't see your point," she shot back.

Basra intervened. "Gentlemen, I suggest that you show Mrs. Qaisrani your handiwork now."

Jamal pulled back the carpet to reveal three adjoining panels made from a dull gray metal. With great effort, he labored to remove the first panel. Pulling a flashlight from the side of the truck, he used it to illuminate what lay beneath.

As Sarah stepped forward, she saw a sarcophagus hidden beneath the van. The lead-lined casket fit between the axles, a few inches above the ground.

"A small but sufficient amount of lead shielding lines the vault. We've also used less dense but effective materials to further absorb any radiation. It is more than adequate to shield against the radiation emitted by the device," Jamal explained.

"You speak more like a physicist than an auto mechanic," Sarah said, her words tinged with contempt.

"I am a physicist, Mrs. Qaisrani . . . a medical physicist. My job is to understand how far radiation will penetrate. In this case, the answer is *not beyond the shield.*"

"How do you know this to be true? Have you tested it?"

"I was waiting for you." He walked over to a large metal cart and pushed it, wheels squeaking, until it was within inches of the van. What appeared to be a scanning device occupied the top shelf. Beneath it was a large hollow cube of lead.

As he turned on the machine, Sarah watched the needle on the meter move slightly.

"This is a scintillator. It is a device for precisely measuring radioactivity—usually in a laboratory setting. Right now, it's picking up a few millirads of background radiation. I'm going to ask you both to step back. A bit further, please."

Once his audience had complied, the man placed the scintillator's probe next to the lead container. The machine clicked a few times as a needle on the meter bobbed up and down. Then Jamal removed the top of the lead container, revealing a small amount of an isotope inside. The needle immediately pegged, as the clicks melded into a constant squeal.

"Cesium 137—it's quite hot." Then donning a lead apron and what appeared to be lead-lined gloves, the man lifted the container from the cart and placed it in the vault within the van. He closed the door, removed his gloves, and began to scan the exterior of the van with the scintillator. Nothing. A few errant clicks from normal background radiation, but that was it.

"The bomb emits far less radiation than the cesium. And the detectors employed by the counter-terrorism organizations are less sensitive than this scintillator. So one can safely conclude that the device will be undetectable once it is in the van."

Rather than concede the point, Sarah shifted the focus of the conversation to a safe in the far corner of the garage. It appeared to be encased by ingots of lead.

"What's in there?" she said, approaching the safe.

"Sections of a spent nuclear fuel rod," the man answered without hesitation.

"Why are they encased in lead?"

"They're hot, very hot. Far more dangerous than the cesium," Jamal warned.

"Open it," she ordered, pointing to the safe.

"I don't think you want me to do that, Mrs. Qaisrani," Jamal protested.

"I'm not interested in what you think. Open the safe."

Jamal looked to Basra for help.

"The material in the safe is hot enough to kill everyone in this room," Basra explained.

"What are you talking about?" Sarah demanded.

"Radiation sickness. It only takes a brief exposure to the rods. After several days, maybe a week, you would experience an agonizing death."

"Then why do you have them?"

"We plan to use them as a counter-measure to help minimize the threat of detection once we deploy the weapon. The rods throw off enough radiation to make the detectors employed by Homeland Security scream with excitement."

"Where did they come from?"

"Tariq Kuni helped us procure them. They are from an underwater storage facility at the Indian Point Nuclear Power Plant—a plant about thirty-five miles north of here on the banks of the Hudson. Two of my men stole them."

"Where are these men?"

"In their graves. It was a suicide mission due to the level of exposure they received."

"Think of it as an insurance policy, Mrs. Qaisrani," Basra began. "There are four pieces of spent fuel rod in that safe. Each piece will be placed in the trunk of a car driven by one of our members. On New Year's Eve, each car will canvass a different part of the city—from the financial district to Times Square to upper Manhattan."

"But they will be detected," Sarah objected.

"Yes, that is our intent—a diversion. CTU will be inundated with alarms from fixed radiation detectors throughout the city. They won't have the resources to easily contain four simultaneous threats without a significant diminishment in manpower. It won't fool the Americans for long, but even a few extra minutes may prove to be precious."

"What keeps the drivers from receiving a lethal amount of radiation?" Sarah's question was directed to Jamal.

"Nothing. The men will be exposed to many times the lethal dose of radiation. If they are not killed in the blast, they will die soon after."

Basra spoke, "They understand and accept their fate. They know what awaits them in paradise, and they give up their lives gratefully."

Now directing her questions to Basra, Qaisrani asked, "Why not use this material to create four dirty bombs? Would that not add more horror to the destruction we will be unleashing?"

"We considered it but ruled it out. We didn't want to prevent an occupying Islamic force from taking over New York by rendering it uninhabitable."

"What happens next?" Sarah asked.

"In five days, you and I will leave from here in the van and rendezvous with al-Bakr in Calais, Maine. We will leave at 4:30 AM and return that evening. We will deliver the van with the nuclear core to this garage where three new guests will be waiting for us."

"The gentlemen from the west?" Sarah asked.

"Yes, Kansas. Tariq, Abdul, and Habib will complete the final assembly of the weapon once the core arrives. Ali and Jamal will ensure that they have everything they need. Once given instructions on arming and fusing of the weapon, the men will complete their work. Then the panels concealing it will be welded into position."

"Why is that necessary?"

"Again, a mere precaution to buy time. Even if it were discovered, agents would have to cut through the lead panels to access the bomb," Jamal explained.

"You've thought of everything, then?" Sarah said more as a question than an affirmation.

"Yes," Basra assured her, knowing that no other answer would suffice.

CHAPTER THIRTY-TWO

December 24
Washington, D.C.
Burlington, Kansas

A TRAIL OF SMOKE ERUPTED from its wheels as the 54,000-pound Gulfstream touched down at a private FBO at Dulles International Airport. Hart waited for a green light from the cockpit before opening the hatch and dropping the stairs. In less than ten minutes, he was speeding toward Langley.

He parked in the underground complex, took the elevator up to the ground-level, and passed through the security turnstiles. He was closing in on the DDO's office when Dottie flagged him down.

"Mr. Kahn asked me to clear his calendar, Commander. He's quite eager to talk with you."

"Thanks for the warning."

"I know it's Christmas Eve. Would you like me to call Dr. Wilkins and let her know that you'll be running late?"

"That won't be necessary, but thanks for the offer, Dottie."

Hearing the conversation in the reception area, Kahn walked out to greet the commander.

"Welcome back, Commander. I'm eager to hear about your trip." With his hand on Hart's back, an unusual touch of warmth from the DDO, he steered him toward his office.

Hart spent three hours methodically recounting every detail of what had transpired at Turnbridge Manor. Kahn saw the abrasions on Hart's knuckles, which were in line with the commander's description of the interrogations.

"I'd suggest you keep those hands out of the president's view the next time we meet with him. He still believes espionage is a gentleman's game."

"From what I've heard, it once was."

"Those days are long past, Commander. Let's move on. Tell me, what is your confidence level in the intel coming out of Turnbridge?"

"Extremely high, Sir. The situation is ugly, no matter how we spin it. Al-Bakr will likely succeed in bringing a nuclear core into this country. If so, he will build a bomb that has the potential to destroy much of New York City. We have until December 31 to find it."

"What about the Arctic Fox? Where has she led us?"

"I just received an update from Tom Levin at NYPD's CTU. Unfortunately, they lost Sarah Qaisrani."

"What?" Kahn walked over and shut the door to his office. "What the fuck are you talking about, Commander? How difficult can it be to surveil a middle-aged woman, for God's sake? I knew we shouldn't leave this in their hands."

"It was domestic surveillance, Mr. Kahn. According to the law, we had no choice, Sir."

"Don't be a god damn Boy Scout, Commander. I know perfectly well what the law says. And I know the difference between the intent of the law and its words. Our job is to protect the people of this country. A single failure, like misplacing a psychopathic jihadist who can lead us to a nuclear bomb, may cost us a million lives."

"Yes, Sir. Mr. Levin is quite aware of the magnitude of his team's mistake."

"Mistake? No, it was a complete fuck-up, Commander," Kahn spit out the words, shaking his head in disbelief.

"I think it is time for me to have a few words with the courier who delivered the message to Qaisrani on Matheson Island," Hart responded.

"That's going to be difficult, Commander."

"Why? I'm ready to get started right now. The FBI did find him, right?"

"Yes, they did. Well, they found his decomposing body. There was a single gunshot wound to the back of the head. Very professional. And smart on their part. They knew he represented a potential leak they could ill afford, so they took the man out of service. I think we're shit out of luck, Commander."

Kahn took a moment to collect his thoughts before speaking again. "There may be another path to locating al-Bakr." His voice was low but steady.

"And what would that be, Sir?"

"We received a call from Stan Hawkins at the FBI. Apparently someone contacted their field office in Boston to report a suspicious activity. The call came from a foreman at McKennon Machinery in Worcester."

Hart felt the hairs on his neck begin to rise. It was his intuitive early warning sign of impending trouble, something he had come to rely on.

Kahn continued, "The man was concerned about a six-foot by three-foot steel case that McKennon fabricated and shipped to an address in Kansas. Apparently, when he saw it in final production, the foreman realized that the tube looked a lot like a bomb casing. He's former military—Air Force to be precise—and has seen his share of nukes."

"When did the Bureau receive the call?"

"A few days ago."

"What?"

"Yes, Commander, they sat on it. The Boston office saw no reason for concern . . . not until they received the photo dossiers and briefing on the impending nuclear threat. That's when they decided that it might warrant attention."

"I thought they had learned something from their spectacular mishandling of the 9/11 bombers."

Kahn didn't respond. He knew the commander was contemptuous of people who pledged to protect America and then failed to deliver on their promise.

And there was a huge personal cost to Hart on 9/11. His middle brother, Corey, was in the Towers when they came down.

"Nothing we can do to change the past . . . we need to pick up the ball and run with it. I'm sending you to Kansas," Kahn told the commander. "I know you just returned, and I know it's Christmas. Tell Liz I'm sorry. The Agency will make it up to her."

"She never complains, Mr. Kahn. But Kansas? That sounds more like an exile."

Ignoring the remark, Kahn continued, "Two KBI agents will meet you at the home of Tariq Kuni. They've already determined it's empty."

The name failed to register in Hart's memory. "Who is Tariq Kuni?"

"He's an engineer at the Tallgrass Prairie Nuclear Power Plant. He immigrated to the U.S. in 2001. From what we've been able to learn, he's a model employee. There have been no signs of radicalization, not even a hint."

"Until now," Hart corrected him.

"Yes, until now. It may prove to be nothing, but Kuni did request time off beginning in mid-December. He is not scheduled to return to Tallgrass Prairie until after the New Year. He told his boss that he was going to visit relatives in Pakistan."

"That should be easy to check out," Hart commented.

"Agreed—the Bureau searched all airline reservation files, but came up empty."

"It sounds like the only relatives he plans to visit are the ones awaiting him in Paradise," Hart responded.

"I would prefer that he spend his remaining time in a jail cell, Commander, not in a fiery blaze of glory for the United Islamic State."

"Have you considered that we may be dealing with a methodically constructed sleeper cell? Where there's one, I trust there are others. If my geography is right, the Advanced Defense Works plant is nearby in Kansas City. That could prove handy to a would-be nuclear terrorist."

"I'll have someone run it down right away," Kahn promised, a bit chagrined that Hart was a step ahead of him.

"Just not the Bureau, please."

"Commander, you've got to adjust your attitude about our brothers in arms. The Bureau does some impeccable work," Kahn reminded him.

"Yes, Sir, as does NYPD's CTU."

"Point taken, Commander."

"I trust they've not contaminated the scene," Hart continued, his attitude unchanged.

"No, that's one thing they've done right. CSI will accompany the KBI agents who are meeting you at Kuni's house. Tear it apart if you have to, but find out what the hell is going on with this guy, and do your damned best to identify anyone else involved. Any further questions, Commander?"

"When do I leave, Sir?"

"Tomorrow—Christmas Day."

"Why not tonight, Sir?"

"You've earned a night with Liz, Commander."

"She will understand, Sir."

"Enjoy Christmas Eve together, Commander. That's an order. Dottie's booked you on a non-stop out of National at 7 AM tomorrow. It's a two-hour drive from KCI to Burlington. She's also reserved a rental car and a room at the Moon Mist Motel just outside of Burlington."

"Sounds like a hell of a place to spend Christmas," the commander said with a forced smile. "For God and Country, right, Sir?"

Kahn dismissed him. The meeting was over.

As Hart left, Kahn summoned Carl Johnson to his office.

"I need you to contact the senior security officer at the Advanced Defense Works plant in Kansas City. We need a list of all employees taking an extended holiday this Christmas, plus full personnel files on any employee who is a Middle Eastern immigrant."

"Mr. Kahn, it's Christmas Eve. The plant is shut down," Carl advised.

The DDO did not need to speak. The look he gave Johnson was sufficient.

"I'll get on it immediately, Sir."

CHAPTER THIRTY-THREE

December 24
Washington, D.C.

HART HAD BARELY SET FOOT IN THE DOOR when Liz grabbed him by the tie and pulled him down to her eye level. With a long, adoring kiss, she welcomed him home.

"Missed you, cowboy."

"Missed you, too, darling."

"How was London?" she asked, relinquishing her grip on his tie.

"A non-stop party," he responded, slipping off his naval officer's jacket. "You know how I love hanging with jihadists."

"I've poured you a drink." Liz cocked her head, then lifted a glass of Macallan from the coffee table before retrieving her glass of chardonnay.

"I'm half a glass up on you, so you'd better catch up," she advised him.

Hart wanted to get the bad news out of the way and hoped it wouldn't spoil their night.

"Uh oh, I know that look. What is it, John? Did someone park too close to your BMW?"

"Very funny. No, I've got to leave town again."

The humor drained from her voice. "When?"

"Tomorrow morning. I'm catching a flight to Kansas. I'll be back on the 26th."

"Going to Kansas to party without me?" There was no point in making John feel badly about things out of his control.

"Something like that. Kahn even had Dottie book me into a palatial resort . . . a place called the Moon Mist Motel. I'd bet on tiny rooms, peeling wallpaper, and the smell of mildew. I think I'll pack some of the Macallan."

"I'm envious," Liz retorted.

Hart set down his drink and grabbed Liz, pulling her into his arms and kissing her until she could barely breathe.

"What's that for?"

"A thank you for understanding. Now, how do we make tonight special? I have some ideas, if you'd like to hear them."

"I can only imagine. You may be brilliant, my dear, but most of the time, you're only thinking about one thing."

"Guilty as charged, Doctor. Would you have it any other way?"

"No, cowboy, I wouldn't. Now, before you get too excited, remember that we are going to church tonight. Midnight Mass. If we're not too tired later, we'll have a little rodeo. Sound okay with you?"

Hart grinned.

The service at the Cathedral was reverent and awe-inspiring—an essential reminder of the good that permeated the world and helped dispel the darkness. As the choir began to sing *Silent Night*, an acolyte carried a single candle through a darkened sanctuary. When he reached the altar, the young boy touched the flame to the wick of a candle held by the senior pastor, who in turn passed on the divine light. Soon the flame spread throughout the sanctuary as the light of Christ was passed to more than a thousand candles in the hands of devout worshippers. As Liz touched the flame of her candle to John's she said, "May the light of Christ be with you."

"And with you," he responded.

Once back in the apartment, John hung up their coats before setting a course for the refrigerator, where he extracted a bottle of Prosecco that had been chilling for hours. He teasingly pointed the cork at Liz, pretending to loosen it.

"Hey, cowboy, you're not supposed to point a loaded weapon at someone."

"Not unless you are prepared to fire." With an upturned eyebrow, he raised the bottle toward the ceiling and popped the cork. It ricocheted and landed in a crystal bowl.

"Heck of a shot, if I do say so myself," Hart grinned.

"Yeah, right. Let's see you do that one again."

"How about we drink a toast instead to our last Christmas together as an unmarried couple." He raised his glass, but Liz didn't stir.

"That sounds a bit morbid . . . how about a toast to our wonderful life ahead, and a joyful, yet uneventful holiday season?"

John clinked her glass. "Hear, hear."

CHAPTER THIRTY-FOUR

Washington, D.C.
Burlington, Kansas

THE BUZZER ON HIS ALARM CLOCK CUT through the deep fog of sleep, summoning Hart back from some distant land. It was 5 AM, twenty minutes shy of the time he needed to be out the door. He kissed his half-awake fiancée, ran an electric razor over his face, and put on his Navy dress uniform, which he had carefully laid out the prior evening.

Grabbing a small overnight bag, he waved a final goodbye to Liz, who managed to open her eyes just long enough to tell him to be careful.

Hart boarded the two-hour-and-forty-minute flight at 6:40 AM. It was scheduled for an on-time departure at seven o'clock. Upon landing at KCI, he took a shuttle to the car rental lot where a spiffy candy-apple red Mustang awaited him. "Note to myself," he thought, "Thank Dottie for arranging a little fun on my trip through the prairie."

Hart had flown over Kansas innumerable times, never planning to stop. His total knowledge about the Sunflower State came from *The Wizard of Oz*. Yet it wasn't a flat, lifeless prairie that greeted him but undulating hills . . . some dotted with livestock . . . others sown with winter wheat. There was a clear charm to it. Hart could see that now.

Unlike D.C., there was no traffic. One could travel fifty miles in less time than it took to get from Tyson's Corner to Langley. That was a welcome change.

Hart arrived at Kuni's property in Burlington ahead of schedule. Rather than risk getting scolded for poking around a potential crime scene, he waited patiently for the cavalry. Fifteen minutes later, two agents pulled in beside him.

"Nice wheels," one of the men remarked as Hart extracted his long legs from the Mustang. "Standard CIA rental?"

"It beats the hell out of a Taurus. Oh, sorry, boys, I didn't see you were driving one."

It was the obligatory exchange of smart-ass remarks whenever Agency and Bureau personnel collided. To a casual observer, it might look like enmity, but for the field agents, there was rarely any malice.

"I'm Travis Duncan," a heavy-set agent said, extending his hand to Hart.

"And I'm Lester Moore," his leaner partner followed suit.

"I'm John Hart."

"Your reputation precedes you, Commander. We're all grateful for what you did—shutting down that damn bug they released," Moore said.

"All in a day's work. Speaking of which, I'm eager to take a look in the house, as well as that out-building."

"CSI just pulled up. Let's let them secure the site and tell us when it's cleared to enter."

"Of course."

The CSI team arrived in two vans. A female agent emerged from the cab of the lead van, then disappeared into the rear of the vehicle. When she re-emerged, she was holding three polybag suits of varying sizes. As she handed one to Hart, she remarked, "I'm sorry, Sir, we don't have one in Kong size."

"Very funny, Agent . . . ?"

"Agent Fine, Gloria Fine."

"*Fine*? Yes, I'd agree with that," Hart's eyes surveyed the attractive blond.

Not amused by his remark, the agent turned away and instructed her team to follow. The three men were to wait until instructed before entering either building. CSI wanted to ensure that any evidence was preserved in a pristine state, beginning with the basics—fingerprints.

Once properly garbed, Hart approached the out-building. Before he could enter, Agent Fine stepped out and placed her hand squarely on his chest, stopping him in his tracks.

"Not so fast, Commander."

Bemused, Hart raised his arms in surrender. Agent Fine summoned a technician, "Please find a respirator for the Commander." A moment later the technician handed Hart a full-face respirator.

"You can put your arms down, smart-ass."

"And why do I need this, Agent Fine?"

"We don't know what they manufactured here. There's evidence of what appears to be beryllium. You really don't want to inhale that stuff. It does a number on your lungs. While you are in there, remember not to touch anything, Commander. I know that probably goes against your grain, but let my team do our job."

Hart pulled the respirator over his face and gestured for Fine to lead. After donning her respirator, the agent showed him into the out-building, pointing to the fine residue, as well as other points of interest.

"There were three men here . . . probably for a couple of weeks. We're running the prints, though I doubt we'll get a hit."

"Don't be so sure," the commander advised her.

Hart carefully noted all the empty boxes, packing materials, and address labels. It would be in the KBI report, but he didn't want to be at the mercy of the Bureau waiting for information. Satisfied that he had learned what was important, he stepped out of the building, yanked the respirator off his face, and took a deep breath, filling his lungs with the pristine prairie air.

There was tranquility to the land, its natural beauty skillfully augmented by the nurturing hands of Tariq Kuni. Out in the country there were no honking horns or blaring sirens—only the rustle of wind passing through the trees. How could the same man who created this refuge, sculpted this garden, also sow the seeds of unimaginable destruction, Hart wondered.

It took six hours to completely process the scene. As their work was wrapping up, Fine approached Hart, who was kibitzing with Agents Moore and Duncan. Holding up a print-out, she said, "We got hits on the other two men who were here with Kuni."

Hart reached for the paper, wondering how they had been identified so quickly. The answer became obvious when Hart learned that the three men held Top Secret security clearances, which required that their fingerprints be on file with the DOJ.

A quick background search revealed that Tariq, Abdul, and Hassan were uniquely skilled in their chosen disciplines.

Together they possessed the requisite skills to build a nuclear bomb. All they needed were the ingredients—most importantly, a core of highly enriched fissile material.

Hart turned to the agents. "Issue an APB stat on these three," but even as he gave the order, Hart sensed its futility.

Hart called Kahn on the way to the Moon Mist Motel. "Sir, we've got an ID on the men who were at Tariq Kuni's house."

"Let me guess. One of them is Abdul Rana."

"How did you know?" Hart asked, "Did the Bureau contact you?"

"No, Carl tracked down all employees who put in for extended holiday leave from the Advanced Defense Works plant. Rana fit the bill—Pakistani, immigrated the same month and year as Tariq Kuni, and was responsible for over-sight on a number of the non-nuclear components of nuclear weapons. Who's the third in this unholy triumvirate?"

"His name is Habib Sayed."

"So we know they have a core, and presumably some beryllium reflectors from Advanced Defense Works. Seems like all they're missing are high-explosive lenses and kytrons. This Sayed doesn't happen to work at Pantex, does he?"

"Yes, Sir. He, too, immigrated from Pakistan the same month and year as Kuni and Rana."

"And I suppose he's also on leave?"

"Yes, Sir. Not due back at the plant until January 2nd."

"What time is your flight out, Commander?"

"6:30 AM. With a little luck, I'll be at the office by 10:15, Sir."

"We've been summoned to the White House to brief the president and representatives of the Security Council. I will meet you there." Kahn ended the call.

The Moon Mist Motel was nothing like Hart had imagined. It was not even a motel. It was a B&B in a quaint Victorian home a half-mile from the center of town. When he arrived, there was no one at the reception desk. After he rang the bell several times, an old woman in a gingham dress with a lace collar tottered out to greet him.

"You must be Mr. Hart."

"Yes, Ma'am. I'm here just for the night."

"Well, maybe you'll fall in love with Burlington and want to stay longer . . . lots of our guests do."

Though he appreciated the woman's down-home charm, he knew there wasn't a chance in hell he'd be hanging out here a minute longer than necessary.

"Maybe," he responded. "You never know."

The woman handed him an oversized brass key with a tassel tied to it. She pointed to a plate of cookies. "Help yourself, Mr. Hart. I baked them for you."

"Thank you. That's kind of you. It's been a long day . . . I'm going take a couple of them to my room and call it a night."

"If you're up early, I'll fix you a hot breakfast," she offered.

"Thank you, but I'll be leaving around 4 AM for the airport."

"I said early, Mr. Hart. I'll be up at 3:30. How do pancakes and bacon sound?"

"Really, Ma'am. There's no need, but thank you."

"It would be my pleasure to fix a home-cooked breakfast for one of our nation's fighting men. My husband was in the war. Is it Captain Hart?" she asked.

"Commander Hart, Ma'am. Tell me, what war did your husband fight in?"

"The Korean War. It took quite a toll on him, but he survived and came home to me and our two children. My husband passed away ten years ago, Commander. I'm not sure why I stay in this little town. My daughter keeps asking me to come and live with her in Atlanta. I guess there are just too many memories here to let go of."

Letting out a breath to expel old ghosts, she said, "I'll see you bright and early, Commander. Your room is at the top of the stairs on the left. Let me know if you need anything."

Though there were five rooms, Hart was the only guest. Early the next morning, he awoke to the smell of frying bacon. As he entered the kitchen, the woman was adding a strawberry garnish to a plate of steaming hot pancakes topped with sliced bananas and syrup. A small pitcher of warm maple syrup was already on the table.

Having skipped dinner the night before, Hart was ravenous. He fought the urge to shovel the food into his mouth like his Marine buddies were prone to do. He didn't want to rush off. He could feel the woman's loneliness. He wanted to linger as long as possible to repay her kindness.

At 4:25, he knew he would be in jeopardy of missing his flight if he didn't head out.

"Thank you, Ma'am, you've been too kind."

"Katherine," she said both in introduction and parting.

"Thank you, Katherine." Hart took her diminutive hand in his, covered it with his left, and gave a gentle squeeze.

"I hope to see you again, Commander."

"John," Hart corrected her.

"I hope to see you again, John."

"And I hope to see you, Katherine."

CHAPTER THIRTY-FIVE

December 25

THE APB ISSUED BY THE KANSAS BUREAU of Investigation put in motion one of the largest manhunts in history. The majority of the effort was concentrated on roads running eastward from Columbus, Ohio. That required surveilling thousands of miles of interstate, state highways, and secondary roads.

Photo dossiers of the three persons of interest, as well as a description of their cargo, were distributed to state troopers, city police, and FBI agents. Law enforcement personnel swarmed the Mid-Atlantic states and East Coast, interviewing convenience store clerks and gas station attendants. Other officers stopped and searched vans, trailers, and small trucks. Mobile radiation detection units were brought in to scan and monitor the critical access points leading to New York City, causing traffic to snarl along I-70 and I-80.

Despite Hart's earlier reservations, the efforts appeared to be paying off when a potential hit was scored in Zanesville, Ohio. A surveillance video captured three men stopping to fill up an SUV with a U-Haul in tow. The images were grainy, making it difficult to resolve the detail of the men's faces. Unfortunately, a time stamp indicated that the tape was forty-eight hours old.

The video was sent to the Agency for image enhancement, after which it was compared to photos of Kuni, Rana, and Sayed. Facial recognition software showed it to be a perfect match. One more piece of the puzzle had fallen into place. Now they had to locate the men before the threesome disappeared into the same void that had swallowed up all traces of Sarah Qaisrani.

The streets of Brooklyn were quiet. A blanket of pristine white snow covered the tiny lawns and dulled the sharp edges of cars parked along the streets. It was early, and most of the children remained tucked in their beds, not yet aware that it was Christmas.

Three men, road-weary after the long drive from Kansas, had just arrived at Al's Garage. They were towing a small U-Haul trailer behind their F-150 pickup. In it were the housing and vital components required for a fifteen-kiloton nuclear bomb.

Ali stepped out to greet them. He spoke in a hushed tone, his voice further dampened by the snow.

"As-salaam'alaykum."

"Wa 'alaykum salaam," came the reply in unison.

"I'm grateful that Allah granted you safe passage. Now it becomes my job to protect you and the gift you have brought," he gestured to the U-Haul.

"If you back the trailer up to the garage, we can unload it from there. We'll transfer the device into the van before dawn breaks. I've got three cots set up for you. There's a bathroom in the back. I'm sorry it's not the most comfortable accommodations."

"We'll be fine; we're just tired," Tariq managed a smile.

It was the final leg of the men's journey—a journey that had begun sixteen years earlier in Pakistan and would culminate in one of America's most beloved cities being reduced to ash. There will be much to celebrate, Tariq thought, as the New Year is ushered in.

"We still have a great deal of work ahead of us. I doubt we'll be sleeping much."

A man emerged from the darkness of night and approached the men. Tariq reached for a gun tucked into the waistband of his pants, but Ali stopped him.

"It is only Jamal. He is here to help."

"My apology for startling you." Jamal folded his hands, lowered his eyes, and bowed. "As Ali said, I'm here to help."

"Are you a nuclear engineer?" Tariq asked.

"No, simply a physicist."

"We can use an extra hand."

Tariq's eyes swept across the garage, taking stock of the tools that were visible, before locking onto something in the far corner. It was a safe embedded in lead ingots.

"The spent fuel rod?" he asked Ali.

"Indeed, and shielded as you instructed."

"You understand that, once unshielded, the radiation from that rod will kill quickly."

"Yes, Jamal made that abundantly clear."

"And the men who will be chauffeuring pieces of it back and forth through the boroughs of New York . . . do they understand the consequences?"

"Yes. They gladly give their lives to Allah to protect our sacred mission. I leave you to your work, gentlemen. Jamal will remain with you."

"One more question," Tariq's voice caused Ali to stop and turn.

"And what would that be?"

"Is it safe . . . here in the garage . . . with so many people nearby?"

"You are not in Kansas anymore, but it is safe," Ali reassured him.

CHAPTER THIRTY-SIX

December 27
The White House

THE SUN WAS JUST CRESTING OVER THE CAPITOL as Hart cleared security at the west entrance to the White House. An aide escorted him to the Situation Room, where a single seat next to the president remained open. A nuclear sword of Damocles was hanging over America, and everyone in the room knew that it might fall at any moment.

Rising from his chair, Conner wasted no time engaging Hart. "Commander, people are eager to hear your news."

"I'm afraid it's not good news, Mr. President." Hart's eyes remained locked on the Commander in Chief, communicating the intensity of his concern. After a moment, Hart broke his gaze and broadened his focus to the full audience.

"Ladies and gentlemen, based upon what we have discovered in Kansas, coupled with information gained through a series of investigative interviews, our fears of a nuclear attack are well-founded. The nuclear core for a fifteen-kiloton device is on its way to New York. It may have already arrived."

"Who did you interview, Commander, and how reliable are the sources?" the Director of Homeland Security questioned.

"Sir, the people I interviewed are directly connected to the case, as well as to al-Bakr."

"And they willingly provided you with information about a forthcoming bombing? If my sarcasm isn't evident, let me make explicit, Commander. Why would they do something so foolish?"

"They required some encouragement, Sir, before agreeing to share information. I'd prefer not to get into the details."

Conner stared into his coffee. He didn't want to hear what had transpired, particularly after Hart promised a degree of gentility when dealing with suspected enemy combatants.

As though to calm the room, the Secretary of Defense asserted, "Commander, a core is not a bomb. It requires sophisticated components to transform it from a lump of uranium or plutonium into a weapon of mass destruction."

"Yes, I'm aware of that, Mr. Secretary. From what we can determine, a UIS sleeper cell was established more than fifteen years ago with the express purpose of one day assembling a nuclear device. The cell was comprised of three men who were selected based upon their unique talents. One resided in Kansas City, Missouri, another in Burlington, Kansas, and the final man in Amarillo, Texas. And, Mr. Secretary, the core is uranium. As you know, that makes it far more difficult to detect."

"Why those locations, Commander?" the Director of DHS asked.

"They are the locations of the Advanced Defense Works plant, a nuclear generation facility, and Pantex," Hart responded, wondering why that wasn't obvious to the secretary.

"Thanks to their employers, the men had access to everything they needed except a core and casing. The core will arrive courtesy of al-Bakr. The casing was shipped to an address in Burlington, Kansas, by a custom fabrication company in Worcester. Its dimensions perfectly accommodate a twenty-six-kilogram core and its non-nuclear components."

Hart looked at the faces surrounding him, men and women hanging on every word, waiting for a vestige of hope. "I'm afraid that all that remains is for al-Bakr to put together the pieces."

"You make it sound as simple as a child's jigsaw puzzle," the secretary persisted.

"Mr. Secretary, for three highly trained nuclear engineers, it should be child's play."

Hart was relieved to hear the president's voice break through.

"And our efforts to locate these three men?"

"We have an APB out for them, Mr. President, but I don't think we'll find them. We obtained a video showing them at a gas station in Ohio, but it was several days old . . . giving them ample opportunity to reach New York."

"What about the Arctic Fox? Has she led us anywhere?" Conner probed.

"The teams surveilling Ms. Qaisrani lost her in Penn Station. NYC CTU is actively scouring locations of known radicals for her. So far, nothing."

"I want you in New York, Commander," Conner declared. "This afternoon if possible . . . tomorrow morning at the latest. You are to assume joint leadership of the CTU with Levin. You will be acting under my orders. Tom won't push back . . . he will welcome the help."

"Yes, Sir. I've already been in communication with Mr. Levin."

"You've got until 9 PM on New Year's Eve, Commander. Then I want you the hell out of there. Marine 1 will be on-station at the CTU with orders to bring you and Dr. Wilkins back to Washington. I'm going to need both of you here to deal with the aftermath. Are we clear?"

"I understand your orders, Sir," Hart replied.

"You never suggested the possibility of evacuation, Commander. Is there a reason why you've not pursued this line of inquiry? Surely we could save tens of thousands of lives, if not more," the Director of Homeland Security inquired.

"I believe that any attempt at evacuation would likely accelerate the timeline for the bomb's detonation. They could also change the target to Washington, Philadelphia, or Boston. I believe the only acceptable course of action is to find the device before it is used against our people."

"Mr. President, I beg to differ with the Commander," the Director stated. "We should begin a rapid evacuation of Manhattan immediately."

Conner didn't miss a beat. "And when the bomb detonates in Brooklyn or the Bronx or Newark? What then? I'm afraid I must agree with the Commander. We've got to pray we find it rather than choosing to run."

Liz was dressed and waiting for him when Hart returned to the apartment.

"I've got to go to New York, darling—not in a few days, but in a few hours. I'm sorry, but I can't take you with me."

"The hell you can't. We've been through this, John, and we reached an agreement. Besides, my appointment to Principal Federal Officer is imminent. I don't take on titles in name only."

Hart pulled her into his office to ensure the privacy of their conversation.

"Liz, this is no vacation. I've got to help Tom Levin find the nuke. There are hundreds of thousands of lives hanging in the balance. You get that. I know you get it."

"Of course I get it." Liz's jaw was set. Everything about her body communicated immovability. "What you don't get, Commander, is that I plan to be at your side. I'll either be there to do what I can to help you avert the tragedy or I'll have a front-row seat for the fireworks, in which case we'll die together."

Hart marveled at her resolve. Playful as a kitten and as fearsome as a lioness, Liz was one of the few women who could make him back down.

"So, cowboy, it's your choice: Take me with you or I'll be on the next train following you to New York."

"Sounds like I don't have a choice."

"Come on then. Let's get packed," she said.

The Acela Express departed Washington's Union Station at 1 PM, arriving at Penn Station at 3:46 PM. From there, it was a short cab ride to the St. Regis, where Hart dropped off Liz with the bags, tipped the bellman, and instructed him to take good care of the lady. He then headed to CTU headquarters, where Tom Levin was expecting him.

"Good to see you again, Commander," Levin greeted Hart with a firm handshake.

"Thanks, Tom. Good to see you. So bring me up to speed since our last call."

"No news at the moment, Commander. We're still searching for Qaisrani, as well as the three engineers. I've got men canvassing dozens of neighborhoods. These people have simply vanished."

"What about Awan Basra?" Hart asked.

"He's high on our hit parade, but we haven't located him. He's not at his known address or the two safe houses that we are aware of."

"What do you mean, *aware of?*" Hart asked.

"We don't know how many safe houses exist or even which boroughs may conceal them. Gilani was shrewd. He wouldn't have left the country without ensuring there were elaborate methods in place to conceal his network's activities. With time, we'll unravel them."

"We don't have time, Tom. We have hours, perhaps days. That's it."

"What do you suggest, Commander? Is there something we've missed?"

"No, I don't mean to imply that. Your folks do a great job. But we need a bit of luck—something to fall into our laps."

"We've cleared out an office for you, Commander. I've also got a badge and photo ID. We had to use an old photo, though—sorry about that. This is your entry ticket into anywhere in the city."

The ID card listed him as Steve Carlson, Senior Agent, CTU.

"Where in the hell did you get this picture from . . . my high school yearbook? And now I'm a Swede?" he asked Levin.

"The staff here know you. But no need to advertise your identity to the rest of NYPD. I can change it to O'Neill if you'd prefer to be Irish or Mandelbaum, if you want to be part of my clan," Levin offered. "By the way, I don't think I know your real name, Commander."

"I'd tell you, Tom, but then I'd have to kill you."

Levin was glad to see that Hart was as he remembered—irreverent and undaunted.

"I understand we now share command of the CTU."

"I didn't ask for it, Tom. I've all the confidence in the world in you."

"That's more confidence than I have in myself, particularly after losing Qaisrani. It's not an issue, Commander. I'm grateful to have you by my side.

"With that said, I'd suggest you go back to your hotel. There's not a lot we're going to accomplish before tomorrow morning. At least enjoy one day in New York."

"Enjoy it like there's no tomorrow?"

"Something like that."

"You'll call me the second anything comes up?"

"That goes without saying," Levin assured him.

"I'll see you bright and early," Hart said as he walked out of Levin's office.

"You're back?" Liz exclaimed, surprised to see Hart at the door.

"I can sit around here just as easily as waiting at CTU for the shoe to drop. Levin's got clear instructions to summon me the moment something breaks."

"And until then?" Liz asked, her eyebrows raised.

"I'm all yours, Doctor," he said. But she could tell that he was not all hers, not that night. He was preoccupied, racking his brain for any missing piece that might turn the tide.

Snuggling up against him on the sofa, Liz asked, "What's your plan?"

"Intensify the search for Qaisrani, al-Bakr, and Basra— I'll settle for any one of the three. Beyond that, pray."

CHAPTER THIRTY-SEVEN

December 28
New York

Hart rolled over and briefly embraced Liz before springing out of bed.

"It's 5:30 in the morning, John," a bleary-eyed Liz Wilkins complained, trying to shake off the last remnants of sleep.

"I'm meeting Tom at the office at six—I can grab a cup of coffee in the lobby on the way. I'll try to call you around noon and let you know what's happening. What's on your agenda?"

Now fully awake, Liz sat up in bed. "HHS asked me to brief Brian Tucker."

"New York's Commissioner of Health?"

"Yes. I've got an unofficial meeting scheduled with him at 10 AM. We've got to decide how to straddle the line between preparedness and keeping all of this under wraps."

"You know what will happen if word of this threat reaches the media," Hart cautioned.

"And you know what will happen if every hospital, health care provider, and first responder is blindsided by the blast."

"Point taken."

Hart walked over to the edge of the bed, leaned over, and kissed Liz. "Bye, darling."

When he reached the lobby, there was no coffee in sight—a mortal sin in Hart's eyes. An attentive desk clerk fetched a steaming to-go cup from the kitchen.

The roads were quiet at this hour. Most of the city was slumbering. Without the distraction of Manhattan traffic, Hart could concentrate on the emerging day. The clock in his head was ticking.

Arriving at the CTU in twenty minutes, Hart used his new ID to gain entry to the secure building. Levin's office was at the far end of the main corridor. But before he could reach it, his cell phone buzzed. Glancing at the screen, he saw it was Marvin Kahn.

Hart broke stride long enough to answer the phone.

"I'm in a hallway in CTU, may I call you back in a moment?"

"Yes, and have Director Levin with you," Kahn's gravelly voice replied.

Levin stood up the minute Hart approached his office. "Tom, we need a private conference room. The DDO wants to speak to us."

Once ensconced in the secure room, Hart put his cell on speaker and dialed Kahn.

"Sir, I am with Mr. Levin. You are on speaker."

"Thank you, Commander. Gentlemen, I have a present on its way to you from Thailand. The captain of the *Jasmine* will be arriving at JFK at 5:30 PM. Have a team there to pick him up and transport him to CTU," Kahn advised.

"If I may ask, Sir, why are you sending him to us? I thought matters were being handled in Thailand," Hart asked.

"The son-of-a-bitch proved tougher than we thought. After three days as our guest, we'd learned nothing . . . despite coming damn close to killing the man. I am confident you will have better luck, Commander."

"Yes, Sir," Hart responded, his wheels already turning. It might be the break he'd been praying for, or it could turn out to be a colossal waste of time—time that they could ill afford to squander.

As soon as Kahn was off the line, Levin spoke. "I'll arrange the pick-up. He will be in your capable hands by 6:15 PM, Commander."

At noon straight up, Hart called Liz's cell, as promised. She answered on the first ring. He could tell from the ambient noise that she was outside.

"Sounds like your meeting has adjourned."

"I decided to take a long walk in the park and try to wrap my head around what we're facing. Tucker and I agree that the city's health care system will be overwhelmed in the first hours following a detonation. Hundreds of thousands of people will die from their injuries before we can intervene . . . mainly from severe burns." Liz paused to collect her thoughts. "There are less than a hundred burn beds in the entire NYC area. We'd need a hundred times that just to have a fighting chance to save people."

"Did you discuss what could be learned from Hiroshima, and how that city managed its casualties?" Hart asked.

"Yes. We know that there were 136,000 casualties, seventy percent of whom suffered a combination of thermal burns, radiation exposure, and blast injuries. Thirty thousand people died the first day. People lay dying in the streets because there was nowhere to take them. Of the 45 hospitals in the area, only three remained functional. Even if they had been operational, ninety percent of the physicians and nurses were injured in the blast."

"And you think that's what would happen here, but on a larger scale?"

"I know that's what will happen, just with a far greater body count." Liz's voice trailed off, before she seemed to regain her conviction, "We're not finished for the day . . . just taking an hour's break. We'll reassemble with the personnel required to implement an emergency response plan. I don't need to tell you how little time we have, and what an extraordinary amount of work remains. It would be helpful if you could find the bastards and their bomb and put an end to this craziness."

"I'm working on it. I'll be entertaining an out-of-town guest this evening. He's due to arrive around 6:15. Let's hope it's not a dead end."

"I'll see you when I see you. Love you, cowboy."

"Love you, too, darling."

The captain of the *Jasmine* was not in the best of shape when he arrived at the CTU. Electrical burn marks were evident on his arms, and his face was swollen from repeated blows. The sedation given him prior to departing Thailand had worn off, leaving the man with a blinding headache. He tried to raise his hands to his face, but they wouldn't move. Slowly forcing his eyes open, the captain realized he was chained to a metal desk anchored to the floor.

"Let me out of here!" he wailed.

"Come now, Captain, is that any way to talk to your hosts?"

"Fuck you!" his voice echoed off the walls of the interrogation cell.

"Yell as loud as you like, Captain. No one can hear you."

The man turned away, refusing to make eye contact with the commander. Hart grabbed his chin and yanked his jaw firmly until the two were eye to eye.

"I believe you saw the work we did on Ahmed Dar."

"Who?" The man's ignorance appeared genuine.

"Let me help you remember." Hart pushed a series of enlarged photos under the captain's nose. They were printed on glossy paper rendering razor sharp images of Dar's ashen face, pock-marked with bullet holes and oozing gray matter.

"The man you had planned to meet," Hart answered.

The captain tried to turn away, but Hart pressed his face into the pictures.

"What do you want of me?"

"Tell me everything you know about your passenger— the small man with glasses."

But there was only silence.

"Do you have a family, Captain?" Hart searched for a way into the man's brain.

"My wife and daughters are strong. They will be fine without me."

Without warning, he reared back and spat in Hart's face.

Acting on reflex, Hart struck the captain full force in the forehead with the flexed heel of his palm. The captain's head recoiled so sharply that Hart feared he'd broken the man's neck. Relieved to find a carotid pulse, he realized that he had simply cold-cocked the son of a bitch.

Slapping him until he regained consciousness, Hart made one thing clear: "Spit on me again, and I'll kill you." He waited for a flicker of acknowledgement before proceeding.

"You think you are protecting them, but you're not. Tell me, Captain, did they warn you about what would happen to your wife and children if anything went awry? Did they buy your silence with threats against your family? Is that why that little brain of yours is telling you to keep silent?"

The captain didn't say a word.

"I have a surprise for you, Captain. These men don't like loose ends, and you and your family are loose ends. Dar was planning to meet you not to invite you to join the United Islamic State, but to slit your throat. Then he would have raped your wife and daughters before slaughtering them."

Letting his words sink in, the commander added, "We did you a huge favor. We killed the animal."

"There are many more animals that you have not killed," the man finally responded.

"We'll protect you and your family. You have my word."

"What good is your word? These men are close enough to reach out and touch my family, and there's nothing you can do to stop them."

"You're wrong. I can have your wife and daughters in protective custody in thirty minutes."

"I don't believe you." He paused. "When you have them in custody, and I am able to speak with them, then you and I will talk." The captain broke eye contact and stared at the floor.

"I'll be back," Hart said as he walked out of the cell.

Hart called Kahn and put the wheels in motion. It took less than thirty minutes for a two-man detail to arrive at the captain's home in Lahore. While one agent worked to calm his wife, the other dialed a number on his satellite phone.

Hart was now back in front of the captain, sitting silently. When his phone vibrated, he reached for it, his eyes never leaving the captain's.

"We're in position, Commander. The woman and her daughters are with us. I'll put her on." The operative handed the phone to the captain's terrified wife.

Hart handed his cell phone to the captain, who raised it slowly and suspiciously to his ear. Speaking in Urdu, he asked if she and the children were alright. A small transceiver concealed in Hart's ear allowed him to hear every word of the conversation. At that moment, the man's wife was sobbing uncontrollably.

"Calm down . . . everything is going to be okay."

The moments between her sobs grew in length until finally there was only silence.

"Have these men harmed you in any way?" the captain asked, ready to lash out at Hart.

"No," her voice cracked, "I thought you were dead."

"I'm sorry to disappoint you, but you are stuck with me for many years, Allah willing."

"A man was shot to death near Bethel Street the day that you went missing. I went to the police, but they refused to help. They told me to go home and wait . . . that you were probably just sleeping it off somewhere. Where have you been and who are these men?" she pleaded.

The captain looked at his captors, studying Hart's face before responding.

"Listen to me carefully," he instructed his wife. "I want you and our daughters to go with these men. They will take you someplace safe. Do what they say."

"What is happening? Why are we in danger? I don't understand."

Hart reached across and took the phone from the captain. Speaking in fluent Urdu, he told her, "Your husband will be fine. Do as he says. He will call you back in an hour." He disconnected.

Turning to the captain, Hart continued to speak in Urdu, "I've upheld my end of the bargain. Now I need to know every detail related to the men and their shipment."

"You speak my language quite well. CIA?"

"Does it really matter who I work for, Captain?"

"No. What matters is that you have the decency to spare my family after I tell you what you want to know. Do with me as you will, but leave them unharmed."

"Nothing will happen to you or your family, other than being reunited. You have my word."

The captain studied Hart for a final time before beginning to speak.

"The small man, the one with glasses and the horribly deformed face . . ."

"Al-Bakr," Hart filled in the blank.

"I only know him as *Ibrahim*. He's not the one who initially approached me. It was a younger man named Zahid. He told me that he got my name from a local who knew I was not too particular about who or what I brought aboard the *Jasmine*, as long as the price was right."

"What did he offer you?"

"He promised me $50,000 to transport him and two others to Mumbai."

"What about cargo?"

"They had a twenty-foot shipping container. They told me it was full of scrap metal. I didn't ask any questions."

"Why not?"

"Why in the hell do you think?"

"I don't know, Captain. Tell me why you didn't push to know what was in that container."

"Do you have a family?" the man asked Hart.

"I had a family."

"And what happened to them?"

"That's not what we are here to discuss."

"Would you have done everything in your power to keep them safe?"

Hart slammed his fist on the table, "I told you that's not what we are here to discuss."

"You've answered my question," the captain responded.

"Zahid showed me photographs of my daughters on their way to school. He also showed me a photograph of my wife in the market. He explained that my family would enjoy a long life—if I kept my mouth shut."

"Did you wonder why they were paying you twenty times the going rate for the trip?"

"It's easier to turn a blind eye than to wonder such things, particularly when one wants to survive to enjoy the fruits of one's labor."

"Why did you arrange a meeting with Ahmed Dar?"

The captain paused as if sizing up the commander. "Because I wanted to avenge my son's death at the hands of the Americans. The man you call al-Bakr offered me a ticket off my pathetic ship and into a life with meaning."

"The life of a jihadist?" Hart questioned.

"A life devoted to fighting for one's beliefs. Belittle it if you wish, but you've experienced how powerful such forces can be."

"What happened to the men and cargo once you arrived in Mumbai?"

"They boarded the *Positano* along with their freight. It departed for Halifax two days later."

"When was it scheduled to arrive?"

"The 28th."

"Today?" Hart shouted in disbelief.

"Yes, I believe it was scheduled to dock in the late evening."

"We're done, Captain," Hart reached up and released the restraints holding the man's wrists.

"What are you going to do with me?" he asked.

"We're going to return you to Karachi . . . to the *Jasmine* . . . like nothing ever happened. Nothing did happen, did it, Captain?"

"No, nothing."

"You promised to protect me and my family."

"And we will as long as you remain silent."

Two men stepped in to remove the captain. Before he could react, the captain once again felt the burn of a needle piercing his skin. Hart caught him as he fell forward.

Emerging from the isolation cell, Hart instructed his colleagues to take the man back to Karachi. "I want a 24/7 detail on the captain and his family—invisible, but close enough to intervene if needed."

Hart looked at his watch. It was 8:05 PM. He turned to Levin, who pulled his cell phone away from his face. "Already on it, Commander. I've got ICE on the line. They are patching us through to the Royal Canadian Mounted Police in Halifax."

The next calls were to the State Highway Patrols in Maine, Massachusetts, New Hampshire, Connecticut, and New York. There was an order from the Department of Homeland Security to shut down 540 miles of Interstate 95. Traffic would come to a standstill as they hunted for a small, heavily scarred man with round glasses and the core of a nuclear bomb.

CHAPTER THIRTY-EIGHT

December 28—13 hours earlier

THE *POSITANO* ARRIVED AT THE PORT OF HALIFAX shortly before 7 AM, half a day ahead of schedule and thirteen hours in advance of when Commander Hart would learn of its deadly cargo.

Al-Bakr remained below deck as the ship docked. He sat staring into a small magnifying mirror attempting to apply the prosthetic devices that rendered his pronounced disfigurement less evident. Twenty-two days at sea had caused his face to grow thinner, and the prosthetics no longer fit as before. It was a small complication, but one he had not anticipated. He finally succeeded in gluing the last device in place.

Leaving his cabin, al-Bakr climbed the steep metal staircase up to the deck, arriving just as the yellow container was hoisted high in the air by a crane. It was then off-loaded onto the bed of a waiting semi. He was pleased to see that Zahid and Yasir were monitoring its movement. Once the cargo was secured, the truck pulled into line for inspection. Barring the discovery of illicit contraband, the driver would receive clearance to leave the port.

The *Positano's* captain stood at the top of the ship's gantry. Al-Bakr approached him.

"May Allah bless you for ensuring our safe passage," al-Bakr said as he handed him a small suitcase. "Four hundred thousand dollars, as agreed."

The man knew he needn't open the suitcase or count the money. It would only insult the passenger, with whom he hoped to do business in the future.

"I've arranged for you to receive an additional $50,000 for the trouble we created while on board," al-Bakr informed him.

"Trouble? If you are referring to that mad dog that needed to be put down, you have my gratitude. He would have turned on me eventually. I should be paying you."

"Then consider the payment a bonus. We may wish to call upon you again."

Bidding the captain goodbye, al-Bakr made his way down the gantry. As he neared the truck, a heavily muscled man with skin the color of ebony climbed out of the cab and introduced himself.

"My name is Aadan Shire. I'll be driving you to Calais and then on to Bangor . . . just as soon as we receive clearance from the Port Authority."

"Basra told me about you. You're well educated to be driving a truck," al-Bakr commented.

"We do what we are called to do . . . for the Caliphate." He pointed to a waiting area just beyond a large gray building. "I'll pick up the three of you over there after the truck is scanned. Don't worry, they won't identify the device."

"No hurry. God's work will wait an extra few minutes," al-Bakr said.

He had traveled more than 7,000 miles in the past month. So, too, had a ball of metal, no bigger than a softball, yet capable of reducing America's greatest city to smoldering rubble. A new world order was about to be ushered in.

Clearance in hand, the men were on their way. It would take five hours to reach Calais, Maine, via the Trans-Canadian Highway and NB-1. The drive was spectacular. Rugged shoreline gave way to towering trees, which were transformed into white giants by a fine dusting of snow. For the three jihadists, it was a welcome contrast to their arid homeland.

A few minutes before arriving in Calais, the driver spoke to his passengers. "It's going to slow down up ahead. There used to be three access points from Canada into the U.S., but ICE reduced it to one. They put in a new facility a couple of years ago, including state-of-the-art detection equipment. Since then, it's been a pain in the ass each time I cross."

Soon they were crawling along in a line of traffic awaiting permission to enter the United States.

"Relax, gentlemen," al-Bakr advised the men, "Allah willing, this will be the final impediment on our long journey. Only glory awaits us."

Forty minutes passed before the truck pulled up to the inspection point. As the customs agent approached, he motioned the driver to roll down his window.

"What's in your load?" he asked, while carefully monitoring the driver's face for traces of deception.

"It's full of scrap metal. It was off-loaded from the *Positano* this morning in Halifax. We're on our way to Jersey."

"Pull it into Bay 3," the CBP agent ordered.

The driver nodded, rolled up his window, and steered the eighteen-wheeler to the outside inspection bay.

"What's that?" al-Bakr asked, pointing to a gantry that lay ahead.

"It's bad news. That's a Rapiscan Eagle® M60 mobile inspection system. State-of-the-art radiographic imaging and radiation detection."

As they spoke, the truck ahead of them cleared the device and a red light turned to green, signaling Shire to proceed fully into the bay.

"What are you going to do?" al-Bakr demanded of the driver.

"I'm going to take my sweet time, as instructed, and hope that Allah is smiling upon us."

As it passed through the gantry, a high intensity beam of radiation fanned out through the truck's cargo. The device was designed to ensure that the cab and its occupants were spared exposure to the 6 MV x-ray beam—a level of energy capable of penetrating up to thirty inches of steel and causing serious injury.

Beyond x-ray imaging, the M60 employed a second level of protection against smuggled nuclear contraband. A gamma ray and neutron detection system monitored the truck for any signals of clandestine fissile materials. When the detection equipment had completed a sweep of the truck, the second light turned yellow, indicating the driver was to proceed to a holding area and wait for the scans to be analyzed.

"Is that it?" al-Bakr asked.

"No, now they analyze the pictures and data they captured. The core may or may not show up."

"Will they recognize it as core?"

"They will see only a dark shadow where there was a higher level of x-ray absorption. That only happens with a short list of very dense materials . . . denser than steel. At the top of the list are uranium and plutonium. They'll know it's not plutonium due to the lack of neutrons picked up by the detector."

Almost nothing rattled al-Bakr, but this was an exception. He could feel his heart pounding in his chest. He'd come too far . . . they couldn't fail . . . not after so many years of planning.

Inside the CBP facility, an inspector waited patiently for the sophisticated software platform to transform thousands of data points into decipherable images that would indicate any illicit material. If the image showed anything aberrant, additional inspections would be performed . . . beginning with a physical inspection.

The man picked up a phone, spoke a few words, and then returned to the image. Moments later, a second inspector joined him. Pointing to an almost imperceptible shadow in the truck's twenty-foot container, the inspector asked his supervisor, "What do you make of that?"

"With no corroborating gamma or neutron emissions, I make nothing of it. Let it go through."

"How about if I run a CAFTA scan . . . or at least do a physical inspection?"

"Let me go have a look," the supervisor offered. "I could use some fresh air."

The CBP agent approached the vehicle. "I need you to step out of the truck, please, and open the container. May I have your port clearance papers?"

Physical inspections were a rarity at a border where it was crucial to maintain throughput of the unmanageable volume of vehicles entering the United States. Such an inspection was a first for Shire. As he stepped out of the vehicle, the passenger door started to open.

The inspector's right hand moved reflexively to his holster.

"Tell your passengers to remain in the truck," he instructed.

Al-Bakr closed his door. The inspector removed his hand from the holster and proceeded to the back of the truck where the driver had climbed to the height of the bed.

He reached for the handle on the container's door and flung it open.

A cloud of burnt-orange dust emerged, engulfing the men in rust. Coughing and covering their faces, they waited for it to dissipate. When the air cleared, the officer could see mangled pieces of rusted metal crunched tightly together.

"The shipping manifest says stainless steel," he said, bemused.

"It's from Pakistan. I guess their definition of *stainless* is different than ours," the driver said with a shrug, "It's getting melted down . . . that's all I know."

The inspector climbed into the back of the container with a printed copy of the radiograph in hand. He used it as a map, leading him to the approximate location of the dark object. Maneuvering carefully between rows of jagged scrap steel, he visually scanned the container for anything unusual.

Nothing. Not until his flashlight caught the edge of a small metal box that was sandwiched between large pieces of scrap. He traced it with the light. Its contours matched the size of the object identified by x-ray. Rather than approach the box, he backed out of the cargo container as carefully as he had entered it and then stepped down from the truck.

"Sorry for the delay. It looks like you're good to go."

The driver thanked the man and started the lumbering diesel engine. As they began to roll, al-Bakr demanded to know what the inspector had said.

"He said that we were 'good to go.'"

"But he was holding the radiograph in his hand. Are you telling me that he didn't find anything?"

"He saw only what he chose to see. Remember, he works for us."

As the truck drove out of sight, the supervisor entered the main building and walked over to the console, where a radiograph of the truck was still on the first inspector's screen.

"It was nothing but a bunch of rusted metal that some-one is trying to pass off as stainless steel," he explained to the man, who nodded his head in agreement, "So I let them go."

A large sign welcomed al-Bakr and his accomplices to the United States. They were two hours from Bangor, Maine—where Sarah Qaisrani and Awan Basra would be waiting.

"You will have to direct me," Shire instructed al-Bakr, "I was not given the rendezvous point, only that it would be in Bangor."

"Exit I-395 at Robertson Boulevard, then turn off on Coffin Avenue," al-Bakr instructed.

"Coffin Avenue?" the driver repeated.

"It seemed fitting," al-Bakr responded, "Stay on that road past Littlefield until it dead ends."

There was little traffic on Robertson Boulevard, and none whatsoever on Coffin. As they approached the dead end, a white van came into view. Slowing the truck to a crawl, Shire pulled within a few yards of the van before shutting off the engine. Al-Bakr jumped down from the cab as Sarah hopped out of the van, then each consciously slowed their steps so as not to betray the intimate nature of their relationship.

While al-Bakr greeted Sarah, Basra asked the driver if there had been any problems in Calais.

"It depends on what you call a problem. Be thankful for the supervisor. Despite what was detected, he cleared us after a physical inspection."

"And your passenger . . . how did he manage the delay?"

"Let's just say he is in a much better mood now."

It took little time to off-load the core and transfer it to the van for transportation to New York City. As Basra, al-Bakr, and Sarah Qaisrani headed for Brooklyn, Yasir and Zahid accompanied Shire in the semi to a refinery outside of Newark, where the remaining contents of the container would be melted down. As the miles ticked by, they bantered about their homes far away, family they'd not seen in years, and what lay ahead. The three men were united by a common ideology and a profound hatred of the West.

The driver navigated through a series of fenced gates before pulling up to a loading dock. As he turned to open the door, there was a loud hiss as a subsonic bullet passed through the man's right temple. Two more shots followed. Al-Bakr had been clear—regardless of Basra's confidence in his man, there were to be no points of potential vulnerability.

Yasir and Zahid moved the body to the back of the cab and covered it with blankets. They unhooked the cab from the flatbed portion of the truck and headed for Newark Airport. They parked in a long-term lot and caught a shuttle to the international terminal, where they boarded United Flight #12 for London. It would be days before the stench of Shire's decomposing body drew the attention of airport police.

Basra was closing in on New York when he felt compelled to share some difficult news with al-Bakr.

"I spoke with our leader earlier today," he said in reference to Sheik Gilani, "He informed me that your associate in Karachi has been killed."

"You're speaking of Ahmed Dar?"

"Yes."

"What happened? How do you know it was an assassination?"

"Two bullets shattered his skull at close range. His body was dropped into a dumpster and covered with a red coat."

"And what of the man with whom he was to meet?" al-Bakr asked.

"We know nothing about the man," Basra confessed.

"When we get to the house, I must make a call. How long will it be until we get there?"

"Less than an hour."

Basra's time estimate proved precise. He, al-Bakr, and Sarah Qaisrani returned to the city just shy of the allotted time, thanks to the absence of rush-hour traffic. Twenty minutes later, I-95 was shut down.

They drove straight to Al's Garage, where Ali, Jamal, and the three engineers awaited them. Ali opened a gate, allowing the van to enter. Qaisrani and al-Bakr emerged from the van and greeted the men.

Basra opened the rear door of the van and lifted the panel concealing the bomb's core.

"It's hard to fathom the power we possess," Basra said, touching the core as though it were something sacred.

Al-Bakr stepped forward. "Let's allow these men to complete their work." He gestured to Ali and Jamal to take charge.

One of the engineers stepped forward and hesitated before addressing al-Bakr.

"What is it?" he asked impatiently.

"I need you to confirm the precise date and time of detonation. We will then complete the assembly of the device, as well as fuse and arm it."

"11:59:59, December 31," al-Bakr responded in a staccato burst, then turned toward Basra, "A millisecond before the dawn of the New Year."

Before leaving for the safe house, al-Bakr reaffirmed, "We will return in two days, on the thirtieth, to claim the van."

When he arrived at the safe house, al-Bakr excused himself. Once in his room, he pulled out an encrypted phone and called Hassan.

"You are safe?" The relief was evident in Hassan's voice as he awaited instructions from al-Bakr.

"Yes, I am safe, as is the package we will soon deliver. But there is something that needs your attention."

"Tell me how I may serve you."

"I told you weeks ago that there might be an important role for you in Karachi."

Flattered, al-Bakr's bodyguard eagerly awaited the details.

"Go there, now. Find the captain of the *Jasmine*. His services are no longer required. Let me know when you've taken care of business." Al-Bakr chided himself for having been so foolish as to bring the captain into his confidence. Why had he done it, he wondered. There was little to gain and much to lose.

Across town, Saad Rahmani, one of Basra's most trusted men, was checking into the Sheraton at Times Square.

"Good evening, Mr. Rahmani," the desk clerk said as he handed the man an electronic key to Room 236. "We have you confirmed for three nights, checking out on December 31."

"That is correct," Rahmani confirmed.

"You will be leaving just when the fun is beginning," the night clerk commented.

"It's too much excitement for me," Rahmani professed, "and I'll be eager to return to my family as soon as I've finished my business."

"I understand, Sir. It will be quite a zoo down here. I hear they are expecting just over a million people. Well, have a good night."

Rahmani visited the room only long enough to ensure that it was acceptable. He then carefully slipped out of a side entrance, avoiding the front desk and the night clerk.

CHAPTER THIRTY-NINE

December 29
New York City

HOUSED IN SEPARATE ROOMS, Sarah Qaisrani and Ibrahim al-Bakr slept like the dead. Neither awakened until after 8 AM, at which time the two most wanted fugitives in America made their way to the kitchen, where Basra met them. As they sipped cups of steaming tea, another man entered.

"This is Saad Rahmani," Basra said, "He will be joining us on our drive into the city."

Rahmani bowed his head slightly, "It will be an honor."

When they were finished with their tea, the group departed. The first stop was the Fast Park Garage, operated by Metro Park. It was located at 210 West 48th Street, with a second entrance at 212 West 49th Street. Al-Bakr was pleased at the proximity to Times Square—477 feet, to be precise—but then something caught his eye, and the smile vanished from his face.

A sign at the entrance to the parking facility stated: "No Vans."

Sensing his passenger's escalating anger, Basra spoke up: "No worries . . . that's standard policy at most parking garages in mid-town. The valets are happy to make an exception—for a $200 tip. We have a space reserved for tomorrow, with a pick-up scheduled for January 2. We've told them that the van will be delivered at 8 PM."

Basra watched with relief as the tension flowed out of al-Bakr's face.

Rahmani eased the car away from the sidewalk and into traffic. His destination was the Sheraton, a few blocks away. Pulling into the circular driveway, he stopped long enough to point out both entrances to the hotel.

"If you enter or leave the building via the side exit, you will bypass the front desk and its loquacious registration clerk. You will also be closer to the elevators."

"What room?" al-Bakr asked.

"Room 236. It's a one-bedroom suite with a pull-out sofa bed. Check-out is at 11 AM on December 31." Rahmani handed al-Bakr the key card.

"Any questions?" Basra asked.

"No. You both have done an excellent job. Sarah and I thank you."

With that, Basra instructed Rahmani to return them to Brooklyn.

CHAPTER FORTY

December 30
New York City

THE HARD-WON INTELLIGENCE DETAILING THE ARRIVAL of the *Positano* and its nuclear cargo proved useless when the ship docked thirteen hours ahead of schedule. Al-Bakr had slipped into the country hours before an alert could be sounded, aided and abetted by a cadre of jihadists. Forty-eight hours later, his location, as well as the location of the nuclear core, were anyone's guess.

Hart was climbing the walls. There were no more leads to chase down . . . no stones left unturned. Armageddon loomed on the horizon—one day away.

"I've got to clear my head, Tom. I know we're running out of time, but staring at the same facts hoping for a different picture to emerge is making me crazy."

"Why don't you take a break for a few hours . . . come back fresh. I can reach you if anything changes."

"Abandon ship, Mr. Levin?"

"Hardly, Commander. Just a brief shore leave. Get out of here. Take care of yourself. You are no good to us if you can't think straight."

Walking into his borrowed office, Hart called Liz, who was between meetings. "Darling, can you get away for a couple of hours?"

"Are you serious, John?"

"I'm not making any headway here. That means zero progress . . . as in dead in the water. I'm hoping a distraction will let me refocus, maybe bring something to the fore that I can't see at the moment."

"How are you going to turn off the incessant voice in your head that warns that D-Day is fast approaching?"

"I don't know that I can. If I begin to feel like Nero fiddling, I'll know it's time to get back to CTU."

"Alright, Commander. I'll see you at the hotel in about forty-five minutes."

There was no warm-up, no loving foreplay. Hart starting unzipping Liz's dress within minutes of stepping into the hotel room.

"Slow down, cowboy," she instructed, but he wasn't listening.

Their love-making was a frenetic attempt at escape, but even the hottest sex on the planet would have proved incapable of dispelling the image of an exploding nuke from Hart's mind.

Lying with her head on Hart's wide shoulder, Liz broached the subject she'd been careful to avoid. "You haven't mentioned a word about al-Bakr, but I feel like he's here, in the room with us. I know he's always on your mind."

"Not always . . . not for the last hour."

"Give me a real answer, John. What's happening? What do you know?"

"I don't know anything more than I've shared with you. Without any knowledge of al-Bakr or Sarah Qaisrani's whereabouts, there's not much I can do."

"And if they are found?" she asked.

"I don't think you want to go there, darling. That's the part of me you'd rather pretend doesn't exist."

"That was before the last attack. Now . . . I hope you do whatever it takes to stop them."

He patted her back, "Yes, darling. But I'm not inviting you to the interrogation."

"On that note, I'm taking a shower," Liz said as she sat up in bed.

"And I'm going back to work."

As Hart and Wilkins returned to their respective agencies, al-Bakr and Sarah Qaisrani were leaving Al's Garage for mid-town Manhattan. At 8:12 PM, they pulled into Fast Park Garage and handed their reservation to the valet. He looked at the ticket, then at the van, and finally back at al-Bakr.

"Didn't you see the sign?" the man asked.

Al-Bakr responded, "We were told it would be okay."

"Who told you that?"

Al-Bakr extended his hand, in which a bill was neatly folded. "I believe it was Mr. Franklin."

"Of course, I'll park it myself."

"We'll pick it up on New Year's Day—assuming you are open." Al-Bakr knew that nothing larger than a silver dollar would remain of the garage.

"Twenty-four seven, 365 days a year."

With that, the man and woman began the short walk to their hotel at the corner of 7th and 53rd Street. They used their key to unlock the side entrance to the Sheraton, then walked unnoticed to room 236, reserved under the name of Rahmani.

"I wish we could stay to see the fireworks," Sarah exclaimed as she moved toward her lover, slipping her arms around his waist.

Al-Bakr stopped her, gently pushing her away. "Not now. Let's wait until we have reason to celebrate."

Sarah dropped her hands to her sides, then smiled coyly as she stepped toward the window. "Do you think we'll be able to see it from Montreal?"

The Arctic Fox and her companion were scheduled to leave at 8:11 AM the next morning from Penn Station on the 69 Adirondack, arriving in Montreal eleven hours later. It was but a waypoint on the longer journey to Matagami, 475 miles northwest of Montreal, a place no one would ever find them. A car would be waiting for them at the Montreal airport, parked in stall 771 at the long-term lot.

But Sarah would not be completing the trip. How naïve, al-Bakr thought, that Sarah would believe her machinations and mock attraction to him had gone undetected. Unlike her husband, Babur, al-Bakr was not blind to Sarah's true nature. He had tolerated Sarah's murder of her father and mother, but she had crossed a line with the calculated killing of Babur. Beyond the killings, he also knew of her numerous infidelities and the pseudo-allegiance she swore to Islam. Sarah had served a purpose— acting as an invaluable conduit to Basra's organization. But with all of the details buttoned down, her usefulness had expired. So, too, would Sarah after they crossed the Canadian border.

"Did you hear me?" Sarah asked, annoyed that al-Bakr had not responded to her question.

"I apologize, Sarah. Ah, yes, I've been told that you will see the flash on the horizon—even as far away as Montreal."

As al-Bakr and Sarah Qaisrani slept that night, men in Brooklyn worked into the early hours of the morning preparing four cars—beaters might be a more apt description—for their role in the attack. The four sections of spent fuel rod were removed from safekeeping, instantly exposing everyone in the room to lethal radiation, including Jamal. Each section of fuel rod was surrounded by what appeared to be an explosive device linked to a trigger, though it was a foil. Ali and Basra stayed safely out of harm's way. One by one, the four men stepped forward to receive a portion of the rod. They were heavier than they had anticipated and hot. More than one of the men strained as a rod was handed to him.

There would be no immediate symptoms of the radiation sickness that was to follow. Within twenty-four hours, they would begin to slough off the lining of their intestines. Their bone marrow would be in the process of dying while their nervous system moved toward total shut-down. By then, the bomb would have exploded, sparing the four jihadists the gruesome descent into hell brought about by radiation sickness.

The men dropped their loads into holding containers placed in the cars' trunks. Each man was handed a map and a circular route. They were to repeat the loop until they were either stopped by authorities—which was their primary objective as decoys—or until the nuclear bomb detonated. The hot fuel rods, spewing every imaginable form of radiation associated with the decay of nuclear isotopes, could easily be detected at a hundred feet. If any one of them was stopped, authorities would conclude that it was not a nuclear explosion they had been seeking to prevent, but a dirty bomb.

CHAPTER FORTY-ONE

HASSAN WAS EAGER TO COMPLETE HIS MISSION and please his master. After eighteen hours of non-stop driving, he arrived in Karachi. He headed straight to the port, where it didn't take long to locate the *Jasmine*. As he approached the decrepit ship, he saw a man standing close to the ship's upper railing. He wore a captain's hat.

Hassan silently pulled back the slide on his .40 caliber Glock, chambering a hollow-point bullet and cocking the trigger. Then he moved toward his prey. He stepped onto the gangway, mindful that the wood might squeak under his weight. Reaching the top, he continued up a short set of metal stairs leading to the deck.

Suddenly aware of someone's presence, the captain turned to face the burly man. He seemed neither surprised nor concerned. Hassan clicked off the safety and leveled the pistol's muzzle at the captain's head.

A shot rang out as a sniper, concealed on a rooftop 850 yards from the ship, squeezed the trigger of his Barrett

M107 .50 caliber rifle. With a muzzle velocity approaching 3,000 feet per second, the bullet struck Hassan before he could hear the rifle's report. It hit with such force that he flew mid-way across the deck. Little remained of the side of his head where the anti-aircraft round had entered.

Two men who had been concealed in the shadows stepped forward. Hastily they secured a series of lead weights to Hassan's wrists and ankles, then dragged his body to the side of the ship. Enlisting the help of their comrade, dressed as the captain, they tossed the body into the murky water below and watched as it sank beneath the waves.

Several hours later, al-Bakr began to wonder why Hassan had deviated from protocol and had failed to telephone.

"The Americans," al-Bakr said under his breath. "It doesn't matter. It's too late," he reassured himself.

It didn't take more than a few vibrations of his phone to rouse Hart from a shallow and fitful sleep. Fortunately, it did not awaken Liz, who lay tucked close by his side, exactly where she had fallen asleep. Careful to extricate himself without jarring her, Hart grabbed a robe and headed for the suite's sitting room. He waited until he had closed the pocket door to the bedroom before answering it.

"Commander, it's Tom Levin. We've got a development."

As he started to speak, the door opened. "Who are you talking to?" Liz asked, still in the process of awakening.

"Excuse me for one minute," Hart said to Levin, pushing the mute button on his phone. "It's Tom Levin. I'll come back to bed as soon as I'm done."

Satisfied with his promise, Liz returned to bed, and Hart returned to Levin.

"What's up?"

"We just received a call from the night shift manager at the Sheraton in Times Square. He recognized a man from one of our flyers. He said that man checked in on the 28th. He remembered thinking it was odd that the man would depart on the 31st just when the party was heating up. He identified the man as Saad Rahmani, part of Sheik Gilani's cell in Brooklyn."

"That room is not for Rahmani . . . it's for Gilani's guests." Hart spoke with certainty.

"You mean Qaisrani and al-Bakr?" Tom asked. "How do you know?"

"It's the only scenario that makes sense, Tom. What's being done to secure the location?"

"We have agents in route. ETA is 0719. I've got NYPD watching the floor and all exits until my men are in position."

"Good. I'll be en route to CTU in ten minutes. Call me the second you've apprehended the occupants of that room. I'll need access to them—unimpeded access. Do you understand?"

"Yes, Commander."

Hart disconnected the call and walked into the bedroom, where Liz stretched out her arm, beckoning for him to join her.

"No can do," he said grabbing a black turtleneck and a pair of black trousers. "I've got to go, and so do you."

"What's happened, John?" a now fully-awake Liz asked.

"CTU is about to make an arrest at the Sheraton Times Square. I'd bet dollars to donuts that it's our bespectacled friend and his northern accomplice. Regardless, I need to interrogate whomever they apprehend."

"And you want me to come with you?"

"No, I want you to get as far away from New York as you can. The eastern seaboard is going to be shut down if a nuke explodes. I'd suggest Atlanta. Just please don't fight me on this one, Liz."

"You know I can't do that. The president didn't have me appointed PFO just so I can turn my back on New York. I'm staying right here, with you and five million other people . . . we're riding this one out."

"God damn it, Liz, do you not get it? Look out that fucking window," he said, wildly gesturing toward the massive pane of glass. "Everything within sight will be destroyed . . . and all the people who inhabit it. You are an invaluable asset. That's why you're serving as the PFO. The president can't afford to lose you."

Her arms crossed in defiance and feet anchored to the floor, it was clear that Liz was immovable.

"Fine," John capitulated. "Go up in a ball of fire. I don't know what in the hell you think you will have accomplished. You will just be a statistic—one of the hundreds of thousands of people incinerated through a grotesque act of terror."

"I will be here waiting for you, John. You can say whatever you'd like, but you're not going to get me to budge. So, I hope you stop these assholes."

Hart started to object, but stopped himself. He sighed. "I'll call you from CTU. It may be hours from now. Don't draw any conclusions; just know I'm trying like hell to do my job."

He started to leave, but felt Liz's hand wrap around his arm. "You can at least kiss me," she said, with a look that melted his heart.

"Of course, darling," he said, wrapping her in his arms. "It's not our last kiss . . . I'll promise you that." Then he walked out the door.

Al-Bakr and Sarah Qaisrani were sitting quietly in their bathrobes, sipping coffee, when the door to room 236 exploded inward. Al-Bakr leaped to his feet, his coffee cup tumbling to the floor as he reached for an H&K 9mm pistol a few feet away. Before he could grab it, an excruciating pain radiated through his body as the probes from multiple Tasers embedded in his skin.

With the agents focused on al-Bakr's quivering body, Qaisrani lunged for the weapon. She was blocked by an agent who seemed to appear out of nowhere. Grabbing his handcuffs with one hand, he reached toward Qaisrani, intending to spin her around . . . arms behind her back. But Qaisrani dodged and parried—sinking her teeth into the fleshy part of the agent's hand. He screamed out in agony as she bit him so severely that his thumb was hanging on by a thread of skin. Before passing out from the pain, he punched her with every ounce of his remaining strength. There was the unmistakable sound of her jaw fracturing.

Paramedics, who had been waiting in the hallway with other first responders, tended to the injured agent, carefully bandaging the hand and thumb before transporting him to the nearest trauma center. No medical care was provided to al-Bakr or Qaisrani. They were shackled and rushed to waiting cars.

As he entered the elevator, Hart's cell phone beckoned again. It was Levin on the line, but the call dropped before he could get out a word. Hart punched the button for the ground floor hard as if he could speed the elevator's descent. When the doors opened, Hart leaped out of the steel cage and dialed Levin.

"Sorry, Tom, I was in the elevator. I'm headed to CTU. What have you got for me?"

"You were right. Sarah Qaisrani and Ibrahim Almasi al-Bakr are now in custody and on their way to CTU headquarters."

"Were they arrested without incident?"

"Qaisrani is one vicious bitch. She nearly bit off the thumb of one of my men. He's in an ambulance headed to the hospital. I'm afraid a swift right cross from his good hand may have fractured her jaw."

"It's okay, Tom. I probably would have killed her if she'd bitten me," Hart confessed. "As long as she can talk, we're fine. A little pain might be an added inducement to cooperate. Please tell me you shipped them to CTU separately."

"Of course, Commander. They're in full restraints and will remain that way until you arrive."

"Do me one more favor, Tom, and have them in separate interrogation rooms when I get there. I'm stopping to pick up some supplies."

CHAPTER FORTY-TWO

December 31
New York City

HART WALKED INTO CTU at 7:45 AM, three minutes after al-Bakr and Sarah Qaisrani had been brought in. The terrorists had been taken to soundproof interrogation rooms, where they awaited the commander.

Hart entered the dimly lit room where al-Bakr was being held. He sized up the frail terrorist before saying a word.

"That Hellfire didn't do much for your looks, did it?"

There was no response.

He moved slowly toward al-Bakr, who sat with his arms secured behind his back in a metal chair. A lever on one side of the chair allowed it to recline fully. In this case, into a deep basin of frigid water. A towel rested on the edge of the basin, half-submerged.

"Your thousand-year war has ended. So has your vision for a Holy Caliphate. Put an end to the killing . . . tell me where I can find the bomb."

"Our war is just beginning, and I am nothing more than a foot soldier. The vision you speak of cannot be extinguished. It lives in the hearts and minds of tens of thousands of people . . . oppressed people who long for the day when they can rise up and conquer the infidels. On that day the borders separating these people—my people—will dissolve into a single land governed by Sharia law, and the West will become a footnote in history."

"You will never see that happen."

"Nor will you ever be free of fear. The terror your country has visited upon other nations has finally come home to roost."

"I'm not interested in your ideological ramblings. I need one thing and one thing only—the location of the bomb."

"Do you really believe that I would erase fifteen years of planning and sacrifice when we are within hours of witnessing the incineration of your greatest city? Surely you have more respect for me than that, Commander."

"I have no respect for you. In my mind, you are nothing more than a piece of shit."

"Well, Commander Hart, this *piece of shit* is about to mortally wound your precious country, and there's nothing you can do to stop it."

There was no thought . . . Hart simply reacted, striking al-Bakr's cheek full-force with his elbow.

Al-Bakr's head snapped back, and for a moment, Hart thought the man was about to lose consciousness. Slowly righting himself in the chair, al-Bakr spit out a mouthful of blood.

"Do you think that you can hurt me after what I've been through? Pain, Commander, is my daily companion. I've learned to embrace her like a devoted lover. So strike me as you will. There is nothing more I have to say to you."

Al-Bakr's words were not spoken in spite. They were the honest confession of a man who believes his cause is just and his actions irrevocable. Hart understood the level of his captive's conviction, but he remained undeterred. Wrapping his hand around the chair's lever, Hart pulled sharply, causing it to free-fall into the basin of water behind it. Al-Bakr's face was instantly submerged. Hart looked at the second hand on his watch. After twenty seconds he raised al-Bakr's head out of the water, quickly covering it with the soaking wet towel.

The man struggled to draw a breath, but no oxygen penetrated the heavy, wet cloth. After nearly a minute, Hart removed the towel. Al-Bakr's lungs heaved as he desperately took air deep into his chest.

"Where is the bomb?"

He waited, but there was no response. Not even a hateful look from al-Bakr. That was the worst possible outcome . . . Hart knew the terrorist was resigned to his fate.

"Let's try again." He thrust al-Bakr's head back into the frigid water. This time, he waited until the life seemed to ebb from the man's still body. He raised him from the water, slapped his face hard, and waited for al-Bakr to gasp. As he did, he threw the wet towel across his mouth and nose. He counted to ten before removing it.

Al-Bakr again sucked air into his oxygen-starved lungs. "Talk to me, you son of a bitch, or I swear I will drown you."

"Do as you must, Commander. Drown me if you wish. It will do nothing to save your city. That die has been cast."

Hart started to walk out. Before he could reach the door, he turned around. Once again, he put his hand on the chair's lever. No one would blame him if he pulled it . . . leaving the man to drown.

But he couldn't do it.

"You're weak, Commander. You cannot kill with impunity. That is your fatal flaw." Al-Bakr spoke not with contempt but with resolution.

Hart left without responding.

Tom Levin met him in the hallway, having observed the interrogation from behind a one-way mirror.

"The video is off, Commander."

Levin was giving him license to kill. There would be no record of what happened in interrogation room 3. Only that al-Bakr died unexpectedly during questioning.

"It won't help, Tom."

"It would spare Americans the expense and anguish of a long trial. There would be some sense of retribution."

"And I thought you were the attorney, Tom."

"I've devoted my life to justice. Killing this animal *is* justice, Commander."

"I won't argue that, but there's got to be a way to get at al-Bakr. I just haven't found it." With that, Hart turned away and re-entered the room holding his prisoner.

"Ah, you've decided to join me again, how pleasant," al-Bakr remarked.

"Why would you kill a million innocent people? Why go down in history as the greatest butcher of all time? You are a smart, well-educated man. I just don't get it."

"Was Truman a butcher, Commander? We won't debate how smart or well-educated he was."

"That was different. We were fighting a mortal enemy that had attacked our country. Truman dropped the bomb in an effort to end the war, not intensify it."

"And how are my people different? Are we not also locked in an existential battle with an enemy that has invaded our land for decades . . . an enemy whose imperialistic aspirations rival those of every other nation?"

"You, a visionary whose dream is a world-dominating caliphate, have the audacity to ask me such an absurd question?"

Hart lunged for the man, gripped his neck tightly, and thrust his head under the water until a vacant stared filled al-Bakr's eyes. Only then did he lift al-Bakr out of the water.

Al-Bakr's chest heaved as his body fought for air. After a moment, his respiration slowed enough for him to speak.

"Thank you, Commander, for that brief glimpse of paradise. It was beautiful. Do with me as you will. I know where my soul is destined, and I have no fear—certainly not of a man as flawed as you."

"I'm not going to kill you."

"No?"

"No. But I am going to let you watch as I have a conversation with Sarah Qaisrani. If she fails to answer my questions, there won't be any reprieve."

"I'm losing respect for you, Commander. Do you think I have some investment in this woman? Surely not. She's a psychopathic killer who derives pleasure from the suffering of others. She loves no one and nothing—certainly not Islam. She has served her purpose. The bomb is assembled, armed, fused, and awaiting detonation. Sarah was scheduled to die . . . you've just saved me the need to take care of it."

"And what of the suffering you cause? Do you think you are any less sick?"

"My goal has never been to create suffering for its own sake, but to foment change."

"Qaisrani is pregnant. She carries your child . . . the heir to the Holy Caliphate."

"That's a feeble attempt to extend our conversation, Commander."

"She's been under surveillance since fleeing to Matheson Island shortly after the bio-attack. Do you know that she's been to a doctor in Manitoba several times in recent months—an obstetrician—and that she's filled a prescription for prenatal vitamins? She may be one sick bitch, but that bitch carries your seed."

"If what you say is true, then I will meet my unborn child in Paradise." Al-Bakr's tone was now somber.

"That's not going to happen. On the day of Kiyamat, Allah will judge you by your sins and damn you to eternal hell. There is no paradise for animals like you."

"So you've read the Quran? I'm impressed, Commander, but I know my God, and I know my destiny. Nothing you say or do will change that."

"We'll see," Hart said as he walked out of the room.

He entered the interrogation room holding Sarah Qaisrani and took a seat, carefully staying a few yards out of the woman's reach.

"What happened to your jaw?" he asked in a tone of mock concern.

She wiggled her jaw, causing the broken bones to click as they shifted position. She didn't wince. Instead, she let out an uncontrolled howl that echoed in the room and reverberated in the commander's head.

Collecting herself, she said, "I don't believe we've been formally introduced. I am Sarah Qaisrani. And you are?"

"Your worst nightmare, Ms. Qaisrani."

She laughed.

"Oh, how melodramatic. What are you going to do to me? I can't wait to hear. I'm sure I'm going to enjoy it."

"I'm going to start by breaking your fingers," the commander promised her.

"Here," she said, holding up her shackled hands and extending her right middle finger. "Be my guest."

Hart couldn't do it, and Qaisrani knew it.

"You are too fucking weak, aren't you? It's *Commander*, right? You never did have the courtesy to introduce yourself. Big, powerful Navy Seal. All that brute force, and it did nothing to stop us from killing 85,000 of your countrymen with a tiny virus. Guess what, Commander? It's round two, and we're going for a knock-out. There's not a damn thing you can do to stop us from killing half of New York."

Hart lunged forward, grabbed her finger, and snapped it like a twig.

No pain registered on her face. Laughing at her captor, she baited him, "Only nine more to go."

Hart hesitated.

"What are you afraid of, Commander?"

Hart didn't respond. He knew she'd gotten to him—broken through rock-solid defenses crafted over decades.

In a soft, seductive tone, Qaisrani whispered, "Even Navy Seals have their secret fears. You know, Commander, the ones you bury so deep that you pray they will never be discovered."

Hart turned his back on the woman, fighting to regain his focus. His actions only emboldened Qaisrani.

"Let's play a little game. I'll start by telling you something you are afraid of, Commander."

"Shut up," he ordered, but she continued.

"You are afraid that you won't be able to protect that precious girlfriend of yours. Excuse me, I understand that she's your fiancée now. How sweet. You won't be able to protect her . . . just as you were unable to protect your brother, Corey, when the Towers came tumbling down."

She paused, then dug her claws in deeper. "I understand they never found his body. That must have been tough on the family," she said mockingly.

The Arctic Fox had ignited a raging fire within Hart. Every instinct impelled him to reach across and snap her neck, just as he had snapped her finger.

"You're angry . . . that's good," the woman observed.

"And what of your youngest brother, Matthew? That was his name?"

Hart's eyes blazed. No one had spoken that name since his parents had passed.

"What lake was it, Commander? I can't quite remember where you let him drown."

Hart lunged for her neck. Holding it in his vise-like hand, he began squeezing the life out of her. She tried to reach up, but her hands were shackled to the table. She pounded them furiously, her eyes now wild. Then her eyes began to float back in her head. She was seconds away from death when Hart finally let go.

Choking, the woman struggled to regain her breath.

"I'm disappointed, Commander. I thought you were going to go through with it. But no, you don't have the balls to kill me."

"We're not finished. But I'm not like you . . . a sick animal masquerading as a human being."

"How many people have died by your hand? And you have the audacity to call me an animal? Fuck you and fuck that whore of yours, too. Start counting the hours. Soon you will be part of the roaring cloud of fire rising above what was once New York."

Once again gripping her neck in his powerful right hand, Hart lifted her inches above the chair to which she was chained.

"I'll make you a promise," he began. "If that bomb explodes, you and al-Bakr are going to have front row seats." Thrusting her back in the chair, Hart left the room, slamming the door behind him.

The Commander had descended into Sarah Qaisrani's private hell. He needed air.

Tom Levin stepped in to take on the role of "good cop."

Armed with a splint and tape, Levin entered the interrogation room. He bandaged Sarah Qaisrani's finger before adding, "I'm sorry. My colleague gets a little carried away. I won't hurt you, but I do need to talk with you."

For the first time, Sarah Qaisrani seemed to drop her guard and smile warmly. Not all battles are won by force, Levin thought, as he scooted his chair closer to Qaisrani.

Just as he rested his elbows on the table, Sarah Qaisrani planted her foot in Levin's groin. A sickening pain exploded in Levin's abdomen. The bitch had struck without warning and with blinding speed. Pushing himself out of range of further strikes, Levin doubled over. Hart, having observed it all from behind the one-way mirror, rushed into the room. He bent over Levin, ministering to him, his back turned to Qaisrani.

Suddenly, Hart lifted his right knee to hip height. His leg now cocked like the trigger of a gun, he snapped his foot behind him in a devastating kick. The heel of his boot caught Qaisrani in the nose, reducing it to a mass of smashed cartilage. Blood gushed out. Sarah's eyes rolled back in her head as she lost consciousness.

Hart helped Levin to his feet, leaving Qaisrani face-down, bleeding on the table. For now, the interviews were over.

CHAPTER FORTY-THREE

CARL MARTINSON HAD SPENT FIFTEEN YEARS running down leads as an NYPD homicide detective. He was damn good at it. So good that he earned the moniker of Bloodhound from his compatriots. That's why Levin had made the Bloodhound the point person in charge of investigating potential hiding places for the nuke.

His instructions were clear: Begin with parking facilities proximate to Times Square. Levin believed that such facilities would be perfect for concealing a large vehicle bearing the bomb. Furthermore, the destructive toll of the bomb would increase with every story it was raised above ground-level, since there would be fewer buildings to contain the blast wave.

Armed with a list of more than a hundred public and private parking garages, Martinson's team began a methodical search. Near the top of the list was the Fast Park Garage at 210 West 48th Street.

Moments after arriving at Fast Park, Martinson was on a lift headed to the top of the garage. He was accompanied by the parking attendant and two agents—one carrying a fully-auto MP-5, the other a dosimeter. They were looking for any aberrant sources of radiation emanating from vehicles large enough to harbor the device. It was a pains-taking process as they began a slow march past row upon row of cars, all the while watching the needle on the device.

Without any signal from the dosimeter, Martinson stopped abruptly. He pointed to a white van.

"Your sign says 'No Vans.' That looks like a white panel van to me."

"We make exceptions," the attendant sheepishly admitted, rubbing his fingers together to suggest a bribe.

"Open it," Martinson ordered the attendant.

"It's not locked. We keep the keys in the vehicles."

"Is that smart?" Martinson growled.

"The public isn't allowed access to these levels."

"Even for a little . . . " Martinson replicated the gesture for a bribe.

"No."

Staring at the attendant as if to weigh his truthfulness, Martinson finally took a step toward the vehicle. He carefully opened the rear hatch and peered into the van. Its interior was festooned with dangling electrical cords and racks of supplies. Pushing the cords out of the way, he looked for evidence that something was awry.

He found nothing.

"Bring me that dosimeter," he ordered his fellow agent, who handed over the device and headphones.

He slipped on the headphones and crawled into the back of the van. He began sweeping the van's interior from side to side with the dosimeter's probe. Again, nothing . . . but he still felt uneasy. Martinson had come to trust his intuition during his years on the force. It wasn't rational, but it usually proved right.

He didn't have time to indulge intuitions. He slid out of the back of the van and slammed the door closed.

"There's nothing here," he called out. "Let's move on."

CHAPTER FORTY-FOUR

December 31
New York City

LIZ HAD BEEN WAITING, phone in hand, for hours. She prayed for it to ring . . . prayed that Hart had broken the will of Qaisrani and al-Bakr. When the call finally came through, she hesitated before answering it.

"I'm afraid I don't have good news," Hart began. "They are more than willing to die rather than betray even the smallest detail of their plan."

"Are you holding back because Qaisrani is a woman?"

"I came within seconds of choking her to death. When I had her neck in my hand, squeezing until the blood drained from her face, I realized that, at some level, I'm no different than her."

"She's a psychotic bitch—amoral, devoid of conscience, and hell-bent on killing us all. There's no similarity between the two of you. What about al-Bakr?"

"Same story—anyone who has survived a Hellfire missile obliterating half his face is not going to surrender his secrets. The man was willing to let me drown him before he uttered a word."

"So what now, John?"

"I want you to listen to me very carefully."

"I'm listening."

"If you haven't heard from me by 10 PM, I want you to go to the lowest level of the parking garage. Take cover in the stairwell. That will be your only chance of survival. Otherwise you will die from the thermal blast or initial surge of radiation. The garage may collapse, but the stairwell is reinforced and should remain intact. Remember that the air will be unfit to breathe for a couple of hours. After that, the radioactive fallout will diminish rapidly. It's a pretty grim thing to confront you with, Liz, but it's our reality at the moment."

"I'll do as you say. And I'll pray like hell it doesn't come to that."

"As will I."

It was seven minutes past eight. As Hart hung up the phone, Levin burst into his office.

"It's not over, Commander. We received an anonymous tip. Basra is at the Masjid al Keem mosque. Four agents are en route to apprehend him."

Maybe there is a God, Hart thought.

"As soon as they are on-site, we'll have a live feed rolling from body cams," Levin said over his shoulder, already moving toward the conference room.

Hart leapt to his feet, following close behind Levin. As they entered the darkened room, four video screens flickered as they awaited signals from the body cams. After a painful delay of eight minutes, they finally came to life.

Four CTU agents, armed with suppressed MP-5s, burst into the mosque and surrounded the stunned Basra.

Without a word, they threw him against the ground, then pinned his arms behind him. His hands were secured with a flex-cuff. As the agents immobilized Basra, a small group of men encircled them, inching ever closer. Within seconds the agents were surrounded by Gilani's loyalists.

Without missing a beat, the agents rose to their feet, leveling their sub-machine guns on four of the men. Red dots from their laser sights appeared on the men's foreheads.

"We are going to remove this man from the premises," the unit commander advised. "I'm giving you to the count of three to move to the far end of the building . . . then we open fire.

"One."

No movement.

"Two."

A slight stirring.

"Three."

What sounded like four short bursts of pressurized air followed. Four men in white prayer robes dropped where they stood. Each bore a single hole through his forehead to the back of his head. The holes were small in front and massive where they exited.

Without hesitation, the men trained their laser scopes on the next four. The jihadists scrambled for their lives. During the commotion, Basra was rushed to a waiting SUV equipped with bullet-proof windows and tires.

The unit commander looked directly into one of his men's body cams. "The prisoner has been secured. ETA in thirty. Out."

Hart turned to Levin. "We've got thirty minutes to prepare, and we are going to need every minute."

"What are you thinking?" Levin asked.

"Basra has a wife and a son, right?"

"Two sons," Levin corrected.

"You've been monitoring their home in the unlikely event that Basra would return?"

"Yes, there are two men watching the home 24/7."

"Have his family brought in now," Hart said firmly. "Once they arrive, do not let Basra see them until I am ready."

"But they've done nothing," Levin protested.

"Point noted. All they have done is co-habit with a terrorist who is planning to kill upwards of a million people. Now, if your conscience is at peace, bring them in."

"What are you going to do?" Levin was almost afraid to ask.

"What needs to be done, Tom. No more, no less. Now let's move."

Basra's family was rounded up quickly. Hart's luck seemed to be holding—Basra's eighteen-year-old son and his ten-year-old brother were at home with their mother when agents burst through their front door.

Hart knew he would have one final chance to turn the tide. While he waited for the Basra family to arrive, he tuned one of the monitors to CNN. Anderson Cooper and Kelly Griffin were engaged in mindless banter as they attempted to entertain people waiting for the old year to yield to a new one. Their repartee momentarily stopped as Cooper surveyed the crowd. He estimated that more than a million people had gathered in Times Square.

When Basra arrived, he was taken into interrogation room 2, where he was shackled to the floor and table. Hart had lined up three chairs along the opposite wall. For the moment, they sat empty. Hart stepped into the room and took a seat at the table directly across from Basra.

"We don't have much time, Mr. Basra. I have a series of questions for which I need answers. I'm not going to threaten you. Just do us both a favor and answer the questions."

The man did not acknowledge Hart's presence.

"Where is the bomb?"

No answer.

"I'm going to ask you one more time: Where did al-Bakr and Sarah Qaisrani plant the bomb?"

But Basra didn't stir. He looked bemused.

"I'm glad you think this is funny." Hart gestured to the one-way mirror behind him. Seconds later, a hooded man was brought into the room. An agent positioned him in front of the first of the three chairs, then shoved him down hard into it. Finally, he cuffed the man's ankles and hands before removing the hood.

"What are you doing?" Basra shouted frantically. "My son has done nothing! Bilal, what are you doing here?"

"They took us, Father, all three of us."

Before the shock of his son's words could fade, Basra's wife, Mahnoor, was placed in the room. The guard allowed her to sit unaided before restraining her arms and legs.

"What is happening?" she demanded of her husband. "What do they want with us? Where is Kalil?" She looked to Basra for the answers.

"You will die for this," Basra promised Hart.

"Right now, it looks like we are all going to die, but not before I have a chance to talk with your children. If time permitted, I'd treat you to the niceties of interrogation—a little sleep deprivation, some blaring noise, and, of course, water-boarding." Then, slamming a pistol onto the table, Hart said harshly, "But I don't have time to fuck with you. So I suggest you listen."

"I'm not interested in anything you have to say." Basra spit on the floor.

"Have it your way. I'm going to ask you a question. If I don't receive a truthful answer, I'll put a bullet in your son's shoulder. The first shot won't kill him. Nor will the second or even the third. The fourth goes through his heart. Now that you understand the rules, let's begin."

But before he could initiate the game of guts, Levin's second-in-command interrupted Hart, summoning him to the door.

"What the hell is it, Captain?" Hart asked the officer.

"We're getting hits on the gamma ray detectors."

Hart turned to Basra's family. "We're not finished . . . we've not even begun," then strode out of the holding cell.

Hart followed the captain into a room lined with monitors and equipment. On one screen, Hart saw four glowing green dots . . . all in motion . . . traversing different boroughs of the city.

"What does this mean?" Hart asked, staring at the screens.

Levin had entered the room and was quietly observing Hart and the analyst.

"It means that we have four highly radioactive sources that are mobile and moving through different parts of the city," the sergeant explained.

"I see that, but what does it mean?" Hart emphasized the final word.

"It means that there are four nukes in play, not one."

"Those are high energy sources, correct?"

"Yes, Sir. They're throwing off tons of radiation—gamma rays, neutrons, you name it."

"The kind of radiation emitted by a uranium core?" Hart asked, knowing the answer.

"No, Sir."

"And we are looking for a single uranium core . . . correct?"

"Yes, Sir. "

"So what else emits that kind of radiation?" Hart asked the man.

"Only thing I can think of is a spent fuel rod, Sir."

"Bingo. Captain, tell the officers in the field to apprehend the subjects. Shoot to kill if needed, but not to spend a second longer than necessary near those vehicles."

As the captain stepped away, Levin asked, "How do you know it's fuel rods, Commander?" His voice was low enough not to be heard by others.

"An educated guess, Tom."

"Based solely upon monitoring equipment?" Levin questioned.

"No. I'm basing it on Tariq Kuni."

"Who?"

"The nuclear engineer from Burlington, Kansas, who assembled the bomb. He works at the Tallgrass Prairie

Nuclear Power Plant. The only thing I can't figure out is how he stole one without irradiating himself to death. I'll let you know when I have an answer."

Over the next seventy minutes, all four vehicles were intercepted. Two drivers, who refused to yield to the arresting officers, were shot dead. Their cars were cordoned off, and patrolmen were brought in to keep the public at a safe distance. The remaining two men were taken into custody—one in Queens, the other in the Bronx. They were already exhibiting signs of radiation sickness.

Hart returned to interrogation room 2. Every minute was precious. He raised his pistol and removed the safety. There was no suppressor to dampen the noise. He knew the muzzle blast would be deafening in the confines of the interrogation room. That was okay with him. It might not faze Basra, but it would scare the hell out of his wife.

"Where is the bomb?" he began.

Mahnoor looked pleadingly at her husband. "Tell him!" she screamed, but Basra said nothing.

The sharp report of the gun exploded in the room. Hart had never taken his eyes off of Basra, yet managed a perfect shot through Bilal's right shoulder. Major blood vessels, nerves, and organs were spared, but the boy howled in pain.

Basra lunged at Hart. The chains drew taut but held fast. Mahnoor reached to comfort her son, but the restraints kept her hands just out of reach of her boy.

"Let's try again," Hart said.

"Where is the bomb?"

Silence.

"Wait!" Mahnoor cried out, but it was too late. Hart squeezed off another round. This one struck the left shoulder, throwing Bilal back against the chair.

"I don't want to die, Papa!" the boy managed to cry as he teetered on the edge of consciousness.

"Be strong, Bilal, not like a woman!" his father bellowed before turning his attention back to Hart.

"Go ahead, kill the boy," an emotionless Basra instructed. "He'll die a martyr's death in the name of Allah."

"Okay."

Hart put his next shot through the boy's side. It would shatter a couple of ribs, maybe nick a lung, but it wasn't a kill shot.

Basra sat unmoved.

The boy's shirt was soaked with blood. Hart knew there was a risk of him bleeding out.

Desperate to stop the craziness, Mahnoor pleaded with Hart to put the gun down.

"Your husband can stop this insanity. Your boy's life will be spared. Tell him to answer my question . . . time is running out."

Basra spat on the floor and stared Hart down.

Hart cued the observers in an adjacent room to bring in the younger son, Kalil. The child clearly had no inkling of what was happening . . . until he saw his brother, motionless and soaked in blood. He screamed as he was chained to the remaining chair.

"At the rate he's bleeding, your eldest son has minutes left. I'm not going to be so charitable with Kalil. One shot through his forehead. He'll die, and with him, the Basra name. Now tell me where the bomb is."

The silence that followed was broken only by the labored breaths of Bilal and the gasping sobs of his mother and brother.

Hart gave Basra a final look before leaping from his seat. He grabbed the younger boy's neck in his left hand and placed the barrel of the pistol flush against his forehead. Kalil's eyes brimmed with tears.

"Enough," Mahnoor pleaded. "In the name of Allah, what kind of man and father are you?" she shouted indignantly, but her husband barely stirred.

This time it was Mahnoor who spat . . . upon her own husband.

Furious, Basra did not lash back. He wiped the spittle from his face. "It's a game, Mahnoor. The American won't do anything to Kalil. Just as he won't put a final bullet in our son's chest. Such acts would be reprehensible to his code of justice. Right, Commander Hart?"

Hart did not respond. Instead, he turned his pistol away from Kalil and leveled it on Bilal's heart.

"You're wrong, you son of a bitch." He pulled the trigger. A crimson spot appeared in the center of Bilal's shirt. Basra's oldest son slumped dead in the chair.

Without missing a beat, Hart returned the gun to Kalil's head. Before he could pull the trigger, Basra cried out.

"Stop! You've done enough damage to my family!" Tears streamed down the man's face. His wife's eyes were fixed on Bilal. She was catatonic.

"Promise me that you will do no more harm to my family," Basra demanded.

Hart did not respond.

"There is a van parked close to Times Square," Basra began.

"Where? What kind of van?" Hart could barely get the words out fast enough.

"A white panel van parked at the Fast Park Garage. The bomb is sealed inside the van."

"What do you mean, sealed?"

"It is in a hidden compartment that has been welded shut. There is nothing that you can do to stop it from detonating at midnight."

Levin entered the room, accompanied by two men who would deal with the aftermath of the interrogation.

"A car is waiting for us, Commander. We'll pick up a police escort along the way. With a little luck, we may make it in time."

"If what Basra said is true, it may not matter," Hart said.

He glanced at his watch. It was 10:45 PM.

Hart waited for Levin to get in the car before slamming down the gas pedal. They were soon joined by an escort of four black and whites. As a conduit opened up for them through Manhattan, they rocketed across streets cleared of traffic. They were on pace to reach the Fast Park Garage by 11:15.

"Tom, did you ever see the simulation FEMA did with the help of the Defense Threat Reduction Agency? They modeled the impact of a 12.5-kiloton nuke exploding at a port in New York."

"What did they conclude?" Levin asked.

"Sixty-two thousand dead instantly. Two hundred thousand more dead in the following hours, days, or weeks."

"Thanks for the encouraging news, Commander."

Hart's mind shifted to Liz. He'd promised he would call her by ten. If she had followed his instructions, Liz should be in the lowest level of the hotel's garage now. He dialed her cell. It rang straight through to voicemail. He tried again. This time, though, he left a message.

"God, I hope I see you again."

CHAPTER FORTY-FIVE

A PHALANX OF POLICE AND EMERGENCY VEHICLES swarmed the Fast Park Garage. As they reached the drive, Hart jumped the curb, careening past startled revelers on their way to Times Square—then slammed on the brakes inches away from the attendant. Hart leaped out of the door and grabbed the dazed man, who stood frozen in the car's headlights.

"There's a van parked here . . . a white panel van . . . take me to it now."

Paralyzed by fear, the man failed to respond. Hart shook him violently.

"Talk to me!" he screamed, not relinquishing his grip until the man reacted.

"Okay, okay," the man squawked as he tried to pry Hart's fingers from his arms. Then he gestured to a lift. "It's on the top level."

"Let's go." Hart ordered the man forward. Before entering the lift, he asked, "Where are the keys?"

"In the van."

"Your sign says 'No Vans.'"

"We make exceptions."

"For whom?"

"Not for whom, for what—a $200 tip."

Hart found the words reassuring. Parking was at a premium in New York City, but no one in their right mind was going to ante up that kind of cash to stash a van in a parking garage close to Times Square . . . not for the sake of a saving a few blocks' walk.

As the lift opened, Hart saw it. The van was parked five cars down on the right.

Levin, fighting for breath after running up five sets of stairs, shouted to him, "Commander, it may be booby-trapped!"

"Who parked the car?" Hart stared intently at the attendant.

"I did. I was working that night."

"Any chance that the people dropping off the van had access to it after that?"

"None. That's one rule we don't bend . . . even for a tip."

Wasting no more time, Hart ran to the van, grabbed the keys out of the ignition, and unlocked the back. Levin was right behind him. The van was loaded with an electrical contractor's tools of the trade. Nothing remotely resembling a bomb was anywhere in sight.

"Nothing!" Levin exclaimed, "a fucking wild goose chase . . . that's what they sent us on!"

"Not so fast, Tom." Hart knelt and looked at the under-carriage of the van. He reached into his pocket, removed his cell phone, and activated the flashlight app. It provided just enough illumination to confirm Hart's suspicions.

"There's a metal box beneath that chassis. It reaches almost to the ground." He climbed into the cargo section of the van and tugged on the carpet until it gave way. Under it was the top of a metal container made of three panels of dull gray metal.

"Lead," he told Levin. "They raised the floor of the van to make the lead-lined container virtually invisible."

"Can you remove one of the panels?" Levin asked.

"As Basra said, they've been sealed shut. How much time do we have?"

"Forty minutes."

CHAPTER FORTY-SIX

"You, OPEN THE LIFT DOOR!" Hart shouted at the attendant as he climbed into the driver's seat. "Get in the fucking van, Tom!"

The tires squealed as Hart pulled forward to gain some maneuvering distance, then slammed the van in reverse, backing it into the lift. Hart kept his eyes on his watch as the lift slowly descended and the seconds ticked by. It seemed to take an eternity to reach ground level.

He didn't wait for the lift's painfully slow gate to open before punching the accelerator. With horn blaring, he plowed through it in a storm of shattered wood and headed south from Times Square. Levin, wide-eyed and scrunched down in his seat, was shouting instructions to NYPD on a handheld communicator.

"Target vehicle leaving Fast Park en route to Red Hook," referring to the Red Hook Container Terminal in Brooklyn. "ETA approximately twenty minutes. Clear us a path and say a prayer," he instructed.

The plan had been quickly hatched by the commander. Told by Basra that the bomb was in a sealed sarcophagus, Hart assumed that a detonation was inevitable. The question was, how many people would die as a result. His one hope was to limit the horrific damage wrought by the bomb's destructive force: thermal energy, ionizing radiation, and the blast wave. With no caves within miles, there was only one way to do that—bury it under as much water as humanly possible.

The van caught air as Hart flew through an intersection at 70 mph. It landed in a fusillade of sparks ignited by the metal coffin scraping against the street. Hart looked at Levin and shrugged his shoulders, "We're still here, aren't we?"

Levin said nothing.

It took twenty-two minutes to reach the deep-water pier.

Two CTU vehicles were waiting for them as they tore through the parking lot and headed for the docks. Jamming the gear shift into park, Hart jumped out and ran to the closest CTU cruiser. He ripped open the back door, yanked a shackled man from his seat, followed by a woman. He dragged al-Bakr and Sarah Qaisrani toward the van. Opening the rear hatch, Hart threw them in.

"What the hell are you are doing?" Qaisrani screamed at him.

"Honoring a promise. You've earned a front-row seat to a nuclear explosion."

Al-Bakr broke his silence. "You think you've won, Commander?"

"There is no winning with animals like you."

"All you will have succeeded in doing is to create a martyr of me—a personage to be venerated by generations of Islamists. So I must thank you for your service to the Islamic State."

"Fuck you, you sorry bastard!" he said as he slammed the door shut.

He shouted to Levin as he jumped into the driver's seat, "Program the GPS in the cruiser for the Brooklyn Bridge!" He rolled down the window before throwing the van in gear and stomping on the pedal. A long pier lay dead ahead, followed by black water. The tires rumbled as he sped across the pier's uneven wooden slats, hoping they would support the van's weight for a few precious seconds.

An instant later, the van sailed off the end of the pier, striking the water with a resonant slap. It bobbed momentarily before beginning to sink. Hart pulled himself through the window and swam fifty yards through frigid water until he reached a rusted ladder that descended from the top of the pier to below the water line.

The soaking hulk of a man emerged at 11:51 PM. As he watched the final remnant of the van's roof being swallowed up, he prayed that Qaisrani and al-Bakr would not drown before the bomb detonated. Dead was dead, but there was an additional degree of justice in vaporizing the two perpetrators.

Only a few minutes remained for them to get as far away from the nuke as possible. The water would effectively quell the thermal blast, as well as the initial surge of radiation. But nothing could contain the devastating shockwave that would follow.

Levin was by the car awaiting Hart's orders.

"I'm driving. Have your men follow right on my tail," he said gesturing to the two CTU agents at the scene.

"Where, Commander? You can't outrun this damn thing," Levin told him. He realized with despair that there was no time to evacuate anyone.

"The hell I can't." Hart sped off in a northerly direction. The Brooklyn Bridge loomed in the distance.

"Civil Defense used the base of the bridge as a bomb shelter decades ago. From what I remember, there are still provisions stored there. According to GPS, it's 4.2 miles ahead. It's going to be by the grace of God if we make it."

Levin looked at the GPS. It indicated an arrival time of 12:01 AM. Hart accelerated to near ninety.

At 11:58, Hart smashed through the fence surrounding the base of the great bridge, with the Crown Vic only inches behind him. He dodged deep pot-holes and discarded trash. He headed down an embankment until the car reached a padlocked door, then stopped abruptly.

"Let's move," he ordered, as Levin and the other men followed on his heels. He drew his pistol from its holster and fired three rapid shots into the lock, which fell with a clang. Heaving open the massive steel door, Hart ordered the men inside the abandoned fallout shelter, slamming it behind them.

It was pitch-black. The only illumination came from a minute amount of tritium in the dial of Hart's watch. The next forty seconds would determine whether they lived or died.

At precisely midnight, an unearthly light pierced the darkness, penetrating minute cracks in the tons of hardened steel and concrete. The blast wave, moving far more slowly than the light, would follow.

"Get down!" Hart yelled, dropping to his knees and wrapping his arms around his head.

Seconds later, the shock wave arrived. The men were blown about like leaves in a strong wind. It subsided as rapidly as it had hit. Hart hoped that no one had been seriously injured. The men listened as the bridge heaved, almost singing out in distress, but it held despite the tremendous under-pressure from the explosion.

"Everyone okay?" the commander asked the men.

"Yes, Sir," came three responses in short order.

Hart feared the damage would be unfathomable. He moved toward the entrance of what could have been their tomb and pushed it open carefully. In the crimson glow of the bomb's aftermath, Hart got his first view of the destruction. He saw a huge cloud of fulminating steam roiled against the night-time sky. More than a million tons of water had been carried thousands of feet in the air by the force of the explosion—an explosion that left a crater a half-mile wide and fifty feet deep. He quickly closed the door.

"We are going to be here for a while. The blast will have kicked some very nasty stuff into the atmosphere. Because it's been suspended in water, a lot of it will fall to earth rather than being carried aloft. That's both good and bad news. It's going to be damn hot, so the less we're exposed to it, the better."

"What about additional shock waves, Commander? Are we out of danger from the blast itself?" Levin asked.

"Not until we're sure that any tidal surges have passed. It would be a pity to survive the blast only to drown from a resulting tsunami. We'll be in the clear within minutes, hopefully. You might as well sit down," Hart advised.

"What did you see, Commander?" Levin asked.

"There's not much left, Tom, at least in the direction of Red Hook. From what I could tell, everything looked flattened . . . as if it had been struck by an F5 tornado."

As he leaned his back against the rough concrete wall of the bridge's inner chamber, Hart's mind turned to Liz. Was she safe?

After two excruciatingly long hours, Hart gave the signal for them to move out. He tried to reach Liz by phone, but his cell was dead, a casualty of his late night swim. Borrowing Levin's phone, he dialed Liz's number.

The phone rang, but she didn't answer. Voicemail picked up after the fourth ring. That was a change. When he had tried to call her earlier, before the detonation, it had rolled straight into voicemail without ringing. What did it mean, he wondered. Had she escaped the blast and emerged from the garage? If so, why wasn't she answering?

The shock wave had passed over the cars. They looked like hell, but with a turn of the key, Hart determined the first car was operable. Levin followed suit.

Levin was headed to CTU with the two agents. Hart's destination was the St. Regis.

CHAPTER FORTY-SEVEN

LIZ DIDN'T DEVIATE ONE IOTA from the commander's orders. By 10 PM, she was ensconced in the lower level of the parking garage at the St. Regis, hugging the staircase with one hand and holding her phone in the other. She didn't want to take any chance of missing Hart's call. Had she checked, she would have seen that no bars were showing on the signal indicator. The cell signal reached as far as the first level of the garage, but no farther.

As midnight approached, Liz dropped to her knees and began to pray. "Let this cloud pass over," she supplicated, tears staining her cheeks. An older coupled edged by her on the stairs. Concerned by her pleas, they stopped and turned back.

"Can we help you?" the gray-haired man asked as his wife knelt down beside Liz.

Wiping the tears from her eyes, Liz forced a smile. "Thank you," she said as she rose to her feet. "You mustn't leave the garage. Something terrible is going to happen at midnight. Stay here with me. I beg you."

Sensing the couple's hesitation, she added, "I know it sounds crazy, but you need to trust me."

The man looked at his watch, then at the woman on the stairs. She certainly didn't look crazy. It was two minutes until midnight.

"It's only a couple of minutes," he said to his wife, before turning to Liz. "If it makes you feel better, we'll wait right here with you."

Liz was thankful for the companionship. She didn't want to die alone.

"One more thing," Liz began, "I think it would be best if we sat on the steps and covered our heads with our hands and arms. Even if just for a moment. Please indulge me."

Feeling a bit foolish, the couple nonetheless complied.

When the first bell at the Cavalry Baptist Church tolled midnight, a brilliant light flooded the underground refuge. It was followed seconds later by winds—a violent, tornadic assault that shook the very foundation of the building. The lights in the garage flickered. The ceiling bowed, cracking but not breaking. A sprinkler pipe burst, sending a cascade of water shooting across the roofs of parked cars. Other than the hiss of the water, the only other sound Liz could discern were muffled screams from above.

"My God, how could you have known?" the man asked dumbfounded. "Was that a car bomb?"

"Something like that. We need to see if the stairs are intact and make our way to the top. This structure isn't stable, and we don't want to be buried here." Liz led the way.

John had been right. The first floor of the garage was heavily damaged, but the stairs were largely untouched. The three survivors exited the garage and entered an apocalyptic world. Though the major structures in Manhattan remained standing, the city had endured a catastrophic injury. Acrid smoke covered the sky, and fires could be seen in the direction of Brooklyn. As she filled her lungs with air, Liz tasted the metallic afterbirth of a nuclear bomb. Isotopes, she thought . . . recalling John's warning to stay under cover for a few hours. She quickly expelled the breath.

"We need to get back in the garage. If we wait a couple of hours, whatever is in the air will either settle out or be carried away by the prevailing winds."

"Who are you?" the couple asked in synchrony.

"I'm Liz Wilkins. I'm a physician. And I'm grateful to be alive."

CHAPTER FORTY-EIGHT

JENNY AND GEORGE HURST HAD BEEN LOOKING FORWARD to their first New Year's Eve out on the town in more than two years. They had missed the first celebration due to George's deployment in Iraq. He was discharged in March, but in December, along came Brittany. Unwilling to leave their newborn, the couple had quietly celebrated the beginning of the next year at home.

But this year was different. Jenny's folks couldn't wait for the opportunity to babysit their granddaughter, while giving their daughter and son-in-law a special night out. The couple planned to celebrate with dinner and a movie—starting at Triple Zero in the East Village before ending up at the Hollywood Theater in Fulton Market. They loved thrillers and couldn't wait to see *Eight Seconds to Midnight,* which had just been released. The film began at 10:02 PM, timed precisely so the climactic scene arrived seconds before the dawn of the New Year.

They lounged in the theater's comfortable recliners while sipping glasses of champagne and noshing on a shared dessert of baked Alaska. After a spate of previews, the movie opened. As promised, it proved to be a non-stop adrenaline ride. The time flew by, and George subtly tapped his watch in front of Jenny at one minute to midnight. He leaned across and gave her a kiss.

At precisely midnight, the screen went dark. Within seconds, a 250-mile-per-hour wind ripped through the Hollywood Theater, killing all attendees. A 25-foot wave followed, washing over the theater and carrying away the bodies. Some of the deceased would be found in the Hudson River, others tangled in the branches of trees.

Jenny's parents rode out the storm at their kids' condo in the Village. They frantically tried to reach Jenny and George, but the cell networks were down. All they could do was hunker down with the baby and hope that sanity—and their children—returned with the break of day.

Mary and Sam Hudson hated going out on New Year's, but they loved to entertain . . . particularly small groups of close friends. That night, New Year's Eve, the Hudsons were entertaining two couples in their historic brownstone near Livingston Street.

Mary had been laboring all day in the kitchen. Dinner would feature Cornish game hens, wild rice, and Brussels sprouts, followed by individual chocolate soufflés.

Sam wasn't much use in the kitchen. Mary had assigned him the job of keeping everyone's drinks refreshed and the conversation flowing.

Stuffed from the overly generous portions, the group opted to delay dessert until the New Year. So Sam broke out the champagne glasses and poured six servings of Prosecco. It was five minutes to midnight.

"Why don't we go up on the roof," he suggested, "It's not that chilly . . . if anyone wants to borrow a coat, we have plenty."

With that, the six revelers marched up three flights of stairs and out onto the roof.

"Watch the clothesline," Mary cautioned as one of her guests ducked at the last minute. "Sam, Darling, why don't you give us a countdown with that fancy atomic watch of yours?"

She turned to one of her girlfriends and pointed at Sam's wrist, "I think it's hideous, but he tells me that it's accurate to one second every 300 years. It's a guy thing, I guess."

Sam ignored the banter. A minute later, he began counting from ten.

"Nine . . . eight . . . seven . . . six . . . five"—everyone was jubilant—"four . . . three . . . two . . . "

He never reached one, stopped by a brilliant, almost blinding glow to the south.

"My God, what is it?" one of their guests asked anxiously.

"Let's get off the roof, now!" Sam roared, but it was too late. The shock wave rolled over them like thunder . . . bursting eardrums and crushing internal organs.

Four of the six would miraculously survive, only to face the threat of significant radiation exposure from the fallout that followed. Mary never made it off the roof.

Thousands of miles above the eastern seaboard, satellites belonging to U.S. STRATCOM detected what appeared to be a nuclear blast. Data from the high-flying birds was relayed to Schriever Air Force Base near Colorado Springs, where analysts confirmed a fifteen-kiloton device had exploded in New York City. The order was given for the president be placed aboard Air Force One and flown to Offutt Air Force Base in Omaha, Nebraska.

There, he would operate out of a mobile command center capable of launching a retaliatory strike against whatever country had perpetrated the attack. By law, he was required to remain in Omaha until it was deemed safe for him to return to the White House. How long that would be was anyone's guess.

CHAPTER FORTY-NINE

HART WOVE HIS WAY AMONG A SEA of stalled cars strewn atop the Brooklyn Bridge. Every window and windshield was shattered. There were no traces of life, at least not based on what he could see as he veered right and left to avoid the carnage. As he slowly passed a tan Honda, he saw a family with two young children in the backseat. Blood ran from their ears, and their eyes were open but unblinking. He wanted to stop and search the cars for survivors, but he knew it would be futile. His priority now was to get to Liz.

Thick black smoke filled the sky, obliterating the light of a full moon. The river below was ablaze as thousands of gallons of crude oil that had spilled into Upper New York Bay ignited.

"It looks more like hell than New York," Hart thought. He took a final look back through the haze at Brooklyn Heights. The devastation appeared total. Ahead, South Street Sea Port was littered with hundreds of small boats, ferries, and even a solitary cruise-liner . . . all lying on their sides, beached by tsunami-like waves.

"The death count is going to be staggering," Hart said out loud, though there was no one to hear.

Hart prepared to exit the bridge, then realized that there was no longer an FDR Drive. He continued to Spruce, then over to Lafayette. He stayed the course onto Park. From what he could tell, it appeared that Tribeca, Little Italy, and Nolita had all been hard hit. The devastation didn't lessen until he reached Gramercy Park.

The six-mile drive, which would take thirty to forty minutes in normal traffic, had taken two hours. Finally, he was closing in on 55th, just blocks from the St. Regis.

Liz pulled the phone from her pocket and frantically dialed Hart. There was no answer. It rolled immediately into voicemail. Her mind searched for reasons to hold on to hope . . . but it kept coming up empty.

"Is it safe to leave, Doctor? We've got children and grandchildren to think about," the gray-haired man asked.

"Where are they?" Liz asked.

"Across the river in Montclair."

"They should be okay," Liz reassured the couple, who let out an audible sigh of relief. "It's been two hours. The level of fallout will have diminished by now," Liz said as she stood and prepared to climb the stairs to the exit.

"Fallout?" the man's wife asked, stunned by Liz's use of the word.

"Yes. We have survived an atomic bomb."

As they emerged from their improvised bunker, Liz was relieved to see, despite her earlier fears, that the skyline was still very much intact. The people walking the streets, however, were a different story. If not bearing some form of physical injury, virtually all exhibited a glazed and distant look.

There was a persistent wail of sirens as emergency vehicles rushed past the hotel's entrance. Liz watched as one driver tried to break through the traffic and pull into the drive . . . the horn of his car blared incessantly, causing Liz to cover her ears.

What the fuck, she thought. *Even after a calamity some things never change in New York.*

The car finally broke through, accelerating as it entered the drive. It was headed straight for her. She jumped back from the curb, pushing the older couple back with her. The car lurched to a stop, its driver's door flying open. A disheveled man emerged, steam coming off of his damp clothes in the cool night air.

Liz ran toward him. It had to be an apparition.

The man smiled and said, "Sorry I'm late, Darling. I got detained in Brooklyn."

Liz burst into tears and fell into his arms.

As John slowly released his grip on her, Liz turned to the wide-eyed couple and smiled, "My knight in shining armor." She grasped each of their hands. "Thank you for staying with me. Go home. I'm sure your children are anxious to know you're okay."

A car identical to the one driven by John pulled in minutes behind him. Tom Levin stepped out of the passenger's seat and waited patiently while the commander and Liz were reunited.

"I thought you were headed back to CTU," Hart commented.

"I was . . . until a call from Mr. Kahn was patched through to me. I've got orders to get you to a safe location. Tomorrow morning, you will be meeting with the president.

"Dr. Wilkins, I'm Tom Levin. I'm sorry to be meeting you under these circumstances, but I'm grateful you are okay. What I just told the commander also applies to you, Ma'am."

"We're returning to Washington?"

"No, Ma'am. You will be meeting with the president at Offutt Air Force Base in Omaha."

"What exactly happened?" Liz asked.

John intervened, "It's a long story . . . I'll tell you later," he promised as he directed Liz toward the car.

Liz looked back at the elderly couple who had been her companions as the shadow of death passed over them. They looked frailer than before.

"Tom, please help these people. They've been with me through all of this."

"Of course," Levin said as he radioed in for a black and white.

"A car is on its way to pick you up. The officer will take you wherever you need to go," he informed the couple.

"Who is that woman? How did she know?" the older man asked of Levin.

"That's Liz Wilkins—she's part of our team."

"And who's the man with her?"

"Let's just say he's an angel, sent from heaven to spare the many."

As they rolled out of the driveway, Levin elaborated on his orders. "I'm to take you to a safe facility about twenty-five miles north of here where you will spend the night. In the morning, I'll escort you to the FBO at LaGuardia.

All air traffic is shut down and probably won't resume for several days, but the president has made arrangements for you to be picked up. I believe Mr. Kahn will be awaiting you on the Gulfstream."

"What about Marine 1?" Hart asked.

"It was recalled after the detonation. Everyone assumed you were dead, Commander."

"Even the president?"

"I'm afraid so, Sir. I had the pleasure of informing him that you were still very much alive, as well as what you had done."

"Tom, there's a lot Liz and I can do here to help," Hart offered, not wanting to leave the battlefield.

"John is right. We're both far more valuable on the ground dealing with the aftermath than sitting in a conference room," Liz added.

"I'm afraid you will have to explain that to the president. I have my orders."

"Understood." Hart knew the matter was out of Levin's hands.

Hart, Wilkins, and Levin spent the night near Mamaroneck in a secret bunker built in the '60s to shelter personnel deemed vital to the ongoing security and operation of the government.

"It's not the St. Regis," Levin commented as they approached the outer gate to what looked like a piece of virgin, timbered land.

A small device at the gate was used to scan Levin's retina. Once they were cleared, the gate swung open. Hart estimated that they covered close to a mile through heavy woods before stopping at a clearing.

Liz's eyes grew wide as she watched the grass in front of her part. Hidden beneath a foot of topsoil, which was covered with a carefully constructed blend of native grasses and weeds, was the entrance to Terminus 1. They pulled onto what appeared to be a loading ramp. Once the vehicle was secure, the ramp began descending into the earth.

"I feel like I'm being buried," Liz confessed.

"We all feel that way the first time. I think you'll be pretty amazed, Doctor, by what awaits you."

A naval captain met them. "Commander Hart, Dr. Wilkins, Mr. Levin, welcome to Terminus 1. I'm Mark Dixon. I'll be your guide this evening. My job is to make sure you have everything you need. You'll find clean clothes on your bunks . . . hopefully they are the correct size."

After a brief tour, they were provided with the information needed to make their short stay palatable, then shown to their bunks, two of many lining the massive rooms in the subterranean facility. The air was scrubbed to remove any trace of contaminants—chemical, biological, or nuclear. Water came from a self-contained reservoir, and power was provided by diesel generators.

Before leaving them, Dixon addressed Hart.

"That was an extraordinary act of heroism, Commander."

"I just happened to be at the right place at the right time, Captain."

While Hart's eyes were focused on the captain, Liz's eyes were locked on Hart. There was nothing coincidental about his actions. Hart was among the most deliberate human beings she had ever met. But he didn't crave adulation. That was not what drove the commander.

With the early light of morning came the dark realization that the bombing had not been some awful dream. As they left the facility, headed to LaGuardia, the evidence was abundant. Abandoned cars lined the roads where traffic had ground to a halt and people, frantic to reach their homes, had set out on foot. A single lane had been cleared by the Highway Patrol and National Guard, its use restricted to authorized vehicles. Smoke still filled the sky.

As they approached Dog Park Run, it looked as though a straight-line wind had swept through the area, flattening lighter structures, lifting boats out of the water and depositing them hundreds of yards inland. Dozens of bodies could be seen in the muck . . . some lying face down, others staring lifelessly at the sky. Liz turned away, tucking herself against John.

Though LaGuardia was twelve miles from the blast, significant damage was evident . . . presumably from a water surge in the East River, Hart surmised. In spots, the road was virtually washed out, forcing Levin to push the Toyota Land Cruiser to its limits.

From the moment they left Terminus 1, there had been a sporadic clicking noise coming from the front of the vehicle. The frequency and intensity of the clicks had grown with their southerly movement. Now, the clicks blurred into an incessant buzz.

"What's that telling you, Tom?" Hart referred to the radiation detector next to Levin.

"It's telling me that you don't want to hang around here any longer than you have to. The National Guard is going to get it the worst. It's their job to keep people in their homes. Being indoors cuts exposure by up to eighty percent."

"What's the total body exposure threshold before the troops are rotated out of the field?" Liz asked Levin.

Levin looked at Hart for help.

"She wants a straight answer, Tom."

"Of course I do." Liz was shocked that she might receive anything less.

"There is no limit, Dr. Wilkins. At this level of exposure, after twenty-four hours in the field, they will have accumulated upwards of 300 rads. The water burst spared us the initial flood of thermal and ionizing radiation, but it caused much of the fallout that would normally be carried away by high altitude winds to drop to the ground."

"You do know that 300 rads will prove fatal for fifty percent of the people exposed."

"Yes, Ma'am, I do."

The remainder of the short drive was shared in silence.

LaGuardia was a mess. Small planes were upended and scattered around the private aviation hangers. It looked more like a scrap yard for damaged aircraft than an operational FBO. The Gulfstream awaiting them was untouched, having arrived many hours after the event.

"Thanks, Tom," Hart gave Levin a bear hug before boarding the plane.

"I owe you a hug, too," Liz said, embracing Levin before joining Hart aboard.

As she peered into the aft cabin, Liz saw John already engaged in an animated conversation with Marvin Kahn. Eyeing her, Hart stopped mid-sentence. "Liz, you remember Mr. Kahn."

"It's good to see you, Mr. Kahn." Liz shook the DDO's hand.

"Good to see you, Doctor. Please join us."

"Thank you, Sir." Liz took a seat facing the two men.

"The president asked to meet with you and apologizes for the inconvenience caused by his mandated seclusion at Omaha. He asked Dr. Wilkins to join him in her role as Principal Federal Officer. There won't be a crowd . . . in fact, I don't think anyone else will be present. President Conner wants to hear the details of what transpired prior to the blast, followed by recommendations from each of you regarding next steps. I've never seen the president this shaken . . . not even at the height of the pandemic. He's relying on both of you to guide him through this tragedy."

"Will you stay, Sir?"

"Yes, but only to listen. Speaking of which, I've got less than two hours in which to debrief you. That's time to cover the high notes. We'll fill in the remaining details later. Dr. Wilkins, I have some questions for you, as well."

As the jet pierced 10,000 feet with its nose pointed sharply upward, Hart began to download everything that had transpired, all of which was captured on a digital recorder by Kahn. Periodically, the DDO would stop Hart long enough to gain a parallel recollection of events from Liz's vantage point in Manhattan.

As the debriefing was winding down, Kahn asked, "How in the hell did you remember the moth-balled Civil Defense facility in the Brooklyn Bridge?"

"I don't know, but I know that it is the one thing that saved my ass, if you'll forgive me, Sir."

Kahn let out an uncharacteristic laugh. "Of course, Commander. I'm damned glad you remembered."

For now, the debriefing was over. But the response to this cataclysmic event was just beginning.

CHAPTER FIFTY

KAHN WAS RIGHT. The president looked ashen, forcing a smile as he greeted the commander, Dr. Wilkins, and Marvin Kahn in his makeshift headquarters thirty feet below the tarmac at Offutt Air Force Base.

Conner gestured to two couches separated by a square table and waited for his guests to be seated before joining them.

"I heard about your actions at the Red Hook Terminal, Commander. That was an extraordinary act of bravery."

"Thank you, Mr. President, but it didn't spare the city. From what we could glean, thousands were killed, and many more will die in the coming weeks from radiation."

"True, but the loss is a fraction of what it might have been. I was told that more than a million citizens would have perished in seconds had it not been for your quick thinking."

"Sir, I'm grateful for your support," Hart began, "but I can't take pride in a half-failed mission. Yes, we limited the impact of a catastrophic event, but that's cold comfort to the survivors in New York. Their city is devastated, there are countless dead or injured, and massive reconstruction awaits them. No, Sir, I'm not a hero. A hero would have found a way to foil the attack, not simply muffle it."

"Commander, do you believe you can dispel all of the darkness? Even Jesus Christ couldn't do that. A hero is a man who faces the darkness and doesn't back away. He steps directly into it . . . into harm's way. Right now the nation needs a hero. So, while I appreciate your humility, don't be so quick to deny the role you've played at this pivotal time in our country's history."

"Yes, sir."

"The bio attack taught us a bitter lesson regarding our vulnerability, as you know better than me. It's impossible in today's world to stop every threat. Our focus must also be on damage control. That's what you did: You minimized the carnage that al-Bakr spent years planning. You shut them down."

"I sent them straight to hell, Sir."

A smile emerged on Conner's lips. "Yes, Commander, you certainly did."

"I'd prefer that not become part of the official record, Mr. President."

"Millions would applaud your actions. You know that?"

"Yes, Sir. But I also know that we are a country of laws. That's part of what separates us from these animals. I judged, sentenced, and executed two people on the spot."

"You put down two rabid animals, Commander. I want that to be our understanding. As I said, the record will reflect that the prisoners perished while being transported to a holding facility where they would await prosecution."

"Agreed, and thank you, Sir."

"Dr. Wilkins, the commander doesn't seem to appreciate how much his heroism impacted the course of yesterday's events. I hope you can impress upon him the magnitude of his deeds."

Liz turned toward John, then back to the president. "Yes, Sir. I will do my best to get it through his thick head, but you know that's a formidable task."

Conner smiled briefly, then became serious before speaking, "I need your help. We need to rekindle the spirits of those affected by the disaster and begin the process of rebuilding New York. The city and its people must rebound with astonishing speed. They must demonstrate that, even after receiving a near fatal blow, their spirit is undiminished. If you wish to appease your demons, Commander, then put your energy into catalyzing an immediate response to what has happened rather than recriminations over failing to achieve the impossible."

"What do you envision, Mr. President?"

"I want you to provide oversight of all the governmental agencies and NGOs on the ground in New York . . . with the exception of health care related entities, which I'm carving out for Dr. Wilkins to manage."

"Liz will do a great job, as you know, Sir. As for all the other folks, well, they are good at their jobs. They don't need a counter-terrorism operative interfering with their efforts.'"

"There will be dozens of competing federal, state, and local agencies all trying to help, but each with their own agendas. Someone needs to connect the dots and ensure that these organizations are working synergistically, not duplicatively. Draw the plan, Commander, for the restoration of New York. Request whatever additional resources are necessary. That's step one."

Turning to Liz, he said, "Dr. Wilkins, you've got a massive job ahead of you, working in tandem with Dr. Tucker. I'm working with HHS right now to make certain that the Medical Reserve Corps, National Disaster Medical System, Radiation Treatment, Triage, and Transport System, as well as dozens of other agencies are awaiting your instructions.

"As Commander Hart has so clearly noted, thousands are dead, dying, or injured. New York's health care infrastructure is overwhelmed . . . its resources nearly depleted. In many ways, the task at hand mirrors that of the pandemic, though patient containment is not the primary concern. Without a coherent plan for bolstering rapid access to care, countless men, women, and children will die unnecessarily. You can help stop that from happening, Dr. Wilkins."

"Yes, Sir."

"There's one more thing requiring urgent attention, Dr. Wilkins. Though the bomb's submersion dramatically reduced downwind fallout, we must still coordinate with the Atmospheric Release Advisory Capability Group at Lawrence Livermore National Laboratory. You will also be receiving data from the Aerial Measuring System and Radiological Assistance Program. Together, you and Dr. Tucker must determine the requisite response for those downwind from the bomb."

"Of course, Mr. President."

Directing his attention to both of them, the president asked if they had any questions.

"Two, Sir. What is your timetable, and what is 'step two' that you alluded to a moment ago?"

"Dr. Wilkins may take as much time as required. CDC is making provisions to cover her responsibilities in the BL-4 lab until she returns. As for you, Commander, I'm afraid that you are on a much shorter leash. I want you ready for redeployment after ten days on-site."

"With all due respect, Mr. President, it will take far longer than ten days to even arrive at an accurate assessment of damages, let alone develop a plan for mitigation. I was hoping for six months, Sir."

"Remember, Commander, your job is not to heal the wound, but to prescribe the right medicants. Build a high-level plan, then hand-pick the best people to implement it. After that, be prepared for a trip abroad."

"Step two, Sir?"

"Yes, there's some cleaning up to do in Pakistan. If they can hit us once, they can hit us again."

"Yes, Sir. Is that all, Sir?"

"Your pilots are waiting to return you to Washington. They will then take you to New York tomorrow morning. I'd suggest that you allow yourself a short reprieve before returning to that post-apocalyptic reality."

"I only have ten days, Mr. President. I'd like to get started immediately."

"So would I, Sir," Liz seconded.

"I need you both fresh and thinking at your best. Shut it all off for twenty-four hours."

"That's a tall order, Mr. President. I'm not sure we can shut if off," Liz continued. "We're eager to return, Sir."

Hart smiled, appreciative of her chutzpa.

"Alright then. I'll let the crew know to file a new flight plan. They will drop Mr. Kahn at Dulles, then depart immediately for New York City."

"Thank you, Sir," Hart and Wilkins said in unison.

CHAPTER FIFTY-ONE

AYESHA STRUGGLED TO IGNORE the persistent vibrations from her phone as she finished her examination of a young patient. Finally able to extricate herself from the exam room, she removed the cell phone from the pocket of her lab coat, eager to see who could be so insistent on reaching her. It was Niya Jamali, and it was the third time she had called within the hour.

Navigating the short distance to her office, Ayesha closed the door and told her nurse that she was not to be disturbed. She pressed the redial button. Niya answered on the first ring.

"Thank God, I reached you. Did you hear the news, Ayesha?"

"What news?"

"A nuclear bomb exploded in New York."

"Oh, my God," was all she said before falling silent.

"Are you there?

"Ayesha, are you there?"

"I'm here, Niya. What else can you tell me?"

"We've got CNN up on the monitors. They are comparing the destructive force of the bomb to the one dropped on Hiroshima."

"How many people died?"

"There is no official death count, yet . . . just that casualties are in the tens of thousands. Apparently the bomb detonated under water. Their experts are saying that saved hundreds of thousands of lives . . . but not why or how it happened."

"Who are they saying is responsible?"

"Minutes before the explosion, a video was emailed to the *New York Times*. In it, al-Bakr proclaimed that the United Islamic State was responsible for the bombing and it was the first of many strikes to follow. There is speculation that the email server was located in Pakistan."

"We both know who was responsible. Al-Bakr would never have gotten access to that weapon were it not for my father."

"Listen to me, Ayesha. You did everything in your power to avert this tragedy."

"You are wrong, Niya. There was so much more I could have done if only my eyes had been open." With that, Ayesha disconnected the call.

Niya attempted to call her back, but Ayesha had turned off her phone. Ayesha rifled through her purse until she felt the hard, cold metal gun tucked away in the bottom of her purse. It was a small one that could be concealed in her hand—a gift from her father following her mother's death. She put it back in her purse and walked to the nurse's station.

"I'm leaving. Tell the patients I am sorry for the inconvenience, but an emergency has arisen."

"What emergency?" the nurse scowled.

"Make one up."

It was a twenty-minute drive to her father's office, plenty of time to calm down, but instead Ayesha's anger only grew with each passing minute. She took the first parking place she spotted, one reserved for officers. She dashed up the limestone steps at the front of the formidable stone building and past an armed sentry guarding the entrance, and toward the elevator. She rode it to the seventh floor, turning right as she stepped out of the cage.

Room 700 was a suite, opening onto a large reception area, past which was her father's private office. His aide greeted her as she entered.

"I need to speak with my father, privately."

"I'll see if he's available," the soldier responded.

"That won't be necessary." Ayesha was already halfway to his door.

"Wait, Dr. Naru—allow me to tell your father . . . " but the words trailed behind her. Ayesha turned the handle and walked abruptly in on the general. He rose to his feet.

The aide followed a few steps behind her.

"It's alright, Lieutenant. My daughter must have something important to discuss with me. Please leave us."

The aide left, closing the door behind him.

Ayesha reached into her purse, her father's eyes tracking every movement. She withdrew the gun, pulled back the slide, and chambered a 9mm bullet before pointing it at her father's chest.

"Put that away," the General commanded, "you've never even shot a gun. Put it away before you hurt yourself."

"You killed all of those people," she said angrily, contemptuously.

"I've killed many people in my life, Ayesha. That's what warriors do."

"Answer one question for me, Father."

"And what question would that be, Ayesha? Do you want to know if I have anything to do with the bomb? If I helped kill thousands of Americans?"

Without waiting for her confirmation, he continued, "Of course I helped in the bombing of New York. We are at war with America. Surely you are smart enough to understand that. Terrible things happen during wars. You know that as well."

"Did you kill her?"

"I don't know what you are talking about."

"Did you kill her?" Ayesha repeated as her hand holding the pistol began to shake.

"Did I kill who?" his tone now insolent.

"Did you kill my mother?" Ayesha's glared, her grip on the gun suddenly tight.

"You are trying my patience, Ayesha. You know it was Mughabi's efforts to kill me that resulted in your mother's tragic death."

"No. The president had nothing to do with it. You killed her for spying on you—for betraying you to the Americans."

The general moved slowly from behind the massive mahogany desk toward his daughter. Ayesha removed the safety on the gun. The general stopped five feet short of Ayesha.

"How did you find out about your mother?" he demanded.

"From the Americans . . . Commander Hart, to be precise."

Ayesha sensed a flicker of recognition on her father's face. Did he know Hart? she wondered.

"I didn't believe him at first. I worshipped you. Don't you know that? How do you think it felt when the American stripped me of my illusions . . . made me see the truth?"

"Their version of the truth is a distorted tale that bears no resemblance to reality," Malik countered.

"Oh, Father, at least have the dignity to admit your sins."

"What did you tell Hart?"

"I told him exactly what he wanted to know . . . I shared with him what I knew of your conversations with al-Bakr."

"You foolish girl. You have signed my death warrant."

"Yes, I have, Father," she said quietly, as she squeezed the trigger.

Ayesha Naru fired a single shot through her father's heart.

Clutching his chest with one hand, he reached to grab her, but Ayesha stepped back. The general slumped to the floor, seconds away from death. His aide burst through the door. Seeing the general lying in a pool of blood, he reached for his holster, but it was too late. Ayesha raised the pistol to her head and pulled the trigger. A bullet tore through her brain, her body falling inches away from her father's.

Niya was frantically trying to reach Ayesha when a call came through to the station. It was a senior communications officer from the army command office. He informed the station manager that General Malik, Pakistan's most decorated army officer, was dead. He had died, not in the field of battle, but at the hands of his daughter, Dr.

Ayesha Naru. Moments after killing her father, Dr. Naru had committed suicide. Nothing more was known at this time. A full investigation would be launched immediately.

"Be ready to break the news at the top of the hour," Niya's manager ordered his key reporter.

But Niya wasn't listening. She was consumed by a flood of memories—images from a dinner not long ago, at a quiet restaurant, where the two women first shared their secrets; then the look on Ayesha's face after Hart had confronted her with the truth about her mother's death. She had forged a special bond with Ayesha, only to have it ripped away in an instant. But worst of all, she felt complicit in the woman's death.

CHAPTER FIFTY-TWO

THE SKIES ABOVE NEW YORK WERE PERFECTLY BLUE and unearthly quiet on the morning of January 2. The tranquility above contrasted with the horror below. A single plane dotted the sky, crisscrossing the city at an altitude of 3,500 feet—low enough to take in the damage wrought by the bomb blast. The worst of it was contained to a radius of two miles from the blast site in Brooklyn, but Hart knew that the spread of nuclear fallout extended well beyond.

The pilot made one final loop before lowering the gear and touching down at LaGuardia's FBO. Tom Levin was there to meet them.

"I'm glad to see you." The relief was evident before Levin spoke a word.

"Glad to see you, too, Tom," Hart and Wilkins responded almost in unison.

"Tom, I need to talk shop with you."

"Shoot, Commander. It's going to take us longer than usual to get to CTU. The roads are hell, and there are now a lot of National Guard checkpoints on the way."

"Is your primary concern looting?" the commander asked.

"That, and keeping inquisitive people out of hot areas."

"Have exclusion zones been established?" Liz asked.

"We are in the process, Dr. Wilkins. Most of the area within two miles of Red Hook has been sealed off. But that brings its own problems . . . as I'm sure you remember from your experiences with the quarantine."

"Yes, I remember it well."

"Now we need to figure out how to get them help. It's gut-wrenching to go into that area. I was there with a FEMA team last night. Lots of dead and dying, Doctor."

"We all have our work cut out for us, Tom," Hart interjected.

"It's going to take time, Commander. Lots of time and resources."

"The president assured us that you and Liz will have the requisite resources and time to get the job done. Unfortunately, I only have ten days."

"What are you talking about?"

"Those are my orders. I am to serve as the president's liaison among agencies in the field until we have a solid plan in place for reconstruction. He's given me ten days; then I have to move on."

"To where? What could possibly be more important than New York?"

"Stopping a second attack."

Levin had no reply. The unimaginable had happened. The thought of a second bomb was beyond comprehension.

Though weary, Hart insisted on getting straight to work.

"Round up your key people, Tom. We're meeting in twenty minutes. Also, could you provide me with a list of all the organizations on the ground, along with their field command structure and contact information?"

"No problem, Commander. I assume the meeting is here. What time does it end?"

"It ends when we're finished for the evening. My guess . . . probably around 1 AM. It's hard to hold people's focus much past then."

Then it was Liz's turn to address Levin. "Brian Tucker and I are assembling our team downtown."

"Why not here?" Levin questioned.

"Show me where you'll house sixty of us, and I'll make the call," Liz responded.

"Point taken," Tom acknowledged.

"We'll establish a protocol for communicating with you and John. If we err, let's do it on the side of over-communication. Now, if it's not too much trouble, I would be grateful for a ride."

As Liz departed for Lower Manhattan, a group of twenty was waiting for Hart in the conference room. After brief introductions, the commander got down to business.

"First, let me thank you for the sacrifices you've made for your city and your country. Each of you could have left your post and traveled out of harm's way. You chose to stay, and now you choose to fight for the soul of this city. We've got a daunting task ahead of us, one that will push you to your very limits of endurance. But when you get to the other side of this calamity, you'll realize that every bit of effort that you mustered, even when you were exhausted, made a difference. You won't just return New York to its glory—you will instill a new vibrancy."

He continued, "Mr. Levin and I will be working closely over the next ten days to develop a systematic and executable strategy for the reconstruction of New York. Our first and foremost priority, of course, is to maintain control of the city. That means preventing any type of civil unrest, looting, or hysteria. Everyone in CTU, as well as NYPD, needs to remember that people have been through hell. Cut them some slack while maintaining discipline. We don't need any riots. We need people pulling together, neighbor by neighbor, to rebuild. We will have multiple teams working on infrastructure, including utilities, roads, power grid, airports, cell towers, and so forth. They'll begin with damage assessments and then move to mitigation recommendations. Every team will be asked to present timelines and resource requirements." Hart paused.

"There will be emergent needs, many of which Dr. Wilkins and Dr. Tucker will be addressing in a separate but coordinated initiative. Beyond medical care, which is under their purview, there will be fundamental needs that this team needs to address: potable water, safe food, and sanitation.

"We will need to keep people informed every step of the way. That will make them feel more empowered and raise the level of hope in our community. We will integrate the mayor, governor, and key religious leaders into our communications planning and execution.

"Those are some of the core elements of our strategic plan—a plan we begin tonight with the goal of having a first iteration within the week."

"How is that possible?" one of Levin's key staffers asked.

"We're going to make it possible. There are more than three dozen agencies already on the ground and more on the way. Unless we get everyone on the same page and marching in the same direction, we are going to have mass confusion and a lot of wasted resources. I will spend the next week with you making sure that the plan happens. Our first session is at 1900 hours. Be sure you're well fed and watered before showing up. We'll be here for a while."

Two hours later, Liz was giving her inaugural address to the medical team.

"Dr. Tucker and I have been given responsibility for managing the health-related aspects of the nuclear attack. In the short term, that means trying to get medical help to the ill, injured, and dying in the most expeditious way possible. For those who have succumbed to their injuries, we will need methods for identification of the corpses, notification of relatives, and disposition of the bodies. Of course, we will need to protect against a variety of diseases that often follow on the heels of major disasters."

A woman seated in the second row raised her hand. "We are already close to exhausting the medical resources of this city. How do you propose to fix that problem?"

"Step one is to get a handle on our available supply of hospital beds, medical and nursing staff, and first respond-ers. We plan to tap into not only hospitals, but health clinics, urgent care, and every other permutation of health care facility that remains operational. That information is being assembled as we speak. We surmise that it will be vastly inadequate, so Dr. Tucker and I plan to draw on the Medical Reserve Corps and the National Disaster Medical System. If that's still not enough, we'll call upon the Emergency System for Advanced Registration of Volunteer Health Professionals.

"The Secretary for HHS has opened access to the national stockpiles of medical supplies as needed. As of now, antibiotics, both oral and in the form of ointments for burns, as well as bandages, field surgical kits, pain medications, and other desperately needed supplies are scheduled to start arriving within hours."

No sooner had she finished than another question arose—this time from a man directly in front of her.

"That's good news, Doctor, but what of the radiation victims—beyond the treatment of superficial burns, how do we intervene with those patients exposed to significant doses of ionizing radiation?"

"That's a far more difficult question, I'm afraid. We're going to have to ascertain the probable level of exposure based upon proximity to the blast, whether the victims were in any way sheltered, and any post-detonation exposure that may have occurred."

Liz picked up a stack of paper, handing it to the first person in the front row to be passed on. It had a map of New York City with concentric circles radiating out from Red Hook Terminal. Each circle had a percentage that diminished with its distance from the epicenter. It predicted the level of radiation exposure at increasing distances from the point of detonation.

"Take a look at this map. The first circle represents a two-mile radius from the blast. The percentage, fifty percent in this case, represents the probable mortality associated with everyone living within this distance from the blast. There is a caveat, however. These computations assume an atmospheric blast . . . not one under water. We believe that the number of people exposed at the time of the blast was exponentially reduced because the bomb was submerged in forty feet of water. That's the good news. The bad news is that the water absorbed much of the radioactive materials and carried them back to the ground as water fell like rain."

"You haven't addressed how radiation victims will be treated, Doctor."

"Unfortunately, our ability to mitigate the effects of substantial radiation is limited. Generally speaking, the best we can do is provide supportive care. Anyone receiving a total body dose of three hundred rads has a fifty percent chance of dying. At six hundred rads, the picture gets even uglier. So, part of our care will be purely palliative."

Before any more questions could arise, Liz added, "I think that's enough for now. Dr. Tucker and I will look forward to reconvening this evening at 1900 hours."

CHAPTER FIFTY-THREE

IT WAS EARLY THE FOLLOWING MORNING when Hart and Wilkins finished their respective planning sessions and made their way to a makeshift bedroom at CTU. Exhausted, they fell asleep in other's arms, only to be awakened a short time later by a call from Marvin Kahn.

"I'm sorry to call so early, Commander, but there's been a change in plans."

"I'm listening, Sir."

"General Malik is dead."

"How, Sir?"

"His daughter. Apparently when Ayesha learned about the nuclear detonation, she went to the general's office and confronted him. We're not sure exactly what transpired, but she put a bullet through the left ventricle of his heart."

"We need to get her out of there, Mr. Kahn."

"It's too late for that, Commander. Dr. Naru is dead."

"What are you talking about? Who killed her?"

"She took her own life. Whatever happened in that room, it was a secret they took to their graves."

Hart was quiet for a very long time.

"Are you there, Commander?"

"Yes, Sir."

"She was a jihadist, Commander."

"No, Mr. Kahn. She was a hardworking physician trying to bring light into the world. Isn't that what the president said we were supposed to do . . . dispel the darkness with light? Well, in my book, she was one of God's true servants. That became evident when the truth about her father was revealed."

"I need you in Washington, then on your way to Islamabad, Commander."

"I'm literally just getting started here, Mr. Kahn."

"For the time being, Tom Levin is going to have to fill your shoes. We're accelerating the timetable on intervention. The president and I will expect to see you in the Situation Room this morning at 1000 hours. That gives you four hours, Commander, to wrap things up and make your way to Washington."

"I assumed the president was still in Omaha," Hart commented.

"He returned to Washington late last night."

The president and a small group of trusted advisors sat awaiting Hart's arrival at the White House. As he approached the president, Conner handed him a folder containing dossiers on more than two dozen Pakistanis.

"I'm sorry to have yanked you out of New York so precipitously, Commander, but we're concerned about the stability of Pakistan following General Malik's death."

"Understood, Sir. And the folder?"

"Your priorities, Commander, starting with General Patel. We want very public executions, not people quietly disappearing in the night. Try to minimize collateral damage if possible."

"Why create a spectacle, Sir?" Hart asked. "That's not our normal way of conducting business."

"And these are not normal times, Commander. We're sending a message, resoundingly clear. Strike the United States, and it will strike back with a vengeance. You're up for it, aren't you, Commander?"

"Yes, Sir." For the first time that he could remember, Hart accepted an order with trepidation.

"There's one more caveat, Commander. We want all of the executions to occur over a twenty-four-hour period. Mr. Kahn has already coordinated with our operatives in the region who will assist in cutting off the heads of the hydra."

Conner continued, "When your work is finished, I will place a call to President Mughabi. He will have some difficult decisions to make. That's it, gentlemen. Meeting adjourned."

CHAPTER FIFTY-FOUR

HART LED AN ELITE TEAM of twelve special operatives with orders to take out twenty-four of Pakistan's key military and intelligence personnel known to have ties to the United Islamic State. The assassinations began at 6:20 in the morning, when a bomb planted under the rear seat of a military-issued sedan rocked central Islamabad. With few people out on the streets at that hour, the victims were limited to the vehicle's driver and his occupant—General Patel.

Over the next hour, four more bombings rocked the city. The first—a rocket propelled grenade—burst through a window of the victim's home, eviscerating the target and his family. By 8 AM, the death toll stood at twenty—including twelve civilians.

The city was reeling from the morning's terror, and its leadership was searching for answers. With eight of the victims having been high-ranking government officials or military officers, their colleagues feared who might be next. But instead of more terror, a quiescence settled in. The calm lasted until noon.

As the lunch hour approached, senior staff flowed out of the Army Command Center and headed to nearby restaurants. Perched 500 meters away, a U.S. sniper took aim with his suppressed semi-auto .308 caliber rifle. He had three targets in sight, all of whom were fortuitously clustered. He inhaled, exhaled, then inhaled and held his breath. When his heartbeat slowed sufficiently to steady the rifle's barrel, he squeezed off three shots in rapid succession. They were all direct hits . . . one to the head, the other two striking the officers' chests. He took a deep breath, then pumped an additional round into each man's body before breaking down his rifle and escaping the scene.

Islamabad was paralyzed with fear . . . its inhabitants not knowing whether to flee their places of work or to shelter in place. As night brought a cloak of darkness to the city, people who had been hiding in the shadows decided to make their break. Among them were the remaining thirteen men on the commander's hit list.

Seven high-ranking intelligence officers from ISI head-quarters left together, erroneously believing that there was safety in numbers. They crowded into an elevator in the parking garage complex. When the doors opened on a lower level, two U.S. Special Forces operatives greeted them, MP-5s leveled. Before the ISI operatives could move, the men opened fire on full auto. They emptied their clips, replaced them, and emptied them once more. One hundred twenty bullet casings littered the floor of the garage. The attackers snapped fresh magazines into their guns as they raced up the stairs and jumped into a waiting car.

The remaining men, six in total, were killed one at a time . . . most in their beds lying next to their wives. Some never knew what happened, dying in their sleep. Others bolted awake just in time to see the muzzle flash that would take them to their graves.

Once the targets had been dispatched, the assassins disappeared into the night.

President Conner waited a day before calling Mughabi.

Mughabi threatened his U.S. counterpart the moment he heard Conner's voice. "There will be a price to be paid for your actions, Mr. President. Do you think you can dole out your perverse form of justice with impunity?"

"Oh, spare me your warnings. We merely did a little housecleaning for you. If you had any balls, you would have done it yourself a long time ago."

"Am I on your list, Mr. Conner? Will I be visited by one of your assassins, or will it be a drone?"

"Neither, though either would give me great pleasure. Instead, you are going to welcome the United States military into Pakistan and turn over the keys to your nuclear arsenal. Then we'll determine how to rid your country of its vermin and reestablish legitimate rule. Surely that's something you can support, Mr. Mughabi?"

"How can I support it knowing that India will strike the moment nuclear retaliation is no longer a threat? You know that our bombs have been the only impediment to an all-out war for decades."

"We will control India," Conner assured him.

"You Americans are so arrogant! Why would India capitulate to your demands?"

Conner remained momentarily silent, leaving the president hanging on in silence.

"You have a choice. You can decline my offer, in which case Islamabad and Karachi will be incinerated by the blasts of thermonuclear bombs. Or you can order you troops to stand down while we send in our forces. It's a important decision. I will give you sixty seconds in whic to make it."

An interpreter seated across from President Conne signaled that he was picking up an urgent side conversation between Mughabi and another man. The man sounded as if he were relaying an urgent message to the Pakistani president.

Conner muted the phone. "What is he saying?"

"The Russians have just advised Pakistan's strategic command that their satellites detected five American missile silos in Minot, North Dakota, initiating their launch sequence."

"It looks as though our strategy is working," Conner said, taking the phone off mute.

"Your time is up, Mr. Mughabi. What is your decision?"

"It is not a decision, Mr. Conner. My only recourse is to surrender our weapons to you as demanded and pray that Allah protects us from a neighbor bent on our destruction."

The next morning, Hart was on the *USS San Diego*, 500 feet below the surface of the Indian Ocean, when a coded communication arrived. It was from Marvin Kahn. A helicopter would rendezvous with the Los Angeles-class nuclear submarine at 0900 hours to pick up Hart and ferry him to Mumbai, where a G550 would be waiting. He was coming home.

As the chopper rose from the sea, the submarine disappeared into the impenetrably dark waters. Hart's thoughts turned to Ayesha Naru. If only he could speak to her . . . share with her the thousands of lives that had been spared by her self-sacrifice. But such was not the will of Allah or of his own God. If there was such thing as paradise, he prayed she was embracing it.

Hart knew New York would more than recover . . . it would become even stronger. Areas that had long been blighted would be supplanted with new growth . . . families tied together by tenuous bonds would reaffirm the importance of unity . . . and a country once divided by partisanship would embrace a United States of America.

Hart was headed home. He couldn't wait to wrap his arms around Liz and make the world safe again, if only for the moment.